Atlantic 1948 no. 3

Aubrey Kerr

ISBN 0–88925–718–3

Published by
S. A. Kerr
Calgary, Alberta
Canada

First printing, 1986

Printed and bound in Canada by
Friesen Printers
a Division of D. W. Friesen & Sons Ltd.
Altona, Manitoba, R0G 0B0
Canada

To Elsie

TABLE OF CONTENTS

This intriguing story not only concerns a wild well which caught fire Labour Day 1948, it tells of individuals who were worlds apart in background and temperament, yet fated to be brought together in common cause:

- the mineral rights owner, a son of the soil with Eastern European roots, suddenly having untold wealth thrust upon him;
- the promoter, whose cunning skills, learned from previous ventures, enabled him to snatch a lease from under the very nose of an international major oil company and capitalize on the near-disaster;
- a tool push who, like Cassandra, was not to be believed but was proved right, too late;
- a one-time roughneck, who had fought his way up from the dumb corner to manage a drilling contracting firm, wreaking havoc on the wild well he was desperately trying to control;
- the newly appointed head of a regulatory agency, unfamiliar with the oil patch, hesitant to exercise his statutory authority until he was forced to assume unprecedented powers;
- the "hero", innovative, committed, a leader who, with the combination of experience and authority of an unfettered mandate, killed the well and restored the field to near normal.

And there were the "hands", most of them green, in freezing cold, in summer heat, in snow, mud and oil, risking incineration on many occasions, yet most of them taking the work in their stride. They and others instinctively followed the leadership essential for this uniquely treacherous task.

PREFACE

The idea of chronicling Atlantic No.3 originated with Willis J. (Gibby) Gibson. In Toronto in 1957, he proposed that Imperial Oil[1] give him permission to record this landmark event. He even went so far as to arrange for a short, but most informative, taping session: the late Mr. Carscallen interviewing V.J. (Tip) Moroney, also of Imperial, who had had charge of killing the wild burning well.

Ever mindful of its public image, Imperial turned down the idea, as it could have implied negligence on the part of Atlantic Oil and its staff. It might also have been seen as a back-hand reference to Atlantic's production payment to Imperial to settle the lease dispute.

When Gibby retired as senior manager,[1] he revived the idea with the Alberta Government in 1977. However, this approach fell through when supporting funds were not forthcoming. In the meantime, several files full of Atlantic No.3 data had been discarded, which added to the difficulty of re-tracing the history of the well.

Knowing of my intense interest in the story and the fact that I was directly involved as Leduc District Geologist for Imperial Oil in 1948, Gibby handed me his files in 1981. Over the next four years, I split my time between the Journal of Canadian Petroleum Technology, the Petroleum Industry Oral History Project, my consulting clientele, and research on Atlantic No.3.

My first encouragement to proceed with serious writing came with a start-up grant from the Royal Canadian Geographical Society. I negotiated space in Petro-Canada's Calgary offices and a modest budget for expenses. Gibby continued to make valuable contributions as one of the members of my excellent working committee. I have also had the benefits of a "shadow committee" who have never allowed me to slow down.

Deborah Maw, research assistant, Evelene Watson, secretary and Don Glass, editor, have provided outstanding services. Team work, always essential in any undertaking, took on new meaning, with Maw, Watson and Glass whole-heartedly combining their talents to create the final product. Anne Nesbitt has had important responsibilities in publicizing the book.

Special thanks are due "Glenbow" for its intelligent advice and unflagging help. In 1985, the CBC "spread the word", bringing important contributors into touch with me. Its Ottawa headquarters unearthed an on-the-spot taped account of the fire. The ERCB, both through one of my committee members and other staff, has generously provided much valuable information.

The "Acknowledgements" lists the names of all those who have been involved in one way or another with my project.

What have I acquired as a result of working on this project? A strong element of humility in the daunting task of co–ordinating, dove–tailing and resolving material that I have accumulated. Many of the stories are folk–loric, blurred by the passage of time, yet retaining that nebulous, all–important human quality which breathes life into any narrative. To quote Bernard Ostry, my job has been to unscramble "the vast penumbra of doubt, the extraordinary untidiness and ambiguity of life". This helps to explain why this narrative can never be complete. For those errors in fact, or differences in story versions, I take full responsibility. I have tried to adhere to the Latin dictum suggested by Andy Baillie: *"De Mortuis Nihil Nisi Bonum"* (trans: of the dead, speak nothing but good).

As well, I have tried to capture the temper of the times; the many acts of expediency and human shortcomings, so often offset by heroism and inventiveness. Most importantly, I want to convey, especially to my younger readers, what it really was like in 1947 and 1948: – gruelling work under unbelievably difficult conditions – snow, ice, mud, water, oil, extreme fire hazard, long hours.

I hope I have succeeded to some extent, but I still expect to hear cries go up:

"You've got it wrong",

"Why didn't you mention me?"

My only answer can be: "Give me enough new material...maybe there's a second book..."

ENDNOTE:
1. Gibson's entire career was dedicated to Imperial/Esso as an engineer advancing to senior management.

LEDUC – A NEW ERA

1

Nineteen forty–six. Canada had just started to move away from a war economy that had lasted six long years.

The country's population was about 12.5 million; Alberta's in the range of nine hundred thousand. Leduc's population in 1946 could be measured in hundreds, while Edmonton and Calgary vied for first place, both in the hundred thousand range.[1]

Rail was the main means of transportation both in Canada and Alberta. There were four trains per day each way between Edmonton and Calgary (including a sleeper). The highway between Edmonton and Lethbridge was one of the few main ones that had been "paved" (in part, near Lacombe, by the direct use of McMurray tar sands). The road bed was "crowned", which made it easy to slide off the road when black ice coated the surface. But speeds were slower and the ditches were shallow so mishaps were usually not catastrophic.

Starting in 1913, Alberta was selling natural gas in the main markets (Edmonton, Calgary and Lethbridge) through pipe lines. Medicine Hat was sitting on its own gas field so there it was just a matter of low pressure pipe connections. Reserves were sufficient to supply the market, but there was no economic advantage in servicing the smaller communities unless they were right on the pipe line. Although Jumping Pound gas field had been discovered in 1944, it was lying dormant and would do so until the early fifties. There was no thought of export.

Canada's vehicle registration in 1946 was about 1.8 million (all types); compare this to the 1983 total of 14 million. Alberta was able to supply most of its vehicles' gasoline and oil needs from two refineries in Calgary, gasoline plants in the Valley and a topping unit at Lethbridge that used Montana crude.

Canada's total crude oil production for 1946 was 7.6 million barrels, of which Ontario contributed 1.6%. Turner Valley was the only significant producer: 6.2 million barrels.[2] Wainwright, Lloydminster and Taber measured their output in a few hundred barrels per day each.[3] Canada's dependence on imports was almost absolute: 63.3 million barrels of crude to be refined and 18.8 million barrels of finished products brought in per year for a total cost of $248 million to the economy.[4]

The West Coast got its crude supplies from Peru and Venezu–

ela; Central Canada and the East Coast looked mainly to Venezuela, which at that time had more than adequate resources at low well head prices. These did not translate into competitive plant gate gasoline prices in Montreal, there being no competition. With this kind of economics for the large volume market, there was really no reason then why western Canada needed to be considered as either a potential alternative or as a complete replacement for foreign offshore crude. The situation changed in the fifties.

The corporate mind–set, especially that of Imperial, was: Norman Wells was not a great economic success; no other productive reefs like it had been found; the Lower Cretaceous oilfields of Alberta were both modest in areal extent and pay thickness. So there was no reason to consider Western Canada other than gas prone.

Exploration, geophysical and geological, was supplemented by exploratory wells drilled from the early 1940's through mid–1946. Magnificent failures had resulted from misinterpretation of seismic data in southern Saskatchewan. Alberta exploration had also met with little success. One significant wildcat drilled near Crossfield in 1945 was the tip–off to a Mississippian subcrop play, but this was not discovered until 1951, only a mile or so away. No doubt about it, this mind–set of the companies seemed to prevail, with little encouragement from their U.S. head offices.

It is true that over 100 wildcat wells had been drilled on the plains, but the rarely tested Paleozoic sequences had not provided many clues as to what was really there. This was because the deeper tests had penetrated the Devonian and older beds only on the shelves of as yet undiscovered basins; these shelves had not provided the conditions for significant reef growth.[5] Needless to say, none of these wildcats produced any significant amounts of oil and gas from the deeper, older beds.

This was the state of affairs in Western Canada in April 1946. Imperial Oil and its parent, Standard Oil of New Jersey (later Exxon), meeting in Toronto,[6] were wondering whether Western Canada had any real potential other than natural gas and the McMurray tar sands. To add to the pessimism, the Turner Valley field was declining (it was producing 15,000 barrels a day at the time). The pros and cons of "what to do next" were discussed, while keeping as the trump card a projected construction of a Fischer–Tropsch synthetic gasoline plant in Edmonton.[7]

One school of thought (headed by Lewis Weeks) was that post–Paleozoic (Cretaceous) sands and interbedded shales were the only targets: they contained relatively large amounts of gas but only minor quantities of medium to heavy oil.[8] This group leaned toward shallow drilling.

Another school of thought at the meeting, led by the late Dr. Theodore A. Link,[9] one of North America's greatest oil–finders, pushed for a stratigraphic basement test program[10] across the basin of Alberta. "Doc", as he was affectionately known, had the benefit of his 1946 Questionnaire sent out to all Imperial Oil earth scientists then on staff. One of the replies, by Hank Kunst,[11] suggested the Devonian beds as a potential oil target in Alberta. Perhaps people had forgotten about Norman Wells, the Northwest Territories oil field that produced from Devonian reefs at shallow depths.

Fortunately, Link's proposal carried the day and the first stratigraphic test in the series was chosen. A one–line seismic reconnaissance, run from Breton northeast to Redwater, had already uncovered an amoeba–type anomaly[12] in Township 50, Range 26. Detail shooting reinforced this feature, which appeared to be related to Cretaceous beds. Knowledge workers had postulated the existence of a hinge–line running northwest–southeast through the area. One could expect southwesterly thickening of Cretaceous sediments, normal to this trend, which could provide a gas supply for the proposed synthetic plant.

Up to this time there was no real evidence that reefal reservoirs existed in the area, but dolomitic material identified by Doug Layer[13] in the 1942 Clonmel Bruderheim wildcat provided a clue.

Imperial Leduc No. 1, in lsd 5–22–50–26–W4M, was recommended by the late J.B. Webb, then exploration manager, on the basis of the mild seismic feature and the hinge line theory, but he was not unaware of deeper potential horizons: "...It is more likely that Devonian sediments will be encountered directly beneath the Cretaceous. Nothing is known regarding the stratigraphy of the Devonian in this area...Porosity is generally present where the top of the section consists of dolomite. Many other dolomite horizons and *reef–like* developments possessing porosity have been encountered. The entire Devonian section warrants thorough investigation".[14] It was licenced as a Silurian test[15] and spudded in November 20, 1946. The Cretaceous sands were reached in December; they tested wet gas. In late December, oil stained porosity, in what was later identified as Devonian carbonate was noted in the cuttings. Following coring and drill–stem testing (oil to the surface) Imperial decided to stop drilling at that point. This zone was put on production February 13 and was dubbed the "D–2" (later known as Nisku).[16]

Because of the encouragement in the Lower Cretaceous

sands, a portable rig had been ordered in from eastern Alberta, in late December, to test the downdip possibilities of an oil leg in these sands. This well, Leduc No. 2, spudded in the day that No. 1 was put on production. Drilling was painfully slow and it was not until April that it reached the equivalent of the D–2 discovery zone of No. 1. To the dismay of everyone at Imperial, the D–2 (completely cored) was virtually non–porous, with only traces of oil staining. While officials were thinking that No. 1 may have been just a one–well freak, drilling resumed at No. 2. After penetrating about 150 ft. of green shale (later known as the Ireton), the author noted a speed–up of drilling on the afternoon of May 6. Drilling was halted six feet into the drilling break. Returns showed coarsely crystalline dolomite, with no oil staining. Nevertheless, orders were given for a drill–stem test; oil flowed in seven minutes the following morning. The porous dolomite which No. 2 had penetrated was named D–3 (later, Leduc).[17] It was subsequently shown to be a true reef build–up, the seismic anomaly resulting from draping of younger sediments over it.

From May 1947 on, an unprecedented drilling boom started which was never again equalled in Canada. The knowledgeable oil patch knew it had something big. Land plays, tied to geophysical prospecting, fanned out in all directions. Despite the hectic activity, world attention remained asleep until the Atlantic No. 3 blow–out. To set the background for this event, let us look at the regulatory body (the Conservation Board) that would play such a pivotal role in the events to come.

ENDNOTES:
1. Census taken every ten years (1941, 1951, 1961, etc.) Canada's population had doubled to nearly 25 million by 1981 while Alberta's had increased 2.4 times to 2.2 million. Leduc, at last count, was 13,000 while Calgary and Edmonton are still competing at about half a million each in 1986.
2. This story takes place in the late forties, many years before "SI" was imposed on the oil patch. The older reader should be secretly pleased, the younger people will simply have to get out their conversion charts to switch from barrels (the first example), cubic feet of gas, pounds per square inch, inches, feet and miles.
3. Canada's 1983 production was nearly 500 million barrels or 65 times that of 1946. Alberta contributed 415 million barrels (83%).

4. Canada's 1983 refining capacity had grown to 740 million barrels or nine times total imports in 1946. It is impossible to make direct comparisons because of the current complicated import/export flow of crude and products. Refining capacity is about the only way that one can tie these together.

5. Conditions for reef growth are ideal where clear sea water at warm temperatures circulates through the coral animal colonies, providing nutriment. Growing reefs can be observed today in the Caribbean Sea, the Red Sea, the Great Barrier Reef of Australia, and other places.

6. Reported by Doug Layer, former Exploration Manager, Imperial Oil, deceased; author of privately circulated "Documentation of Leduc Oil Discovery", 1979, Esso.

7. The process was developed by the Germans during World War II, producing gasoline from coal to fuel the Luftwaffe. The plant was actually under construction in Corpus Christi, Texas, to process 50 MMcf/d of gas to yield 5,000 b/d of gasoline. A drilling program in 1945 and 1946 in the general Viking–Provost area was identifying large gas reserves to supply the plant.

8. Gas in Provost–Kinsella area east of Edmonton, oil at Taber (400 b/d) in southern Alberta, Wainwright (500 b/d) and Lloydminster (900 b/d) in east central Alberta.

9. S.A. Kerr, "Ted Link: Larger Than Life", *The Journal of Canadian Petroleum Technology,* 19, 3, (July–September, 1980), p. 18, 20, 22.

10. Drilling to go "to the granite". Basement equates to interface between Phanerozoic sediments and the underlying Precambrian granite (which outcrops on the Canadian Shield).

11. Senior Geologist with Imperial Oil until 1971, now retired in Kelowna. Kunst worked with Carl Chapman, then geophysicist, to produce the report on the Leduc seismic anomaly.

12. An indication, from the plotting of "arrivals" (time $\times$ velocity = depth) that a formation lies at shallower than normal depths over a given area.

13. See endnote 5.

14. Webb, J.B., October 1946 memo to Walker Taylor.

15. The Silurian salt target appears to have been chosen because it was considered to be the deepest horizon having oil or gas potential. Ironically, beds of this age are now known not to exist in the subsurface west of Saskatchewan. The projected depth, 7000 ft., qualified the wildcat for tax relief ("deep, difficult").

16. A widespread biostrome (coral reef), 150 ft. thick in the Leduc area, which is variable in its reservoir characteristics.

17. A bioherm (coral reef), limited in areal extent but of great thickness, often having significant reservoir capacity because of its usually excellent porosity and permeability. There is an active water drive from the underlying Cooking Lake dolomite aquifer.

THE CONSERVATION BOARD

2

The Petroleum and Natural Gas Conservation Board,[1] created in 1938 by an Act of the Alberta Legislature, was an outgrowth of many attempts to control the waste of natural gas and reservoir energy in the Turner Valley field. It took over the responsibilities and the staff of the Petroleum and Natural Gas Division of the Department of Lands and Mines. Regulatory bodies had been set up before, shortly after the province had received its minerals from the Dominion Crown in 1931,[2] with a view to controlling all aspects of the oil and gas industry. Turner Valley, at that time too, was the main focus of attention. In the bizarre atmosphere of the early thirties, where waste was not necessarily a dirty word,[3] how could one achieve equality of interests? The dilemma was compounded by the down–flank "discovery" of crude oil in the Turner Valley wet gas field in 1936.

The Board was not quite nine years old when Leduc was found. The then chairman, Alex G. Bailey left shortly thereafter for the private sector.[4] Only a few D–3 wells had been completed in the Leduc field so Bailey had no reason to realize that the presence of gas in the Viking sand and loss of circulation in the D–3 dolomite were potentially dangerous. With an uncommon prescience, he called for an examination of Leduc field casing and completion procedures. The Alberta Petroleum Association,[5] along with operators of Leduc leases, were asked to study the matter and report to the Board with recommendations.[6]

Following Bailey's departure, D.P. (Red) Goodall continued in the capacity of acting chairman.

A native of Petrolia, Ontario, Red Goodall had graduated from the University of Alberta in 1926 in geology. He had worked at many tasks in Turner Valley. No doubt about it, Red had gotten his hands dirty gaining invaluable experience, having to earn his opportunities as he went. It was while he was on a hard–rock assignment down east in 1937 that he received a wire from Charlie Dingman, Director of the Petroleum and Natural Gas Division, Provincial Department of Lands and Mines. A vacancy had been created in the Turner Valley office due to Vern Taylor's moving to Royalite. Goodall took Vern's job. As a labourer back in 1929–30, he had installed the very gas meters that provided the data he now had to

*Photo furnished by George Warne,
ERCB.*

analyze. In 1938 he moved into the Board offices in the "old"
Telephone Building on 6th Avenue S.W.

Not given to eloquence, Red could be said to have been one of
the most, if not *the* most, taciturn Board official. He was a keen but
silent tribune at Board hearings and his rulings were respected.
Well thought out responses were usually limited to a simple yes or
no! Goodall provided the all–important administrative link from
Bailey's departure to the re–organization of February 1948.

Goodall, not wanting the chairman's job, must have been
relieved on February 2, 1948 when Ian McKinnon, Assistant Deputy
Minister of Lands and Mines, assumed the Chairmanship of the
Board (on a part time basis).[7] Goodall became Deputy Chairman.
On February 7th, Dr. George W. Govier [8] was appointed a Member.
He also acted in a part time capacity, dividing his time between the
new 514 – 11 Avenue S.W. Board office in Calgary and the University
of Alberta in Edmonton. G.E.G. (Goldie) Leisemer was Chief
Engineer, having joined the Board in 1941.

McKinnon was a product of Scotland. He had articled as an
accountant and emigrated to Canada in 1929. His early work was
with the Alberta Government in the Department of Lands and

Mines. During World War II, he served in the RCAF, re–joining the Department upon discharge.

Photos furnished by George Warne,
ERCB.

In retrospect, McKinnon is difficult to describe. From the time Atlantic No. 3 first became a visible problem (March 8) until Moroney took over (May 14), we see McKinnon preoccupied with the brand new job he had just taken, dividing his time between Edmonton duties and coping with "pressures" from his superiors in Edmonton and from some sectors of industry. One could say that he was unprepared to cope with such a sudden event, largely because of the fact that he had no previous operational experience. Fortunately, Red Goodall provided invaluable stabilizing guidance because he knew how things were done in industry.

Govier's first link with the Conservation Board had been as a post–graduate student proceeding to his Master's degree under Dr. Boomer at the University of Alberta. He spent one summer with the Board at Turner Valley and then went to Ann Arbor to work towards his Doctor's degree. According to Red, George had been investigating gas conservation because it bore directly on Turner Valley. He was certainly a man for the times in the sense that, after the Leduc discovery, when gas started to become surplus, he was a natural for his new responsibilities at the Board. He became a respected expert in the behaviour of natural gas, not only in reservoirs, but under flowing conditions. His judgment in solving mathematically related problems came to the fore when formulae had to be developed for many contingencies. It is very likely he assisted in working up the pro-rationing formula for Leduc crude in May 1948.

As with other fields, the Board posted engineers to monitor the activity and ensure that required reports were made.

Until 1947, the main field office of the Board was in Turner Valley, with outposts in Vermilion and Medicine Hat. When the

Nate Goodman and Ted Baugh in front of the Board's first "office" (12' x 18' skid shack) in Leduc town (1947).
Photo furnished by Alex Essery.

Leduc field was opening up, the Board sent Nate Goodman, a graduate petroleum engineer, there. Nate's was a keen mind and he was a sharp observer. He soon developed a solid rapport with industry personnel and maintained good communications with everyone. His diary is an invaluable link with the well tour reports and was of much assistance in putting together this story, especially as it relates to details of the Atlantic No. 3 blow-out. Nate was later joined by Bill Kinghorn and, later still, by Alex Essery, both of whom were bottom hole men and experienced Board employees. Len Henderson, a gas measurement expert, also came to Devon.

Goodman kept records and visited the well site frequently. A decision to hire Myron Kinley appears to have been made by the Board, with Denton and Spencer and McMahon probably also involved. McKinnon was reported to have said: "We were caught in a bind and needed to obtain outside advice".

ENDNOTES:
1. The name was altered first to the Oil and Gas Conservation Board. When coal, electric power and pipelines were added to its mandate in 1971, it took on its present title, Energy Resources Conservation Board.
2. Premier Brownlee and the United Farmers of Alberta, government at the time, were the driving forces behind the transfer.
3. S.A. Kerr, "Feds vs. Province 1931–1981", *The Journal of Canadian Petroleum Technology,* (April–June 1981), 20, 2, p. 32.
4. Bailey (June 4, 1947) formed Bailey Selburn Oil and Gas and associated companies, ultimately selling out to Pacific Petroleums.
5. The Alberta Petroleum Association became the Western Canada Petroleum Association, which evolved into the present day Canadian Petroleum Association.
6. See Chapter 8.
7. McKinnon became full–time Chairman in 1951 and resigned in 1959 to chair the National Energy Board in Ottawa. Gordon Connell, well–respected senior engineer now retired from Gulf, was hired by Charlie Dingman in 1937, several months after Goodall. He moved to the Board in 1938 and later to Royalite. Gordon recalls that McKinnon asked him if he would be interested in the newly vacated Chairman's job in 1947 because, according to Gordon, Ian was not anxious to take on the operational responsibilities and wanted to stay in Edmonton.
   One can speculate as to what could have transpired if Connell had accepted: he might even have moved on, as Ian did, to head up the National Energy Board in Ottawa. He spent the later part of his career as resident NEB contact for Gulf.
8. Govier became Chairman in 1959 and retired from the Board in 1978.

THE REBUS FAMILY – SOIL TO OIL

3

A cairn on the grounds of the Polish Catholic church (south side of Nisku–Devon road), commemorates those hardy pioneers from Western Galicia[1] who settled in the area. Those named on the plaque, who had acquired title to their minerals, would not know of their good fortune for 50 years.[2] Of these, the Rebus family were the first to have riches suddenly thrust at them in 1947. Ironically, the benefits of this sudden wealth were to be fragmented by disputes within the family, over which, even to this day, a curtain is still drawn: "We just want to forget about those things".[3] Of extreme concern at the time of the Atlantic blow–out was the constant threat of fire through the summer of 1948; their farm could have been their funeral pyre, fuelled by their own crude!

Let us go back to 1897, when Stanislaw Sarnecki was sent by his countrymen to scout out Western Canada. He liked what he saw in the area west of Nisku and recommended emigration to those who lived in his home District of Jaroslaw and wanted a better future. These families soon realized that instead of the few acres they occupied in Europe, they could acquire 160 acre tracts for their very own. Bronislaw Rebus and his wife Rose, one of these families, dwelt near the village of Radymno, south of the town of Laszki where their fellow travellers, the Baras,[4] lived. Joseph Rebus, one of Bronislaw's sons, in a 1986 interview, was told by his father that the group sailed on the Stefan Batory to Halifax in 1898, then travelled by CPR train to Strathcona, then the rail head.

Bronislaw Rebus filed on a quarter section of Crown land in what was then the Northwest Territories when he arrived in Western Canada in the summer of 1898. The location was 7 miles west and a little south of Nisku siding (20 miles southwest of Strathcona). The CNR and GTP rail lines had not even been thought of. Roads were non–existent and trails which cut through the forested area were the only access. Fortunately, the district had been surveyed. Witness posts and pins guided the settlers to where they should be.

Bronislaw lost no time in building a log dwelling, 14 ft. by 22 ft., in November. In order to qualify as a homesteader, he was required to file application papers for citizenship. By 1902, Bronislaw had become a naturalized British Subject; this allowed him to make formal application for his quarter section Crown homestead, which was approved late in that year.[5] He valued his house at $100, and stated that he had six head of cattle, four horses and six pigs. Two other farmers confirmed the above by sworn statements: Stephen (Szczepan) Bara (Reginald's and Norman's grandfather) and Anton Stachnik. As Joseph Rebus recalls, the homestead quarter was disappointing, being low lying and swampy. So Rebus Senior looked around, signed an agreement to take over a quarter section from Fred Berthiaume and assumed an unpaid balance in 1904.[6]

Mrs. Berthiaume,[7] Fred's mother, was a successful entrepreneur and at one time the owner of a sawmill and hotels. In 1901, Fred had purchased from the CPR the northwest quarter of 23–50–26–W4M for the price of $3.00 an acre, but still owed on it. All minerals except coal went with the title. This was the same year in which the CPR received a patent on the above and other parcels in the township from the Dominion of Canada.

This quarter, one mile east of the homestead, was on higher ground, better drained and sloped north. These features were to become critically important in 1948 when the huge oil run–off was directed to the northwest corner by gravity and collected behind dykes. Of much more future significance to the Rebus family was their move from a quarter section in which "all mines and minerals" had been reserved to the Crown to a CPR[8] tract which included oil and gas in the title. The transfer to Bronislaw was confirmed in October 1911.[9]

No further activity on Bronislaw Rebus' title occurred except for numerous mortgages and tax notices which were discharged as the years went by. Curiously enough, there is no mention of mineral taxes which, even in the dirty thirties, were payable at the rate of one–eighth of a cent per acre graduating up to ten cents.

According to C.T. (Bill) Webb, retired "Mr. CPR", some farm-ers in the Leduc area in 1938 were willing to relinquish their miner-als rather than pay these taxes. What an opportunity *that* would have been, but how would anyone know then what riches lay beneath the soil?

The will of Bronislaw Rebus, drawn up in 1939, lacked an Executor. Whether this was by design or by neglect is not known. Joseph claims that Father Roziecki had helped his father draw up the document. But Joseph did not want to be present at the signing, and the will was witnessed by Messrs. Mike Bara and F. Sank. Bronislaw bequeathed to his wife Rose (Euphrosina on the grave marker), the northwest quarter of Section 23 (no other tract was mentioned) and instructed Peter, one of his younger sons, "to care for it". Upon Rose's death the tract was to go to Peter. This seems to be contrary to Polish–Ukrainian custom by which the eldest son would automatically inherit the assets of his parents' estate (this would have been Michael). By this time, the family consisted of seven boys and three girls. They all became participants in the 1947 windfall.[10]

When Bronislaw Rebus died on August 3, 1940, Michael and Joseph applied to the Court to become Administrators of the Will and were duly appointed by the Court on November 26 of that year.[11] Administrators do not have the powers of Executors, a fact of which the appointees were possibly unaware.[12]

Late in 1944, Peter, the heir apparent to the quarter, had been discharged from the Armed Services for medical reasons and presumably was not interested in "caring for the land". He abrogated his future right by conveying what would have been his interest on his mother's death back to her.[13] Perhaps his failing health was the reason.

The next critical link in the chain of title was forged on January 14, 1945 when the widow assigned her title to her son John.[14] Rose still kept a life interest. John had, by that time, moved onto the land with his wife Hilda and his mother.

There is no record of any of these title changes having been questioned by the Administrators. Their role appears to have been negligible in the affairs of their father's Estate until the fall of 1946, when Imperial was getting ready to drill its wildcat, Leduc No. 1. Company landmen were trying to pick up as many freehold leases as possible in Twp 50 R 26 W4M. Jack Webb, then Exploration Manager for Imperial, confined the landmen's acquisitions to within that township, keeping in mind the scattering of Crown acreage which had previously been "permitted" by Imperial under the 1945 provincial regulations.[15]

When leasing, Imperial Oil would send out two men, one to draw up the lease and ensure that the Dower Act had been signed; the other person to witness the landman's signature. There is uncertainty as to who approached the Administrators and concluded a lease with them in October 1946. It is quite possible that it was Johnny Jackson,[16] now retired. Jackson had started in the oil patch south of Calgary working with Ivone St. G. Burn and Pete Baptie, surveyor. Gordon Hawkins was rod man. Burn had a long history of employment with Imperial and Royalite as a draftsman, surveyor and landman. In spite of the fact that Imperial signed up the Administrators on October 22, 1946, its caveat was not registered until March 25, 1947 (March 27 according to the final lease), over a month after the discovery. Like other 1946 deals, the terms were a "princely" $5.00 signing bonus for the entire 160 acres (about 3 cents an acre), a 21 year lease and a 12½% royalty.

But several fatal errors were made. Firstly, Imperial Oil was responsible for ensuring that the consent of all the beneficiaries had been obtained prior to the Administrators signing the lease and there is no record of this. Secondly, the 1940 "Letters of Administration" did not give the Administrators the power to deal off any lands since the will had given their mother, who was then living, a life interest in the NW quarter of Section 23. Thirdly, the Administrators should have been aware of the transfer of title, albeit unregistered, of the NW quarter of Section 23 to John Rebus. There is no evidence that either Imperial or the Administrators sought beneficiaries' consent prior to signing a lease.[17]

In the meantime, uncommitted acreage suddenly became very valuable after February 13, 1947. Just how sudden and how valuable was amply demonstrated six days later on February 19. Jim Lowery, head of Home Oil, *purchased* Bill Sycz's quarter section for $58,400 (less the one–eighth royalty to Sycz) to set up a field office. Bill was permitted to live in his house and farm the land.[18]

The Administrators of the Rebus estate now realized that the lease that they had signed October 22, 1946 with Imperial Oil now had a value much greater than the original 3 cents per acre. They went to their solicitors; Harvie and Yanda, to make "Application for Transmission" of "the land now standing registered in the name of the deceased (Bronislaw)".[19] That firm should have checked with Michael and Joseph as to their responsibilities. The over–worked Registrar's office OK'd the transmission without questioning the transaction of October 22, 1946. Strangely enough, Michael and Joseph not only had the NW quarter of Section 23 on this document, they included the SW quarter of Section 23 and the SW quarter of 26, neither of which had been cited in the will of Bronislaw Rebus. Title passed to the Administrators on March 5, 1947.[20]

In the course of reciting the chain of title in the first section of this chapter, we have referred to a document which shows John Rebus receiving title to the NW quarter of Section 23 from his mother on January 14, 1945. John must also have also realized that he might have a position in the minerals. When W.E. Simpson, K.C.,[21] who had already been involved in several "clouded" titles, was approached by John to register his caveat, he must have seen at once that the Administrators were on the title. But at the same time, he was very likely satisfied that John had a better claim than his brothers. Consequently, he accordingly registered a caveat on behalf of John March 27, 1947.[22] The Registrar accepted it on the basis of documentation. This instrument recites the assignment of Rose to John, January 14, 1945 and appoints W.E. Simpson as

John's agent. John's wife Hilda, a school teacher, also filed her caveat April 17 to comply with the Dower Act and to further reinforce John's claim.

To further complicate matters, Peter filed *his* caveat on June 7, 1947.[23]

So at that time there were two, or possibly, three distinct, separate claims to the title. John Rebus was relying on his mother's assignment of January 1945 and had Simpson to back him up. Peter must have thought that he still had a glimmer of a chance, going back to the original mandate given to him in his father's will. What fertile ground to create a family conflict!

Law firms in Edmonton were now doing a roaring business searching titles that had previously been of no interest except for surface rights. The Land Titles Office was in a turmoil, with promoters and landmen going through the records, looking for unleased land or parcels with "clouds" over them. Two of these people were Art Mewburn, son of a pioneer family and George Cloakey, a thorough land researcher "with a blood–hound's nose for a promising lease". Did either of them detect flaws in the "lease" between the Administrators and Imperial? Did either of them bring this parcel to the attention of Frank McMahon? There is no written record of any negotiations whereby McMahon became aware of the Rebus mix–up but it would appear that W.E. Simpson, K.C., might have been the tip–off person.

Frank McMahon, originally a mining promoter, with his brother George, had dabbled in Fraser Delta gas, Flathead Valley oil and Turner Valley, using different corporate vehicles. His latest, Atlantic Oil Company Limited, was to provide the means by which he became wealthy. At that time he had Pat Bowsher and Len Youell in the Toronto General Trust Building office, plus Lyle Caspell as field production person.

One can say that, with the innate sense of the born promoter, Frank could not help but be impressed by the opportunities in Leduc. He had been on the outside (ousted from Pacific in the thirties) for long; a productive parcel in this new boom area could turn his fortunes around.

Enter Norman George Lacey, ("Bus"/"Buster"), easy–going, affable, confidante/chauffeur of Frank's. Lacey had started out roughnecking in the Valley and was now working with "Swede" Hanson peddling Altamud.[24] Bus was well–known, well–liked and could charm the birds out of the trees. He was just the right type to sweet–talk a suspicious farmer such as John Rebus into leasing his land. Lacey's other claim to fame was baseball, and he may have been a baseball buddy of one or two of the Rebus brothers.

"Bus" Lacey
Photo furnished by Sandra LeBlanc

Shortly after February 13, 1947, Imperial Oil naturally wanted to find out just what they had discovered, so they moved out boldly, locating their No. 3 well two miles to the northeast and No. 4 three-quarters of a mile to the southeast. No. 2, one and a half miles to the south, was drilling and would not get down to the D–2 zone until April. Both No. 3 and No. 4 reached the D–3 reef shortly after No. 2 discovered it (all in May) and all were successes. The productive limits of the D–3 were now greatly extended. This meant that the Rebus quarter could be classified as virtually proven unless there was an unexpected embayment along the east edge of the D–3 reef.

Frank McMahon, with this new, positive evidence of proven oil land, moved quickly, his instincts telling him correctly that only an unprecedented cash offer for the NW quarter of 23 would drive off the competition. John Rebus was now more sure than ever that he had good title to his property and that it had a greatly enhanced value. But how could he have had any real idea in terms of barrels of crude and their value to a prospective lessee, let alone his royalty share?

On July 2, 1947, Frank McMahon had Bus Lacey sign an option with John Rebus. The deal gave him and him alone $175,000 in cash plus 25,000 shares of Pacific Petroleums. This bonus was over 40,000 times as much as had been accepted by the Administrators in 1946; 3 cents per acre compared to $1,250 per acre.

What must John's feelings have been — no less than that of a LOTTO 6/49 winner! Lacey is reported to have spirited John and Hilda away to Calgary to the Stampede to keep them away from other potential lessees and the Rebus family. This meant an extension of the option to July 14, and it was not registered until July 28. But word leaked out about this huge sum and the rest of the family was in an uproar. It was one thing to lease rights for a few cents an acre but it was quite another matter to know that over $1,000 an acre was going to John only. John could have signed a lease in October 1946 and the family might not have known, much less objected.

But now, with all that money up front, seven beneficiaries of Bronislaw's estate recalled the $500 bequests which they had never received. They were therefore very much a part of the estate.

After many legal skirmishes by all parties, a lease was finally executed on August 16, 1947 with six parties as signatories who "have now agreed among themselves to settle their various claims and differences":

1. Norman George Lacey, as Lessee
2. Michael and Joseph Rebus, as Administrators
3. John D. Rebus
4. Rose Rebus, Widow (lease explained to her in the Ukrainian language by Dmytro Yanda, Barrister)
5. Peter Rebus, Anna Clark, Catherine O'Staff, Mary Melnyk, Joseph Rebus, Karl Rebus, Wojciech (Alford) Rebus, Michael Rebus and Andrew Rebus (remaining brothers and sisters) as Claimants
6. National Trust, as Trustee

Somebody must have advised the family that, because of dissension, it would be wise for them to appoint a trustee with power to collect and disburse the royalties. The lease document, an excellent example of over–kill, cites the chain of title culminating in John the beneficial owner. It confirms Rose's life estate by granting her $30,000 cash out of the $200,000 bonus. Rose Rebus was quoted: "If we could have had only a small piece of that money 50 years ago..."[25]

As an after–thought (inserted and initialled on page 2–A), it was decided to include Imperial Oil's claim: whereby "The Administrators... *purported* to grant a lease..."

"Whereas the claimants have asserted claims to a certain interest in the said lands as beneficiaries under their late Father's will", established all the other brothers and sisters as 'players'.

As Bill Webb stated: "It was a complete lease, dower acts and all". Finally taking their place in the sun, the Administrators were to receive the $200,000, then distribute it to the "claimants".

Five days later, on August 21, Bus assigned all of his right, title and interest to Frank McMahon, with no mention of consideration. No doubt he was suitably rewarded for his leg work! And two days still later, McMahon turned his interest to Atlantic Oil Company Ltd., recovering only the $200,000 bonus.[26] But by that time he had title to a number of shares by virtue of being one of the promoters.

Imperial Oil's claim had to be recognized by McMahon. And McMahon, not so much the promoter now as the pragmatist, realized that he needed a title with no clouds over it. Atlantic's agreement to a 100,000 barrel production payment to Imperial was signed a few days later.

Walker Taylor's temperament and his way of running things were 180 degrees to that of Frank. We pause here to look at the man who would play an important part in the events of 1948.

Walker L. Taylor, a Major in World War I, started off with Royalite[27] in the Valley. He established a reputation for discipline and organization. When he was in charge of the Canol project at Norman Wells during World War II, these attributes, in the face of harsh conditions, were further developed. He gained respect among the men there. As Don Mackenzie, one of his engineers, put it: "I'd work anywhere for him". It was therefore no surprise to see Walker become Imperial Oil's division manager in the old 606 – 2 Street S.W. office, after winding up Canol.

On August 22, 1947 a "secret deal" was signed by Walker Taylor and McMahon. Both agreed that they would be the losers if they went to court. "Hawks" in the Imperial Oil office wanted to contest the lease. When shown the document, Johnny Jackson said he had never been aware of it even though he was in an office down the hall with Ivone Burn at the time. The deal called for Imperial Oil to receive a 100,000 barrel production payment: 60,000 from 17½% of production, and the remaining 40,000 from 8.75%.[28] [29]

If all had gone as planned, four wells producing 75 barrels a day each or 300 barrels a day total would have netted 17½% to Imperial Oil: 42.5 barrels daily. This would have taken 60,000 divided by 42.5 or about four years and the 40,000 barrel balance would have required a proportionately longer time. However, instead of years, it was *days* to Imperial's pay–out when Atlantic No.3 went wild.

Imperial must have felt that it had a weak case, otherwise why would it have given up without a fight and been satisfied with the production payment? Johnny Jackson remembers being closely questioned by Mike Haider (newly arrived "Jersey" hit man). One of the Youngbloods, Oklahoma leasing experts brought in by the parent to help pick up more freehold, vindicated Johnny's actions and confirmed Jack Webb's assessment: that there had been a lack of homework on the part of Imperial's Legal Department. In other words, the lawyers should have done a more thorough search and detected the two conflicting titles. (See Appendices A, B, C and D for other versions.)

Looking back on this tangled chain of events, could John Rebus have succeeded in an "end run", ignoring his brothers and sisters? Maybe, but their exasperation might have produced consequences which all would have lived to regret.

When the author interviewed the three brothers in Edmonton, July 1981: Joseph, Karl (since deceased) and Alford (Wojciech), the rifts created by the events of 1947 were still evident, judging from their remarks. This despite the fact that these three and the others are sharing equally in the royalties.

ENDNOTES:
1. At that time under Austro–Hungarian rule. Now Polish territory, as it had been prior to 1792.
2. Up to 1887, homesteaders on Dominion of Canada Crown lands received full freehold titles. After that date, all mines and minerals were reserved to the Crown. It was not until 1931 that the ownership and administration of the Crown minerals was taken over by the Province of Alberta.
   Settlers acquiring CPR lands up to 1905 received all minerals "except coal and valuable stone". From 1905 on, the railway reserved "petroleum", the definition of which would generate a land–mark test case in 1948. After 1912, CPR reserved *all* mines and minerals when it sold homestead lands.
3. Hilda Rebus, May 6, 1986 – personal communication.
4. The Baras homesteaded on land just south of Bronislaw Rebus, where Reg, one of the grandsons, still lives and farms.
5. Documents giving these details are on file in the Provincial Archives, Edmonton.
6. Canadian Pacific Railway Land Sales Ledger Book. Contract #16787 (Glenbow Archives).
7. According to Mrs. Berthiaume's grandson Frank, now 81 and living in Winterburn, they had emigrated from France and, after a brief stay in Montreal, travelled west using ox carts. Frank states that the family at one time had four "homestead" parcels but all their records were burnt in a fire. It was his uncle Fred who sold the NW quarter of 23 to Bronislaw Rebus.

8. CPR exacted no homestead requirements: grantees merely paid $3.00 an acre with interest. But there was a stipulation that no logging could be done on the property until the grantee had paid the above and had thus obtained a clear registrable title in the Land Titles Office.

9. The Certificate of Title #4916 AI, dated October 6, 1911 confirms Bronislaw Rebus to be the Owner of the NW¼, Section 23, Township 50 Range 26. There is also a document that Gordon Hawkins, Land Manager for PanCanadian (rod–man with Imperial at the time of Atlantic No.3) unearthed from that company's files. It confirmed Berthiaume as the original owner and was also dated 1911.

10. Will of Bronislaw Rebus (dated October 20, 1939, Leduc). On Rose's death, Peter was to pay to each child (except Michael, John and Andrew, who were bequeathed $1 each) $500 "without interest and when possible". There is no record of Peter or John, (see #14 below) having paid these sums. So those monies were still owing and these seven children could legally claim an interest in NW quarter of Section 23 by virtue of fact that the terms of the will had not been carried out. This was the basis on which they later successfully claimed a part of the $200,000 bonus paid by Bus Lacey to John Rebus.

11. Court Order dated November 26, 1940 in Leduc. (No document number – Edmonton Land Titles Office.) There is no record of the Administrators having first obtained agreement from other members of the family.

12. Prior to any proposed transfer or assignment, the assent of all bene-ficiaries named in the will who had an interest in the land must have been first obtained.

13. "Articles of Agreement dated the 16th day of November, A.D. 1944, between Peter Rebus as Assignor and Rose Rebus as Assignee the remainder of the interest in the said land was assigned by the said Peter Rebus to the said Rose Rebus."
    (Quoted from the August 16 Settlement Agreement, Edmonton Land Titles Office.)

14. Caveat #5382G.G, Edmonton Land Titles Office, dated March 27, 1947. This instrument recites the assignment of Rose to John, Janu-ary 14, 1945 and appoints W.E. Simpson as John's agent. It also mentions "standing in the name of the Administrators..."

15. These regulations granted rights to all the Crown lands within the permit area. By converting to lease by quarters and drilling, the permittee could earn 100% of the permit area. It is interesting to note that Imperial did not add the "Leduc" discovery township (50–26–W4M) to its then existing Crown permit until July 1946. When new regulations were introduced in the fall of 1947, they triggered conver-sion to lease on discovery of oil and forced surrender of half of the permit land back to the Crown.

16. In a 1985 interview, Jackson stated that he signed a lease with John Rebus on the NW quarter of Section 23 but there is no record of this in the Edmonton Land Titles office. What Jackson might have negoti-ated with John was a lease on his *SW quarter* of 23–50–26, dated

October 8, 1946 and registered by Caveat (4001GG) in the Land Titles office, February 10, 1947.

17. W.F. (Bill) Clark, then a very junior landman with Imperial Oil, now retired from Bow Valley in a senior capacity, recalls that after the Rebus episode, Imperial Oil gave strict orders that any land involving Administrators was to be thoroughly screened to ensure that *all* beneficiaries were contacted to obtain their collective assents prior to any move to lease.

18. NW 21–50–26–W4M. The field office would become headquarters for phone calls and "social" gatherings.
    Also *see* Smith, Philip, The Treasure Seekers, MacMillan 1979, pp 105–6.

19. Instrument #982GI, Land Titles Office, Application for Transmission dated March4, 1947.

20. Certificate #4916AI issued to Bronislaw Rebus, dated December 13, 1911 was now "cancelled" as per stamped notice on the face of the title duly signed by the Registrar, showing transmission to "Michael Rebus et al" as of March 5, 1947.

21. In a telephone conversation July 8, 1986, Simpson, then 92, (oldest practicing lawyer in Alberta), remembered the Rebus affair as "...quite a lot of trouble..." but naturally could not recall details. "...So long ago..." He did remember his first Leduc case: Mike Turta's surface rights claim (successful) at Imperial Leduc No.1 well site.

22. Caveat #5382G.G., Edmonton Land Titles Office dated March 27, 1947.

23. Caveat #1272GI, Edmonton Land Titles Office.

24. "Altamud" was impure bentonite mined near Drumheller but it was not widely accepted because of its grit content which abraded pumps, pipe, etc. Most drilling mud came from Wyoming, e.g. "Wyogel".

25. TIME Magazine, September 22, 1947.

26. Petro–Canada is presently the lessee of the Rebus quarter section.

27. Royalite was at that time a wholly owned subsidiary of Imperial.

28. Document on file in Glenbow Archives.

29. Reserves attributable to the NW¼ of Section 23 ranged from 1.6 million to 1.8 million barrels.
    Stan Slipper, director of Pacific at that time, submitted a very optimistic estimate: 3.2 million barrels. This was discounted by Norm Whittall.
    Using $3.00 a barrel as the going price at that time, Imperial's production payment interest was $300,000 while McMahon's working interest was something in the order of 1.4 million barrels. This would be worth $4.2 million at that time, not discounted.
    McMahon obtained his working interest by paying Rebus $200,000 bonus; this works out to $200,000 divided by $1.4 million equals 15 cents a barrel in the ground. Further details as to reserves and reservoir characteristics are to be found in Chapters 4 and 15, and in the Appendix.

MCMAHON: ENTREPRENEUR

4

"Atlantic made us rich." Ask any Pacific former employees who were there in the early days and they will confirm that statement by Frank McMahon, although few of the hands benefitted financially. Atlantic's uncontrolled production in 1948 gave Frank (and his brother George) the leverage with which to build their empire. The exultation with which Frank must have later added: "Atlantic No.3 is producing through a 40–acre choke" confirms him as a flamboyant entrepreneur, never being hampered by facts. Throughout the crisis, he would turn his back on grubby technical details to work on corporate opportunities. He also ignored threats of lawsuits, and as it turned out, none were launched (though several were seriously considered). One could say the brothers led a charmed life throughout the wild well's career, emerging as millionaires, not only in terms of cash from production revenue but also from the appreciation of their large blocks of Atlantic (and Pacific) stock.

Who was Frank McMahon? A native of Moyie, British Columbia, his first job was as helper on a hard–rock diamond drilling crew in the twenties. McMahon's first contact with hydrocarbons was in the Fraser Delta, working on the holes with his own diamond drilling crew and taking a piece of the action with a promotional company that had been formed to drill for gas.[1] His vision, only a dream in the Delta, was to become a reality years later, 700 miles to the north-east, in the Peace River country. But as a result of his experience in the Delta, Frank realized the importance of leverage in a public incorporation; in effect, the use of other people's money.

In the thirties, Frank turned to the Flathead Valley of southeast British Columbia where tantalizing oil seeps can still be observed. Columbia Oils was the vehicle there but this drilling venture was unsuccessful.

Turner Valley next beckoned, with the down–flank oil discovery of 1936 fresh in everyone's mind. A new company, West Turner Petroleums Limited, the creation of Norman R. Whittall, was incorporated and listed on the Vancouver Stock Exchange. This was the forerunner of Pacific Petroleums. Because of his extravagant spending, Frank was asked to resign from West Turner; it was, shortly afterwards, in 1939, converted to Pacific Petroleums.

During the period in exile from Pacific Petroleums, one of his many ventures was Atlantic Oil Company Limited, incorporated in Alberta on March 1, 1945. This company lay dormant until the summer of 1947, when it applied for public listing. The Board of Directors were:

George L. McMahon, President
Frank M. McMahon, Drilling Contractor and Vice–President
Graham H. Morton, Chartered Accountant
G. Maxwell Bell, Publisher (Calgary Albertan)

The approved prospectus showed assets consisting of half interests in, firstly, two quarter sections east of the Leduc field limits and secondly, six quarters in the Camrose area. There were also two reservations in the Hanna–Wintering Hills area in which interests could only be earned by drilling validating wells.

Total capitalization of the company was 4 million shares, of which 1.1 million were held in escrow for properties. 2 million were offered to the public on July 28, 1947 at 25 cents a share. Ross Maguire, then a very junior salesman with Laurence B. Gibson,[2] recalls the commission as 6¼ cents a share, Atlantic netting 18¾ cents to the treasury. There is no record of how successful the selling campaign was.[3]

The timing of the stock offering to the public couldn't have been better. On the same day, July 28, an option agreement had been signed by Bus Lacey (Atlantic Oil) and John Rebus, offering John $200,000 for "his" quarter section. No doubt Frank spread the word that the Rebus quarter would be brought into the company; the effect of this would be nothing less than startling, since only "window dressing" acreage had been noted in the prospectus. The Rebus lease was signed on August 16.

A contract with General Petroleums was made and drilling commenced. There was no question, as the year drew to a close with two wells completed, that producible, bankable oil reserves underlay the Rebus quarter and that they would lever McMahon back into Pacific Petroleums.

Stan Slipper,[4] consulting geologist, was a close associate of McMahon's, having already been advising him on gas exploration in northeast British Columbia. Slipper estimated crude reserves under the northwest quarter of Section 23 (160 acres): 20,000 barrels per acre or 3.2 million barrels, (twice that which was subsequently determined by the consulting firm Link and Nauss as original recoverable reserves).[5] Slipper's value of $4 million (at $0.80 net per barrel) was discounted by Norm Whittall, a Pacific director, to $2.5 million. The Pacific Board considered the exchange of 2.1 million Atlantic treasury shares for 700,000 shares of Pacific's common stock; this was approved at a directors' meeting on December 19, 1947. Whittall's estimate had the effect of making the Pacific stock worth over $3 per share; it was trading on December 17, 1947 at $0.85 per share. This exchange gave Frank a large block of Pacific stock, a seat on the Pacific Board of Directors and restoration of his position after eight years in exile.

According to newspaper stock transaction records, Atlantic started to trade on January 27, 1948 at $0.32 per share.[6] Pacific was then at about $0.90 per share.

As a result of negotiations between McMahon and the Royal Bank of Canada, Atlantic's production was now assigned, the company holding back $1,000 a month to operate the wells. In addition to this, the Bank extended credit facilities of $150,000 on January 20, 1948; this was increased to $255,000 on April 20.[7] By that time, the Atlantic No. 3 well was completely out of control, but there is no indication that the Bank really understood the gravity of the situation and the possibility that Atlantic could have been sued. One of McMahon's main jobs may have been making the rounds so that everybody would have the right perspective on the Atlantic quarter: "going to make lots of money and the Royal Bank need not worry". This was exemplified in a minor way one day when McMahon tossed his hat into one of the bubbling oil sumps and cried out, "now I've got enough money to buy a new hat"!

Stock market records show no reaction to the March 8 blow-out, Atlantic and Pacific trading in the 33 cents and 91 cents ranges respectively.

On May 11 there was the first hint that something out of the ordinary was taking place; Atlantic traded 9,000 shares at 25 cents.

On May 12, Carl Nickle reported in the Calgary Herald that the Leduc oil field would be shut down completely on Thursday, May 13 so far as normal production operations were concerned. This was the prelude to the take-over by the Conservation Board. The stock traded at 25 cents on May 12 but on the 13th there was a reaction both in the newspapers and on the stock exchange. Atlantic traded as low as 21½ cents but closed at 27½ cents on a total volume of 37,500 shares. Pacific reacted in a similar fashion although it was now trading more in the one to three ratio. It closed at $1.03 from a high of $1.17. Ross Maguire vividly recalls the wild trading of May 13, one of the chief purchasers being George McMahon.[8]

Friday, May 14, market activity indicated the growing realization within the knowledgable oil fraternity that the flow of oil could benefit Atlantic. There were 45,500 shares traded at a high of 31 cents, closing at 29½ cents.

On Monday, May 17, 41,900 shares traded, closing at 32 cents.

A story that went around during those days exemplified the conservatism of the Canadian investor compared to the clever and experienced U.S. risk taker. A phone call was received from Los Angeles inquiring as to what was going on up at Leduc.

Is there a well producing 15,000 barrels of oil a day? Yes.

Is the stock of the company publicly traded? Yes.

What is it trading at? 25.

25 cents or $25?

When the answer came back 25 cents, the U.S. speculator at the other end just said, "buy as much as you can".

Information from National Trust shows that Atlantic Oil sold approximately 48,000 barrels of oil out of the pits; this generated royalty revenue of about $17,000. There is no record of how the oil was handled, but the general recollections are that the oil was pumped directly out of the pits in the northwest extremity of the quarter section into a fleet of oil trucks and taken to the Nisku loading racks.

Through June, July and August, the Atlantic and Pacific stocks gradually crept up; by the 3rd of September, Atlantic was trading at 48 cents while Pacific was $1.40 bid. September 6, the day the well caught fire, was Labour Day and the stock markets were not open. But the next morning, the stock sold off to 39 cents with Pacific selling down to $1.30. [9]

The real turning point in Atlantic's fortunes came when it was ordained by both the Conservation Board and the Attorney General's office that Atlantic would be immune to law-suits. The Atlantic No. 3 Act was passed to legalize this move. Once the fire at No. 3 had been put out, it was calculated how much oil had been produced and Atlantic knew it would get the net proceeds after all costs had been paid by the Board for the directional drilling and other related expenses. Thus the stock traded as high as $1.27 later in 1948. In 1949 it reached $1.40; in 1950, $3.40, and by the time it was rolled into Canadian Atlantic in 1951, the new corporation's stock traded at $7.90.

These stock price advances, by now mainly due to other favourable developments, pyramided the McMahons' personal fortunes. Yet the 1949 statement: "Atlantic made us rich" still held true because it was the wild well's production that placed them firmly in the millionaire class.

ENDNOTES:
1. Marsh gas (methane) is common in the sediments of the Delta due to continuing generation of this gas through the rotting of vegetation. It is not in sufficient volume to constitute a commercial source.
2. Ross Maguire is still actively employed with Nesbitt Thomson Bongard. Laurence B. Gibson was one of several local stock brokers flogging the stock.
3. Neither Alberta Securities Commission nor the Alberta Stock Exchange were able to provide any statistics or any other historical data which would assist in filling in the blanks.
4. S.A. Kerr, "Western Canada's First Petroleum Engineer and Wild Well Fighter", *Journal of Canadian Petroleum Technology,* 23, 2 (March–April, 1984): p. 25–26
5. This information was determined by Link and Nauss Consultants in their Report of 1951, attached to a "Canadian Atlantic" Prospectus filing for the Securities Exchange Commission.
6. The Alberta Securities Commission stated that delays between vending and start of trade may be as long as four months.
7. MacKenzie, R.W., retired Royal Bank officer, personal communication.
8. Quotation from the press: "Closing down of the Leduc oil fields (sic) near Edmonton because of a wild well reacted on western oils today with issues showing substantial losses at the opening but these firmed slightly in later trading...Oil stocks had their biggest day since last August as 237,000 shares changed hands. Sensational reports from Leduc unsteadied the market. A number of issues recorded losses...Recoveries were general and the market closed with a firm tone. Atlantic had the biggest fluctuation, a new low of 21 cents was reached shortly after the market opened. The close at 27½ cents was 3½ cents better than Wednesday's close."
9. Quotation from the press:
"Atlantic Stock Drops After Fire
The fire at Atlantic No.3 had a depressing effect on that stock traded this morning. Atlantic dropped from 47 to 49 cents down to a low of 33 cents in early trading today but regained some strength and just before noon was trading at 39 cents. Pacific Pete, which controls Atlantic, sold down from $1.40 to as low as $1.20 but came back to $1.30 later in the morning.
Imperial Oil was not affected and was selling at $17.75. This is a gain of two points in the last week. Prospects of a new oilfield at Redwater, 30 miles northeast of Edmonton, caused the boost in this stock."

THE DRILLING CONTRACT AND CONTRACTOR

5

Although Frank McMahon was preoccupied with other concerns,[1] he knew that the Rebus quarter was his trump card. This practically proven source of future revenue would provide badly needed cash to ease collateral requirements for his northeast British Columbia project. More importantly, McMahon hoped to use these wells as leverage to trade Atlantic stock for Pacific.

He then went looking for a drilling rig.

There are no details as to who McMahon contacted but he must have canvassed most of the contractors. All available "power" (internal combustion) rigs were under contract.[2] Ralph Will,[3] head of Drilling Contractors, does not recall having been approached but he hinted very broadly that McMahon would probably not have contacted him because of a failed transaction which angered Frank. In a similar fashion, Gene Denton,[4] one of the principals of General Petroleums is said to have had no time for McMahon because of previous problems in the "Valley". Nevertheless, Frank was able to cut a deal with G.P., probably because the lease appeared to be proven and the drilling contractor stood a good chance of being paid. Clause 21 of the Contract (see below) provided protection for G.P. It was to be a marriage of convenience with ramifications that would reach out beyond either party's imaginings (or nightmares!).

Steam had been "king" in Turner Valley both because of its extreme flexibility in delivering smooth power and its very low operating costs: water was piped to the rig and natural gas (virtually free) from adjoining wells to fire the boilers. The steam rigs were only partly out of their element in Leduc. Sammy Hector had developed a water supply system similar to his Turner Valley set-up and Imperial had proved up gas in the Viking[5] at Leduc. Although no one could have known it beforehand, steam power became absolutely indispensible when the Atlantic No. 3 rig, with its own boilers shut down, was able to struggle along with steam piped over from nearby Imperial No. 48, which was also being drilled by a steam rig.

It is now time to take a closer look at the men behind General Petroleums. The drilling company was formed in 1941, with Cody Spencer as General Manager and Gene Denton as Managing Director. Three prominent Calgary business men were directors: Ralph Smith (lawyer), Harry Howard (chartered accountant) and

A Rotary Rig

1.	Crown block	8.	Hoist or draw
2.	Traveling block		works.
3.	Hook	9.	Pumps
4.	Swivel	10.	Boilers
5.	Mud hose	11.	Pipe rack
6.	Kelly	12.	Drill pipe
7.	Rotary table		

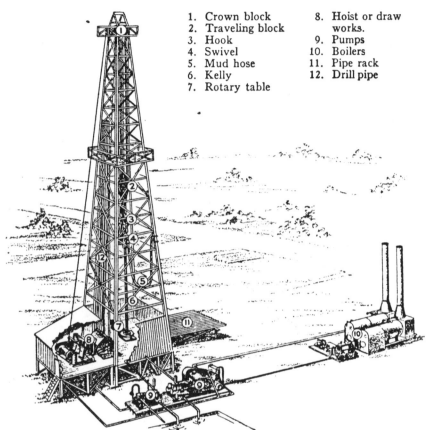

A Rotary Drilling Rig in 1948. Rotary drilling bores a hole by rotating a bit on the end of a string of pipe, called drill pipe, some of which is shown standing in the derrick ready to be "run in" the hole. The draw works at the left is the mechanism that runs most of the job. The pumps in the foreground force mud down through the drill pipe and back up between the drill pipe and the wall of the hole, flushing out the cuttings and plastering the wall of the hole so that it will not cave.

Illustration courtesy This Fascinating Oil Business, Max W. Ball; Bobbs–Merrill.

Colonel Shouldice. The firm started off with a truck mounted power rig which was gradually augmented by purchase and lease of additional equipment. In addition to Rig No. 10 and some power units, General Petroleums had several steam rigs which had been acquired in the Valley. Two of these (Rigs No. 4 and No. 19) were to be called upon to perform the most important and most lucrative tasks of their careers.

H.E. Denton was a petroleum engineer by profession and had worked in Wyoming. He was brought up to Canada by Ralph Will in 1938 and employed by Anglo Canadian.

Cody Ralph Spencer, the drilling expert, was born in Nabisco, Oklahoma in 1909. He started off roughnecking at a very early age and actually came to Turner Valley in 1929 as a member of the Noble–Olson drilling crew. He returned to the U.S., where he ultimately went to work with Ralph Will and the Rocky Mountain Drilling Company in Wyoming and Montana.

Cody R. Spencer
Photo furnished by Westburne

Will had been offered the job of heading up Anglo Canadian Drilling Company in 1937 by Phil Byrne, President. After he was there a year, Cody phoned Ralph to see what opportunities there were in Canada. The boom following the oil "discovery" on the west flank of Turner Valley in 1936 was still in full swing. Ralph knew Cody as an "honest and hard worker", so Byrne gave Will the O.K. to hire him as tool push.

Spencer was a product of the times, tough, demanding and with a mania for speed. He stretched his men and equipment to the limit, the latter, on one occasion, literally. Harry MacMillan, retired in Devon, recalls when he was drilling for Cody on a well in Turner Valley. They had just acquired a new string of drill pipe which got stuck in the hole. Cody was determined to free it and ultimately did after "reefing" on it with eight lines and 100 tons on the weight indicator.[6]

When the pipe was pulled out, a new bit was put on and Harry ran back in the hole. When he got to bottom, there were still two singles which had to be laid down.[7] Cody drove up and told Harry, "You're not on bottom". Harry assured him he was and put weight on the bit to prove it. Cody had stretched the new string 60 ft. in his efforts to free it!

His untimely death, December 27, 1962[8] has not dimmed memories of those who worked closely with him. At the time of writing, Cody would have been 78; he would have been able to help greatly in answering questions for which there are now no easy answers. Despite the passage of time, controversial items still emerge and it would be less than honest not to paint him as he would probaby wish (to quote Cromwell: "Warts and all"). He had his detractors (who hasn't?). It was in his nature to be feisty, impatient and demanding, these characteristics helping shape some of the key events to come.

Jimmy Irwin, retired senior executive of General Petroleums (and Westburne) was one of his devoted hands:

> One of the most remarkable men I ever met in my life...He used to work at different times on two rigs...He'd work a shift on this rig and a shift on that rig...He had one speed and that was high...He was a perfectionist...If someone did something, Cody could do it better...Cody would show up at any rig at two in the morning...He was a great man to travel...He'd get you to drive the car and he would be asleep in two minutes and you would drive half the day and night and when we got to where we were going, he was up and ready to go...He would never ask anyone to do anything that he wouldn't do himself.[9]

This was one of the reasons Cody would often try to accomplish the impossible, and, with this trait, he would sometimes make matters worse. Johnny Yeo, retired chief mechanic for G.P., also a Spencer fan, quotes one of Cody's mottos: "Hurry up, every chance you get".[10]

It took the Leduc boom to really put General Petroleums on its feet, but in the fall of 1947, the firm was still in shaky financial condition. This was due to the latest in a series of difficulties that resulted from a disastrous drilling program in 1945 and 1946 at Cat

Photo taken in G.P.'s Leduc Office, 1949. Back row, left to right: Sandy Stewart, mechanic; Joe Lapichinsky, office clerk; Chris Hartry, driver; Jim Irwin, drilling superintendent; Bill McKellar, lease foreman; Hugh Baker, Joseph Lake production; Slim Swan, "push"; Dave Jeffrey, transport. Front row: Bill Cummer, office manager, G.A. (Al) Wright, field superintendent; Frank Flewelling, drilling superintendent; Johnny Yeo, chief mechanic.

Photo furnished by Westburne.

Creek, Montana. This play was supposed to have been a "lead pipe cinch", but five dry holes later, and the fact that G.P. had taken a participating interest, put the firm only one or two jumps ahead of its creditors. Jack Moore, then journeyman welder, recalled Cody warning him one Friday to cash his cheque that day for re–tubing boilers, rather than wait for Monday.

Turning now to the "contract" (Drilling Agreement) between G.P. as "Contractor" and Atlantic as "Owner", it was carefully thought out. Clause 5 stated: "The contractor shall supply and use adequate and efficient blow–out prevention equipment". G.P. had been using the Hosmer button, a device which had been popular among many contractors but which had definite limitations.[11] In the light of what happened, did the Hosmer meet the terms of Clause 5?

Clause No. 25 was also to be the subject of prolonged scrutiny, interpretation and legal skirmishing: "The contractor shall insure the said rig against *loss by fire* and shall also carry public liability and property damage insurance".

Gene Denton, perhaps with misgivings about McMahon, but more to protect his company's position, realized there was no provision for lost circulation. He wrote an amending letter to Atlantic on September 19 with a key clause (2) inserted: "Day work to be paid to the Contractor after 72 hours of lost circulation". Clause 14 in the main contract spelled out very clearly the "Owner's" (Atlantic's) responsibility for operations after that period of time had elapsed. Despite the wording, it was to become the focus for intense dispute as to ultimate responsibility.[12] There is no correspondence indicating that McMahon/Atlantic objected to either the "Drilling Agreement" (Contract) drawn up by Porter, Allen and Millard (now Mackimmie, Matthews) of the amending letter, coun ter-signed by Frank and George McMahon.

When the G.P. rig at BA Pyrcz[13] was released, it was moved over to lsd 13 Section 23 to drill Atlantic No. 1.[14] [15] Application for Licence to Drill had been signed by the Minister.[16]

A conventional steel derrick was erected by Hislop Rig Builders, with the Kerber brothers as human flies who bolted it together girt by girt. The well and subsequent Atlantic Oil Company holes were to be under the supervision of Denton and Spencer, a consulting engineering firm.

Denton and Spencer was created in 1945 with both Spencer and Denton as directors. What was to become a matter of great controversy was whether the consulting firm acted at arm's length from the drilling contractor. The two directors stated they were "inactive", a point which also became a matter of some debate as conditions deteriorated at Atlantic No. 3.

The man heading up the consulting firm was J.F. (Spi) Langston. A Calgary native, "Spi" had graduated from the University of Alberta in 1936 (Civil Engineering, with Distinction). After a brief stint with a geophysical crew, he went to work for Lane Wells Company. Langston was rapidly introduced to the art of well surveying, experience which stood him in good stead. When Lane Wells folded their tents in Canada in 1941 (they returned in 1950), Langston contacted Gene Denton, who took him on at G.P., which was just getting started. His engineering work was interspersed with drilling and tool pushing for G.P. He also supervised well completions, acidizing and production. Spi became Managing Director in 1945 upon the formal creation of the firm. In 1947, Denton and Spencer became involved in diamond coring through the efforts of Spi. It can be said that he was a pioneer in this endeavour.[17]

Atlantic contracted with Denton and Spencer to locate well sites, run surface casing, core, drill stem test and, finally, run the production casing string. The well would then be kicked off and put on production through facilities which had been engineered by the firm.

Atlantic Oils at that time had a very small staff. One of those involved in Leduc was Lyle Caspell, who seems to have had an undefined role at best. Lyle had grown up in Turner Valley and had worked for the McMahon interests for some years prior on production work. His signed, undated report and two unsolicited letters give him much credit.

Unlike present day practices, where operating companies routinely assign a company or consultant drilling engineer to each well, the responsibility for all day to day operations other than drilling appears to have devolved on Denton and Spencer. Caspell's was not the job of company representative because few can recall seeing him on the site.

At Atlantic No. 1, in lsd 13 Section 23, 278 ft. of surface casing were set, the well having been spudded on October 2. The well was then drilled without incident. The D-2 was diamond cored and found to be non-porous. As was the habit in those days, the well was completed in the D-3 "barefoot".[18] It was put on production early in November with an initial potential of 2,900 barrels a day.

It is instructive to note what Denton and Spencer said in their report on Atlantic No.1 under the heading "Acknowledgements":

> Central Leduc Oils (Pyrcz lease) made available a complete separator hook-up which facilitated the completion of the well and saved considerable expense while awaiting the fabrication of a new unit (and Don Whitney came with it).
>
> Leduc Consolidated (lessees of the parcel offsetting to the east) made available a casing head, string of tubing, tanks, line pipe which could not otherwise be obtained. (This firm later tried to sue Atlantic.)
>
> Imperial Oil loaned their swabbing equipment for the completion of the well.
>
> Mr. Aubrey Kerr, Chief Geologist for Imperial Oil, made available his experience and advice regarding the value of the zones cored and the proper position to locate the casing shoe. The drilling contractor, General Petroleum Limited, through their Superintendent, Mr. G.A. Wright, and toolpusher W.Murray, performed all operations in a workmanlike mannner.

Mr. F. McMahon and Mr. B. Lacey(!) were available at all times either in person or by telephone for advice regarding production equipment and procedures...[19] There is no mention of Lyle Caspell being involved.

Lyle Caspell, Frank McMahon and J.F. (Spi) Langston at Atlantic No.1, November 1947.

Photo furnished by Howard Blanchard.

Langston's "Conclusions and Recommendations", (page 30 of the same report) point up his care and concern for good engineering practices. He elaborates on the flush production which occurred on November 14, the well producing about 120 barrels an hour with back pressure on the tubing of about 300 psi and separator pressure 105 psi. He suggested that rates of flow should be restricted to 150 barrels per day.

...Every effort should be made to produce the well at the maximum rate in line with good practice, bearing in mind that an error on the low side would have no ill effect but that an error on the high side might greatly decrease the value of the property and lower the ultimate recovery during its economic life.

Drilling operations then moved over to No. 2 well site, a quarter of a mile east of No. 1, in lsd 14 Section 23. It was spudded on

November 27 and only 279 ft. of surface pipe were run. Trouble occurred by loss of circulation in the D–3; it was successfully overcome. Langston recalls that he warned Atlantic of the seriousness of this but no special notice appears to have been taken. The well was ultimately cased on December 29 and was placed on production January 9, 1948 with about the same potential as No. 1.

In this history, two or three chroniclers stand out. One of them is Cal Bohme, a native of Vermilion, now senior engineer with Norwest, a Calgary based consulting firm. Earlier, in the summer of 1944 at the age of 16, he had toiled in the local dairy for $33 a month. His next job was better: washing dishes in the Chinese cafe because it paid $12.50 a week for only eight hours a day. When Cal found out that roughnecking paid $6 a day (a phenomenal amount of money!), he started at Borradaile, near Vermilion, with G.P., on very heavy oil. This area was booming because the crude, owned by the CNR, could be burnt directly under the boilers of their locomotives, thus reducing the need for imported supplies.

> ...We would work on the service rigs there, pulling tubing, bailing, and we'd be covered with that black heavy tarry oil from head to toe...but at the end of the day they would give us a wash cloth and a bucket of gasoline and you'd just start washing yourself down from head to toe to get that gooey old oil off. [20]

Cal's first exposure to a "wild well" was at Marwayne. "We encountered a tremendous flow of water at fairly shallow depths and flooded the rig out, pretty near upset it..." [21] It was a G.P. unit with a Hosmer; that tool turned out to be of no use there.

Cal arrived in Leduc in the fall of 1947 and started at Atlantic No.2. By now his G.P. wages were $8 a day less $1.50 a day for board and room in the company camp.

When the weather turned cold, it was necessary to blow out, with natural gas, the water lines which supplied the boilers, so there would be no freezing in the lines. The water supply came from Hector's system which had a sump over in the north west corner of the lease, (later to be taken over by oil). On one occasion, gas got into the boiler house by mistake.

> There was myself and Howard Blanchard [22] inside of one of three boilers that provided steam for the rig and we were cleaning it out with a water hose and scraper rods...I can remember the whole roof blowing off...and the terrible concussion inside the boiler and...Howard stuck his head out first and said, 'There's fire all over. Let's get the

hell out of here' and he went out. The good thing about it, it was a very flimsy structure. It just blew all the tin sides out of the boiler house so we managed to get out of there without any serious injury.[23]

Following the completion of No. 2, the next location was lsd 12 Section 23, the south offset to No. 1. The Kerber brothers recall having skidded the rig over during daylight hours, thus cutting down on rig–up time. After No. 3, the east offset to it, No. 4 was to be drilled, thus providing four producers on the quarter section. But fate now played a hand in the affairs of not only General Petroleums, Denton and Spencer and Atlantic, but also Imperial Oil, the Board and the Rebus family, the mineral and surface owners of the northwest quarter of Section 23.

ENDNOTES:
1. His major plans included the development and transmission of natural gas in northeast British Columbia, and repossession of control of Pacific Petroleums. He had been ousted from that firm in 1939 and had spent the interim "in exile".
2. Few power rigs were in use when Leduc was discovered but those that were, were mostly of the light capacity, semi–portable type, good for about 6000 ft. with $3\frac{1}{2}$ in. drill pipe. Foothills drilling (always deep, using $5\frac{1}{2}$ in. drill pipe) still required steam. Power rigs took òver in the early fifties with innovative designs and increased depth capacities.
3. Will, "Dean of Drillers", retired in Calgary after many years "turning to the right". Interviews November 22, 1985, May 30, 1986.
4. Gene Denton was described by Bill Cummer, then G.P.'s Leduc office manager as "the genius of it all". Unwell in 1948, his premature demise in 1949 left the company "as never being the same after".
5. The Viking sand in the area had proved to be gas productive and Imperial drilled No.10 in Sec. 26–50–26–W4M to tap that zone. General Petroleums used their Cardwell truck rig brought from Lloyd-minister. This well was intended to furnish the needs of the infant community of Devon; later it was also able to supply fuel for G.P.'s rig.
6. "Reefing" – the act of pulling on stuck drill pipe (or anything else in the oil patch).
   Martin–Decker – the trade name for a weight indicator, a clock–like device that shows weight on bit when drilling, obtained by subtracting the desired pressure on the bit from the total weight of the drill pipe. It shows the safe limits one can "reef" on the drill pipe.
7. Most rigs pulled triples made up of three 30 ft. joints of drill pipe.
8. Spencer had gone ranching after his disposal of his company hold-ings to Westburne. He was driving his truck with a load of feed, on top

of which was his saddle. Near Claresholm he checked to see if the saddle was still attached and the truck, still in motion, tipped over on him.

9. Excerpts from a 1984 taped interview on file at Glenbow Archives.
10. Interview February 1986, on file at Glenbow Archives.
11. See chapter on BOP's and Casing.
12. CLAUSE 14: ...FOR the purpose hereof, during such time as the "Day Work Rate" is in effect, the Contractor shall furnish, at its expense, the complete drilling rig and equipment as is presently being used, labor, drilling supervision, fuel and repairs and replacements to its own rig and equipment, and the Owner shall furnish, at its expense, all bits, core bits, water, mud, testing and electrolog equipment and materials other than those aforesaid agreed to be supplied by the Contractor, and all operations during such time shall be at the sole risk and responsibility of the Owner, and the Owner shall be responsible for and indemnify the Contractor against all loss or damage to the well, rig or equipment arising out of or in connection with such operations.
13. In lsd. 12–25–50–26, one mile northeast of the Atlantic quarter; spudded June 3; abandoned September 19, after penetrating hundreds of feet of green shale, just missing the east edge of the D–3 reef.
14. The following press release was premature. There is no explanation for Snyder and Head other than McMahon was anxious to get the lease drilled. It is believed that that firm had already disposed of its rigs.
    "ATLANTIC ANNOUNCES LEDUC LEASE
    Sept. 3/47. Calgary Herald. Atlantic Oils, new company in the Leduc field announced this morning acquisition of a quarter section in the Leduc field. Atlantic officials said the company had bought the lease outright, including Imperial's interest in it.
    The officials said they considered the quarter embraced four proven locations, that the sites already had been surveyed, that Snyder and Head would do the drilling, that equipment was moving in."
15. This clipping in the *Western (Oil) Examiner,* September 6, 1947 (one year to the day No.3 would catch fire!) was also premature.
    "ATLANTIC SPUDS ON VALUABLE LEASE AT LEDUC
    News was released this week that Atlantic Oils, a recent incorporation, had obtained a choice quarter section in Leduc field, the NW ¼, sec. 23–50–26w4. The holding is as near proven as possible.
    Freehold rights are said to have cost the new company $280,000 and in addition, Imperial oil rights in the lease were obtained."
16. Letter dated January 23, 1948 to the Petroleum and Natural Gas Conservation Board from H.H. Somerville, Superintendent of Mining Lands: "Atlantic Oil Company Limited has sufficient funds on deposit with the Department to cover the drilling deposit of $2,500.00."
17. S.A. Kerr, "Diamonds in the Oil Patch", *Journal of Canadian Petroleum Technology, 19, 2, (April–June 1980) p. 16, 18.*

18. The casing shoe is hung above total depth, leaving a portion of the pay section uncased. This eliminates perforating and cuts down on need for acidizing.
19. J.F. (Spi) Langston, "Report on the Drilling, Coring and Completion of Atlantic #1 Well", (November, 1947), Unpublished. On file at the Glenbow Archives.
20. Taped interview by H.S. Simpson, 1986, on file at Glenbow Archives.
21. Ibid.
22. Retired roughneck who confirmed this story in a personal communication.
23. Taped interview by H.S. Simpson, 1986, on file at Glenbow Archives.

WELL CONTROL 6

A procedure which could have reduced (but not eliminated) the danger at Atlantic No.3 would have been the installation of an adequate system of blow–out control (BOP)[1] with appropriate bleed–offs. Nothing could have prevented charging of the shallow near surface sands with oil and gas during the blow–out, since the surface casing had not been set deep enough to cover these porous glacial beds. Cretaceous sands down to around 2,000 ft. also became charged during that time.

But, in those days, the Conservation Board had no BOP requirements and the drilling contractors installed them only if or when they feared losing their holes.

The composite catalogues[2] of the twenties advertised many devices, because blow–out prevention was a concern in certain areas of the U.S. A 1929 ad (illustrated) dramatizes the vaunted(?) superiority of the Hosmer... ...''split seconds''...''swift-est''...designed for Santa Fe Springs, California. The Hosmer appears to have been developed by a small firm, then licensed out to various tool companies: Baash–Ross, McEvoy and Houston Oil Field Manufacturing Co. (HOMCO). It was well known and one of its users was General Petroleums.

Blow–out prevention and surface/intermediate casing pro-grams are interdependent. The following discussion is in this con-text.

The earliest wells were drilled with cable tools; the holes were virtually empty. One ''string'' of casing after another had to be run in every time a ''vein'' of water (or gas, or oil even) was encountered or when the hole was caving. So one started off with 20 in. casing and could end up with 6 in. This resulted in as many as five ''strings'' run inside each other, each succeeding one extending from surface to a greater depth. Blow–out problems were usually automatically solved.

Royalite No. 4 wet gas discovery of 1924 in Turner Valley[3] became a notorious exception when it blew out from the Mississip-pian limestone reservoir and caught fire.

With the advent of rotary drilling in the late twenties, holes in Turner Valley were started with cable tools and finished by rotary. The upper part of the hole was adequately cased and rotary rigs drilled faster with the hole full of mud. The resultant hydrostatic

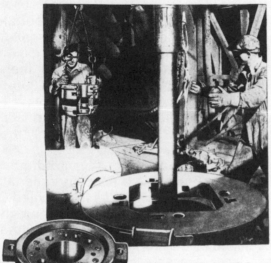

Advertisement in Petroleum World, February, 1929.
Photo furnished by Mr. Vestal, Long Beach Collection/Long Beach Public Library.

head usually prevented any loss of control and blow–out preventers were not necessarily installed. Rigs were set up with little room between the derrick floor and the ground. Shallow cellars were dug to allow for the casing bowl and mud flow line, but little else and certainly no clearance for an elaborate BOP. The Hosmer took up very little vertical room above the casing bowl.

Gordon Webster, engineer for Home Oil in the Valley and now retired from that company, categorically stated that blow–out pre–venters were not used in Turner Valley. On one occasion he wished to install one and Ralph Will, then Contractor for Home, was dead against it. Will recently confirmed that there were no requirements for them.

At least 500 ft. of surface casing were run in the Valley, in some cases 1,000 ft. for certain Royalite wells. In readiness for drilling ahead with rotary tools, a hole would be cut in the 13½ in. surface casing for flow line attachment. When completing, a 7 in. long string would be picked up with the elevators and the bushings would be pulled, with the 13½ in. cut off to take the 7 in. with slips and the casing head.

Garnet Edwards, retired drilling superintendent, also says that there were no BOP requirements in Turner Valley and surface casing was run only after the surface hole had gotten down into firm bedrock.

Despite the fact that faulted and folded beds had to be pene–trated on the way to the Mississippian "pay", drilling there was fairly predictable; there were no horizons such as thief sands or high pressure zones that would cause any problems. So the 500 ft. of surface casing, according to another source, was an industry choice. Furthermore, consolidated bedrock was almost always reached by 500 ft. Drilling became routine to the point where a contractor would "turn–key", delivering a hole, cased to the Mis–sissippian, ready to be put on production. Barefoot completions were the norm (perforating guns being uncommon). A technique which utilized some acid plus a compressor improved "kickoffs" of wells.

The Princess blow–out, northeast of Brooks, in 1940 was a warning that problems could exist on the plains. Nevertheless, most wildcats used only 150 ft. of surface pipe. When at Imperial Grassy Lake No. 3 in 1945, a "basement" test (total depth 6,400 ft.), the author posed the question concerning blow–out prevention to Art Branscombe, Royalite drilling engineer. He said there was no BOP on the wildcat. This seemed to represent the attitude of industry that there was very little in the way of potential pay zones, let alone high pressures, in the deeper horizons east of the Foothills.

Imperial Leduc No. 1 (the D–2 discovery well), at first glance, suggests a change of philosophy because 497 ft. of 13⅜ in. surface pipe were run; but the reason for this seems to be that it was scheduled to be a 7,000 ft. Silurian salt test.

It still sends shivers down the author's spine to be reminded that at Imperial Leduc No. 2, only 248 ft. of 8⅝ in. surface casing, set with 70 sacks of cement was run, because, unlike No. 1, it was only meant to go to the Lower Cretaceous. The hole was said to be still in glacial drift at surface casing depth. This well was drilled with a Franks portable power rig using 3½ in. drill pipe. It is possible that a longer string of surface pipe, or larger diameter drill pipe could not have been handled by that light portable mast.

After No. 1 found D–2 oil, it was felt safe to alter the drilling program at No. 2 to deepen to the D–2 with the above surface pipe. When the D–2 proved to be non–porous, drilling was continued into a brand new zone: the D–3. Had the D–3 there been anywhere near as permeable as at Atlantic No. 3, disaster would have struck immediately! The short surface pipe and the relatively small pumps would have been no match for the D–3 in its wilder moments. Then, tempting fate still further, a full hole packer was run to drill stem test the D–3. Just think of the swabbing action of that packer as it was being pulled up a 5,300 ft. 7⅜ in. hole past the Viking zone! The author cannot recall whether there was any blow–out prevention equipment installed at that well.

Garnet Edwards cites the Imperial Leduc No. 10 Viking gas well as having been drilled with a truck–mounted rig with no BOP. This ties into the generally accepted practice in the Vermilion–Lloydminster area, where no surface casing was set; the conductor pipe being used to handle the mud returns.

Gordon Webster knows of no blow–out prevention requirement in Leduc, although he recalled if people installed a Hosmer as a BOP they were "going all out". He maintains that 300 ft. of surface pipe at Leduc was the "best practice in those days".

Garnet Edwards says that 300 ft. wasn't enough for his Leduc Consolidated holes. He also knows of no regulations regarding surface casing or for BOP's. Bill Maughan had instructed Edwards to install a single Shaffer BOP which they had bought from Newell and Chandler. Its rams were actuated by a wheel. It lay rusting on the derrick floor until they had that Viking gas blow–out during a drill stem test of the D–2. It was only then that the BOP was installed, but this took some doing because it was plugged up with cement and hadn't been used for years.

In 1947 the Board had moved Nate Goodman to Leduc to oversee engineering operations. He was also quite conversant with blow–outs, having parked his car by the Leduc Consolidated well (half a mile east of Atlantic No. 3) and getting it covered with mud.

Still unaware of the dangerous potential for blow–outs in Leduc, but thinking ahead, Messrs. Alex Bailey and D.P. Goodall of the Conservation Board, in May 1947, reviewed with industry the question of surface casing. They did not consider blow–out pre- venters in their deliberations. It was not until 1949 that the Board formulated such regulations. Two suggestions (not orders) resulted: a minimum of 250 ft. of surface pipe was to be used, and production casing was to be cemented up past the Viking zone.

Up to the time of Atlantic No. 3, the average surface casing was 300 ft. so Atlantic Nos. 1, 2 and 3 were not out of the ordinary in their programs. The Globe Leduc West holes to the north were being drilled using a Reagan "bag" which could be inflated around the drill pipe for blow–out control, if necessary. The Board's Schedule of Wells shows that, shortly after Atlantic No. 3 got out of control in March 1948, all D–3 development wells drilled by Imperial Oil began setting up to 600 ft. of surface pipe, a prompt reaction by Visser and Moroney. Imperial was also in the forefront in buying its own Hydril[4] BOP's, which were installed on its wells. Home, Globe Leduc West and other operators continued to set 300 ft., as did Imperial on its D–2 holes.

With the growing spectre of Atlantic No. 3 preoccupying their minds, the Board convened a meeting April 26, 1948 at which Leduc operators expressed their opinions. J.F. (Spi) Langston acted as secretary. Surface and production casing, plus lost circulation material were discussed, but there was no recorded discussion on BOPs. The Board's attitude seemed to be "laissez–faire", the operators having their choice as to whether to run the 250 ft. minimum requirement or more.

Perhaps we can take Frank Manyluk's[5] word that the Board made no move to "lay down the law" after Atlantic No. 3. One may state with fair certainty that the industry regulated itself.

In the course of research for this history, the following com- ments on the Hosmer were gleaned:

G.A. (Al) Wright, field superintendent for G.P., now retired after a long career as one of the top hands in the industry, defended the Hosmer (for use in conditions less severe than Leduc D–3?) "The trick was to seat and latch the button into place..."

As Tip Moroney described it:

> ...a very simple type control gadget which consists
> of a bowl with a locking device...a packing element which

is hinged and you just slapped that around the drill pipe. It has a trigger lock or latch which you close. Then you lower the pipe into hole until the first tool joint pulls the packer down into the bowl and it packs off.

Hughie Leiper:

...it certainly served a purpose, the problem being trying to get the button in place to start with because it had to be properly centred...the hole[6] was a little crooked and of course the drill pipe was hanging to one side of the table so even on a trial run, you had to...centre it properly in the table in order to get it in and you fitted it under the upset of the drill pipe and of course you can imagine when the well blew, blowing thousands of barrels a day through that table, there was no way in the world to get the button in...

Howard Blanchard, one of the roughnecks on Atlantic No. 3 put it very succinctly: "try to put a Hosmer button into an open hole blow and you will find it likes coming back and saying hello!... What a bugger they were."

Last but not least, Lyle Caspell:

Great concern was felt by Caspell and Matthews[7] in the use of the Hausmer (sic) button instead of the conventional hydraulic blow-out preventer. The Hausmer button has a very limited use, it's a monster piece of equipment and the inventor should be drowned in mud. The split circular hinged slips fit around the drill pipe with no ability to rotate in the set position.[8]

Lou McCullough and Paul Bowlen, having considerable drilling experience, were consulted after the March 8 blow-out:

Hosmer efficient if sufficient warning is given to permit raising of drill pipe. A modern valve-type hydraulic preventer should have been installed so as to operate it inside or outside the derrick.

In summary, whether or not the Hosmer provided "adequate and efficient" prevention as specified in the Drilling Contract was a moot point. There certainly wouldn't be any argument as to its inability to qualify by today's drilling technology.

ENDNOTES:

1. Any device that "packs off" (seals off) the hole and prevents formation contents from escaping (i.e., blowing out).
2. The oilman's bible, containing everything pertaining to drilling and production, published annually.
3. S.A. Kerr, "Royalite No.4, Diamond Jubilee", *Journal of Canadian Petroleum Technology,* 23, 5, (September–October 1984), p. 17, 18, 20. Royalite was a wholly–owned subsidiary of Imperial Oil Ltd. until 1948.
4. A BOP having hydraulically actuated rather than wheel operated rams.
5. Conservation Board staff engineer later appointed as Member, since retired.
6. At Atlantic No. 3.
7. Clarence Matthews (deceased), engineer with Denton and Spencer at the time of Atlantic No. 3. He played a controversial role in the decision to "drill dry".
8. Lyle Caspell, Leduc Oil Field. On–hand story of the rogue well Atlantic #3; undated signed report.

THE DRILLING OF ATLANTIC NO. 3

7

Atlantic No. 3 was dogged from the very beginning. The well was spudded January 21, 1948; 300 ft. of 15 in. hole drilled and 10¾ in. casing run to 296 ft. This was insufficient surface casing for the location because at total depth, the hole was still in unconsolidated sands and glacial material. There is some question of an adequate cement job; only 150 sacks were used. Additional cement (7 sacks) was batched in to fill the annulus on January 23. There must have been enough cement to bond otherwise the wild well should have hydraulicked the casing out of the hole later on.

Atlantic's (G.P.'s) boilers were fired with Viking gas, augmented at times by solution gas from the Atlantic tank farm. Nevertheless, drilling was slowed by periodic shortages. When the D–2 was reached, coring and testing revealed non–porous dolomite. It was thirty–four days from move–in to reaching the D–3 on February 18.

A Schlumberger electric log was run at 5,267 ft., just into the D–3. This was to provide a valuable guide later on. The SP and Normal curves indicated the presence of gas in the Viking sand (there were no sonic or radio–activity logs in those days!). As "Tip" Moroney was to reflect many years later: "We may not have had a blow–out if the Viking had not been gas–bearing".[1] The D–2, being non–porous, was not a factor in later operations.

To give a proper perspective of the D–3 reservoir at Atlantic No. 3, it was encountered at –2,909 ft. subsea[2] (5,265 ft. drilled depth), some 71 ft. above the known gas/oil interface of –2,980 ft. (5,336 ft., drilled depth). The program called for drilling to 5,354 ft. and a long string to be hung at 5,349 ft. (–2,995 ft. subsea). This would leave 5 ft. of open hole "barefoot", which would be in the middle of the oil zone. Successful completions at Atlantic No. 1 and 2 had used that technique to eliminate perforating and cut down on acidizing costs. The oil/water interface was at –3,018 ft. subsea (5,376 ft., below surface) but no hole would normally be drilled that deep.

Drilling had only just resumed after logging when the mud level in the hole dropped out of sight, despite the use of gel–flake, sawdust and oats. The D–3 was showing signs this would be no ordinary "lost circulation situation". Other D–3 holes in the Leduc field had been trouble makers (even Atlantic No. 2) but circulation

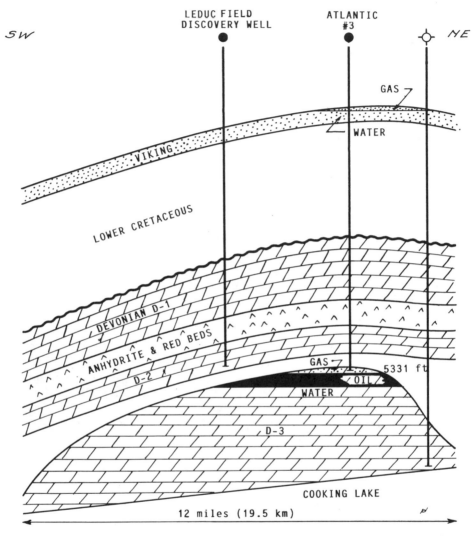

Diagrammatic southwest to northeast cross section across Leduc Oil Field. Lithology patterns continued through zones: Viking Sandstone, D1 Dolomite, D2 Dolomite, D3 Dolomite.

Drawing by P.A. Dykstra

had been restored in a matter of hours. Home–Leduc No. 1 had a gas blow–out but Ralph Will killed it and ran 7 in. production casing "right now". This meant he also had to run a 5½ in. liner and cement it at the desired completion depth. This procedure would have been Atlantic No. 3's safe alternative.

The risky path lay in trying to maintain circulation and "make a run for it", with the hope that the remainder of the D–3 section would not be so porous and circulation could be maintained to casing point.

As noted in Chapter 5, the contract stated that "lost circulation was Owner's (Atlantic/McMahon's) responsibility after 72 hours".[3] Bill Warnick, G.P.'s mud man, recalls Cody Spencer re-assuring him: "Don't worry about it, we'll be on day work in the morning." Had Frank McMahon, as Owner, wanted to be absolutely sure of a satisfactory completion, he could have ordered Spencer to run the long string then and run a liner at total depth, in spite of the extra cost of the liner and the cement job.

Did Spencer warn McMahon of the danger? Did McMahon insist on Spencer trying to make a run for it so as to avoid the cost of the liner? Spencer was certainly enough of a gambler and he may have lulled Frank into a false sense of security.

The decision reached was to try to re-establish circulation and make hole. Partial circulation was restored with sawdust, oats, gel-flake and several cement plugs but no hole was made because full circulation could not be maintained.

On February 20, a 50-sack cement plug was run. Several things happened: the plug disappeared, probably into the D-3 and the mud level dropped, allowing Viking gas to come up the annulus, exerting 55 psi at surface. As Dave Gray explains: "the cement plug, being fully displaced, was over-balanced, causing the hydro-static pressure to exceed the bottom hole reservoir pressure and forcing the plug into the D-3".

Dave Gray was one of the key players, an engineer seasoned in the Middle East where he had worked on a 30-month contract. He was born in Vancouver and graduated from the University of Oklahoma in petroleum engineering. He signed up with Denton and Spencer early in 1947, working in Lloydminster. Dave's contribution to this story is in the form of copious notes, replete with details of how they tried to restore circulation with cement plugs, trying different mixtures. He later left Denton and Spencer to form the consulting firm: Murray, Mitchell and Gray in Edmonton. In recent years, he has been an independent operator.

By the fourth day, February 22, the well was "alive" after a second plug had been run. The annulus was blowing gas from the Viking. Then was the first, but not the last, time the Hosmer button would be deployed. 115 barrels of mud were pumped down the annulus in an attempt to stop the gas flow. No hole had been made since February 17, three cement plugs had been run, and the drill pipe was sticking, so it wasn't surprising that the bit had become plugged and had started to "grow roots".[4]

On the 23rd, the Hosmer was again dropped in. Mud was

Atlantic no. 3
Sketch of Wellhead Assembly

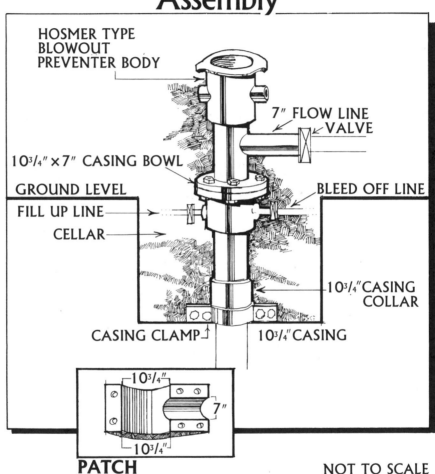

HOSMER TYPE
BLOWOUT
PREVENTER BODY

7" FLOW LINE
VALVE

10³/₄" × 7" CASING BOWL

GROUND LEVEL

BLEED OFF LINE

FILL UP LINE

CELLAR

10³/₄" CASING COLLAR

CASING CLAMP

10³/₄" CASING

10³/₄"

7"

10³/₄"

PATCH   NOT TO SCALE

pumped down the annulus at 500 psi through the fill–up line but circulation was not regained. With the pressures present, the shallow beds were almost certainly now being charged with Viking gas. A string of "macaroni" (1¼ in. tubing) was run inside the 4½ in. drill pipe to drill out cement that had "flash–set" in the drill pipe. This succeeded in opening up the ports of the bit. The drill pipe came loose, but after pulling ten stands (900 ft.) off bottom, the well started to flow again. Once more, the Hosmer was installed and mud was pumped down the drill pipe. It was during one of these episodes that the old valve on the 7 in. flow line was found to be seized; it could not be closed except with a very large wrench to which was attached a "snipe".

From the 26th of February to the 2nd of March, a succession of cement plugs was run, none of which controlled the gas flow or restored circulation. However, on March 2, firm cement was encountered at 5,210 ft. during drilling. None was present at 5,258 ft., but it was again encountered at 5,266 ft. At this point, more cement was run, with similar results. The interval 5,258–5,266 ft. appears to have been a major thief zone. However, production casing could probably have been run at this time, and the well saved.

The hole, up to March 8, was continually losing mud into the D–3, yet the mud level, as Cody stated, was remaining constant at about 1,100 ft. from the surface, allowing the Viking to blow out, but still containing the D–3. This is a very important point to keep in mind in understanding the background of the decision to drill "dry".

Howard Blanchard:..."it was nothing but trouble. It was on top of us or ahead of us from start to finish...we had some of the most experienced men...but no use, it simply kept getting worse..."[5]

Carl Moore, one of G.P.'s most respected drillers: "They did things there we all knew wouldn't work but still we had to go along with it".[6]

The evening of March 6 marked a turning point in the affairs of Atlantic No. 3 when a "Summit Conference" took place. Unlike other historic events, there is no written record, only memories (some of them faulty) of where it took place, who was there and what they said.

Lloyd Stafford, G.P.'s tool push on No. 3, was there. He was at the first oil well in Western Canada as a small boy. His grandfather was a driller at "Oil City", Cameron Creek at the turn of the century, in what is now Waterton National Park. Lloyd started in Turner Valley, working with cable tools on the Spooner lease. He went on to rotary drilling and was employed by several outfits before going with G.P. Stafford is regarded as the unsung hero of the draw-works.

Clarence Matthews, Denton & Spencer engineer, was either in Edmonton in his hotel room or out at the meeting, according to Bill Warnick. Cody Spencer may or may not have been there. Howard Blanchard said he knew about the get–together but thought it was too high–powered for him and went back to his bunk. He recalls Clarence being in favour of drilling "dry". According to one source, Lyle Caspell was ordered up to Leduc by Pacific's treasurer, T.O.

(Ted) Megas on March 9, "the day after". Caspell's report states: "Drill ahead was instruction received from an author(it)ative exec-utive sitting behind a big walnut desk."[7] Dave Gray said that he (Dave) was away on days off, but somebody else thought that he was there.

Don Whitney, production foreman at the Atlantic tank farm, met Stafford on the road after the decision to drill "dry" was made. He quotes Lloyd as saying, "it's the best (decision) we could do (make) and we hope we can get through (to casing point)."[8]

Drilling "dry" meant drilling ahead while pumping water down the drill pipe without actual circulation. It was felt that this would be safe as the production zone (probably meaning the oil zone) was expected some 30 ft. deeper.

They decided to go ahead on this basis. Jack Pettinger: "I do remember that Lloyd Stafford was 'dead against it'. I remember him saying 'the least that can happen is a blow-out'."[11]

Upon the decision of March 6, to drill "dry", a water line was rigged up to the standpipe so that water could be pumped directly down the drill string. Daylight tour on March 7 made 19 ft. and the afternoon tour 22 ft. of new hole with no returns. The graveyard tour of March 8 had drilled 17 ft. to 5,331 ft., still 23 ft. short of the projected total depth for running the production casing when the well blew out completely at 4:15 a.m., flowing large amounts of oil and gas from both D-3 and Viking.

Bill Kinghorn, now retired at the Pacific Coast, had been brought up from the Valley as mentioned before and was one of the Conservation Board's "bottom hole" men taking pressure surveys. He said he had pleaded with Red Goodall to not let them drill "dry".

Jack Pettinger,[9] now retired from Halliburton, set down in a letter of May 1981 his recollections of March 6 discussions:

> On the Atlantic 3 job, total frustration eventually set in...I remember sitting in on a conversation with Cody Spencer, Clarence Matthews and Lloyd Stafford...–Clarence was of the opinion according to geological information...that there was still...30 ft. of the 'Lost Cir-culation Formation' to penetrate and it was suggested that they drill ahead 'dry' and then try to control circula-tion over the area in one operation.[10]

(This *may* help resolve the Spi Langston account which follows.)

There is another item which is difficult to explain although there was a motley assemblage of mixed grades of casing on the Atlantic racks. Spi Langston had a special casing shoe which had

Atlantic No. 3, shortly after blowing out from the D–3, March 8, 1948.
Photo furnished by Howard Blanchard.

been flown in from the U.S., ready to run on the long string. This was a Larkin, which had a set of petals opening up below the ports when the shearing ball was pumped down. This would partially shield from the D–3 the scouring and lost circulation effect of the cementing. Spi said he was ready to run casing with this special shoe. Because of a possible mix–up in drill pipe measurement (an extra single picked up?) 30 ft. of hole were inadvertently drilled, according to Spi. This could have happened during the struggle to get cement plugs set and regain circulation from March 2 to March 8.

Information gathered shortly after the D–3 blow–out from those parties having responsibility, is summarized:

– Dave Gray had suggested drilling be continued. He had seen "dry" completions in the Middle East through a limestone in which it was particularly difficult to maintain circulation. The technique was to drill ahead with water, reach the required total depth and cement the drill pipe in place as production casing.

– Lloyd Stafford and Nate Goodman telephoned Gene Denton and Cody Spencer to discuss the proposal. Nate also contacted the Board's Deputy Chairman, Red Goodall and further discussions were held in Calgary between Denton and the Deputy Chairman, as to the advisability of drilling "dry".

– Red Goodall confirmed that Nate Goodman was in constant attendance during the time circulation was lost and did not object to the procedure outlined, having in mind the drilling experience up to that time.

– Goodall mentioned that the annulus should be kept full 'in order to counteract a possible blow–out'. (This was impossible to achieve.)

– Clarence Matthews had contacted Atlantic Oil Co. and made his recommendation to them to drill "dry". He was then reported to have received their approval by telephone. Clarence then conveyed the word to Lloyd as to how he was to carry on: if cement did not hold at 5,265 ft...."dry" drilling was to be proceeded with.

Cody's Spencer's experience in Wyoming in the thirties may have been a factor in deciding the course of action. According to Ralph Will, then with the Rocky Mountain Drilling Co., and Spencer's boss, a field on the southwest flank of the Big Horn basin was characterized by a depleted but extremely porous and permeable sandstone known as the Frontier. It had to be penetrated to reach the deeper pay zones. Ralph instructed Cody to drill through this thief sand with pumps running very slowly, adding sawdust all the time. Once the zone had been penetrated, normal drilling could be resumed.

Tom Wark, tool push on Imperial Leduc No. 48, says if those in charge had only listened to Lloyd Stafford the blow–out would never have happened. But Lloyd was over–ruled.

Hughie Leiper, now a senior officer with an oil company, is another chronicler who has contributed to a better understanding of events. Leiper, a native of Didsbury, moved to Turner Valley in 1929 with his family. His father had obtained a job first on the steam rigs and then with the "Purity 99" Gas and Oil Products refinery.

Leiper recalls that during World War II, the tool pushes would line up at the high school Friday afternoons and induce the husky lads to work weekends. This put extra cash in Hugh's pocket and enabled him to consider studying Petroleum Engineering (he ultimately graduated from the University of Oklahoma). He enrolled in Mount Royal College but finances forced him to leave temporarily. It was during this time that he started his roughnecking career with Dick Harris. Hugh recalls having had to pay his way out to Manyberries to work for Bob Wark, then with Can–Tex Drilling. When he was in Princess, he was approached by Frank Flewelling of G.P. who offered him a job. That is how he got to Leduc. He was on Rig #10, first at the BA Pyrcz well and then on the Atlantic wells.

Leiper remembers that he was an underling on the job and was in the cookhouse when the pow–wow was on which resulted in the drill "dry" decision.

> You know, Stafford was so damn mad he quit – did you know that? He says, 'Well, that's the decision, boys. I want no part of it, I'm quitting.' And he walked out. But being the dedicated and conscientious man he was, the minute the damn thing blew out he was back into the thick of things again.[12]

Let's hear Lloyd's version of the meeting in a recent interview with Gibby Gibson and Harry Simpson:

> As I recall, Cody Spencer and Clarence Matthews were there. Dave Gray was there and he was the one who suggested drilling "dry". But I wasn't in favour of it because I knew if you lost circulation...in a bad zone...you are going to lose it all. And the gas will bypass you because the first part is your big bubble of gas, your high pressure...right at the start. And the expansion of that gives you your blowout. Keeps moving up...till it gets away, then it is too late. Nate Goodman was along at the time...in the doghouse with us...they said they were going to drill "dry" and they were going to let the water run in, pumping a little down the drill pipe – that water lightens

up your fluid column and any wells we ever drilled were mostly killed with water but they had to be weighted up after. I decided to...get ready to go ahead and "dry drill". But I didn't start the crews. I roamed around thinking and wondering about it, then went over to a Commonwealth rig and talked to the tool pusher over there and I wasn't happy. I didn't want to start that drilling because I didn't think I could handle it. I went back over sometime about midnight. There was a phone call. It came from the Mac-donald Hotel in Edmonton. It was Clarence Matthews. He wanted to know if we had started to drill. I said, "No, we hadn't." "Well," he said, "you had better set it on bottom and turn it to the right." I still wasn't happy about it so waited around a while and finally I said "Well, we will start it." I told him at the time, "I'll call you back and let you know which way it is going". We started drilling fairly steady. So I went down to camp, I had a coffee and I laid down just across in the cabin there...I had my coat and everything on just like I had come in. I fell asleep and somebody called me that the well had blown out. I went back up to the rig. They had shut off all the fires and boilers and the well was blowing. It was a nice well. I called Matthews and I told him, "It's a dandy and it's headed southeast", and it was.[13]

Lloyd then returned to the rig and had the crew fire up the boilers. He plugged his ears with cotton batting. Stafford knew the kelly hose wouldn't be able to withstand the mixture of oil and sand and shale fragments. He took the brake and pulled the kelly up to the top of the derrick to get the hose out of the way of the main blast. This made it possible to at least pump down the drill pipe. Oil was running back in around the rig so Lloyd ordered bulldozers out to pile up the snow and ice and create a wall.

Hugh Leiper, then derrick man, on graveyard tour March 8 picks up his version of the story from 4 a.m.:

We were down in the cellar thawing out a line and all of a sudden there was a blurp of mud, and lost circulation material spewed over the drilling nipple and that's when I said to Cliff (Covey, cat-head man), "Let's get the hell out of here", so we...got out of the cellar. We ran out to the west from under the rig and just about 20 ft. in front of us, one of the rotary table master bushings landed in front of us. This had come from the "Oilwell" 26½ in. steam rotary table...Two men could not pick up one of these...It was still dark and of course, later on, we never did find the other half...I yelled at Cliff to run down to the boiler house to tell the firemen to shut the boilers off...and I ran up the steps and through the dog house out onto the rig floor...and I stayed with Bill (Murray, the driller) who had already dispatched Frank McKelvie and Bob Curle. We brought that string off bottom and hoisted it as high as we could...Bill and I, after chaining it down (locking the brake tight with a chain fastened to the floor) ran down through or past the engine on the draw works into the pump house and went out the side door...There were coming out of the well itself, showers of shale and gravel. The rig had been winterized using tin and the shale would penetrate that tin just like you turned a machine gun on it. So we hid alongside the stacks of mud and shale...and when it let up a bit, Bill and I took off for the boiler house and it was a frightening sight. By this time, it was starting to get daylight and although you couldn't talk to one another because of the noise, it was hitting the top of the crown and spraying as far as the eye could see...Bill sent Frank McKelvie down to the camp to wake up Lloyd Stafford. The night before, I had been a witness in the cookhouse to quite an argument about what to do with this well...A decision had been made to drill ''dry'' and I can remember Lloyd certainly opposed to this whole exercise and he did make the comment that from there on in, he didn't want to be involved so we didn't know if he had quit or...if he was joking or just what...Lloyd came up and there nothing anybody could do. We had shut all the boilers off...We got in there with 2x4's and 2x6's, knock-ing off as much of the tin sheets as we could so we could get air into around where it was blowing. They eventually got word to Cody Spencer and he arrived...[14]

Later in the morning, it was discovered that the blow–out had knocked off a nipple on the stand–pipe leaving a "Dutchman" (threaded portion left inside the fitting)...Jack Moore, then welder, now resident of Anchorage, recalls the task of removing the bro-ken–off piece:

Cody, Clarence Matthews and, I think, Gene Denton arrived at the lease in mid–morning, and Clarence asked me if I had a brass diamond point chisel and hammer with my tools. There was a Dutchman broken off in the stand–pipe and they wanted to compound several Halliburton and Dowell cement trucks to regain circulation...With a derrickman's harness buckled on me, I crawled across the floor to the stand–pipe with a rope held by Matthews and Murray at the dog house door, to pull me out of trouble if required. I had almost finished the task when several jerks of the rope caused me to turn my head – in question. There was Cody motioning me to get back to the dog house. I indicated 'almost finished'. With that, he pulled me across the floor to the dog house. To offset the roar of gas he cupped his hands and yelled in my ear, "Do you want to get your uncle in trouble?" Whereupon, he took the tools from me, put on the harness and finished the job himself. That was indicative of Cody.[15]

In a recent interview, Cal Bohme was asked, in view of the experience he had gained since 1948, what the main causes of the Atlantic No. 3 blow–out were and how it might have been avoided. His reply was that the decision to drill ahead 'blind' "was a very seriously flawed decision, especially with such a short section of surface casing".

The most pressure that one could expect the surface pipe to hold would be about 300 psi, equivalent to the overburden pressure. But the bottom hole pressure at total depth was over 2,000 psi so this meant that as soon as they drilled into the D–3 with little mud in the hole that this pressure could be exerted against the shallow formations just below the surface casing shoe.

Even with the Hosmer button, it might have been possible to keep the pressure bled off through the 7 in. line by pumping mud down the drill pipe and attempting to fill the annulus with fluid. But even so there was the dilemma: killing the well, then losing circulation, then the well starting to blow out again on you. Cal described it as a cyclic situation: "...build up enough pressure to kill the well, then lose it into the lost circulation zone."[16] There was no error on the crews' part; they drilled ahead in good faith, believing that the people who gave the orders knew what they were doing. Bohme recalls his being on tour when they finally succeeded in landing the Hosmer button:

>   ...I can remember when we spent the entire shift pumping a slug of mud down the drill pipe and the flow would slow down enough that we could get up to the well with the Hosmer button and try to latch it and I think we made five or six attempts and every time we would try, the flow would be so great, you couldn't even hold on to the button. It would blow it out of our hands and as I say, it

would blow it up in the air and we would get out of the road quick...[17]

Stafford recalls he had just pushed the Hosmer into place and the pressure on the surface casing was building up

The morning of March 8, 1948. Note the heavy snow cover.
Photo furnished by Howard Blanchard.

MA AND MYRT

It is through the eyes of individuals such as Myrtle Collins that the events and especially the personalities of Atlantic No. 3 assume a unique and somewhat romantic patina. As cook's helper to Ma Ferguson, Myrt was privy to a side of the workers that was, in many cases, different from their strained and anxious behaviour exhibited while working at the well. Ma was respected for running an excellent cookhouse, and a stop to eat a meal of her fine cooking was what kept many a rig hand going. Myrt recalls that there was nothing Red Adair enjoyed more than a slice of cheese with Ma's apple pie.

Myrtle Collins was born in Saskatchewan at the beginning of the Great Depression. In 1941, she moved with her family to Black Diamond where, at the age of fifteen, she went to work for General Petroleums.

Myrt recalled that she "peeled a lot of spuds, and did dishes and helped with just about everything there was to help with!" With three crews of workers to feed, Myrt found that with "the guys coming in off a shift and the guys going out...we were up quite early in the morning and when we finished at night, we usually went to bed".

Chow time at the camp. With cooks like Ma Ferguson and Myrt Collins, who would want to miss dinner? Do you recognize yourself?
Photo furnished by Myrtle Collins.

These homemade meals included the preparation of a mid-night lunch. Ma was known for her firmness in insisting that the men clean up the counter after their meals.

The fact that the cookhouse was viewed as both a meeting place and a refuge was "sweetened" by the fact that Ma's baking was always left out to attract the hungry. At the time of the drilling of the Atlantic wells, Myrt remembers that, although John Rebus (who lived on the land and sold his fresh milk to the cookhouse) never came to visit, his brother Michael Rebus "used to come out all the time...He'd come in [to the cookhouse] and have something to eat and josh with us quite a bit". Michael Rebus's friendly ways were also remembered at the time that Atlantic No.1 came in; in Myrt's words: "when the first well blew in, he brought out cases and cases of rum, Crown Royal and turkeys and we had a big feast and everybody got a bottle of Crown Royal".

In response to the interviewer's questions as to whether Myrt also received a bottle, she replied: "Yes I did and I saved that sack for a long, long time but I didn't ever...know what happened to the whiskey!"

At the time of the Atlantic No. 3 blow–out, Myrt was among the personnel permitted access within the area of the rig. She recalls, in particular, Carl Moore, Lloyd Stafford and Bill Murray among the well hands who were willing to explain to her the technical aspects of the blow–out. Myrt provides us with the following description of one of her visits to the rig: "I remember I went up there one time and walked on the planks to get up to the rig and it was oil...bubbling all over the place and it looked like oatmeal, oatmeal bubbles...that was the way the oil was coming up."

Myrt's recollections of Atlantic No. 3 also included the reloca–tion of the G.P. camp at the time "the well blew wild". During the move, Ma broke her leg and Myrt's mother (Hilda Collins), who had never cooked in a camp, was recruited to fill the bill. Myrt explained that if it had not been for the help of Lloyd Stafford and Cody Spencer, she and her mother would never have gotten through this difficult time. Undoubtedly, in spite of their fine efforts, Ma's famous chow was surely missed.

In June of 1948, Myrt and her mother left the camp to go to Vancouver. Although a few years later, Myrt did return to the oil patch to work at other camps, her memories of Atlantic No. 3 are still vivid.

D. Maw

...We were standing there – all the valves closed – all of a sudden a sizzling underneath...the weld had begun to open up where the 7 in. flow line was welded into the 10¾ in. casing. The hissing was getting louder and all of a sudden it just went bang. A bunch of shale had blown up around the bottom of the head and just plugged the annulus off solid. Cody had one of these big hats on and he looked at us and started saying, "God damn, God damn", jumping up and down. He threw the hat off and he jumped on that a couple of times. I pulled my old clothes off and I was going to throw them in the boiler but the boys said, "No don't. We will clean them." They had one of those old steam boxes there. I was soaked with oil – if anything had caught fire it would have been goodbye for all three of us that were there.[18]

The morning of March 8 saw curious local residents and oil workers coming over to the wild well for a better look. Paul Fandrick recalls the oil spraying over his farm three miles to the south, blackening the snow which was still 2 ft. deep. This oil spray was to continue through the summer, and when the wind blew from the southeast, it would settle on Devon clothes lines, one of them being Elsie Kerr's. The frost was still in the ground, except for the mud pit, which had thawed. The violent force of the oil and gas flow, along with shale, made it nearly impossible to deploy the Hosmer, let alone get near the rotary table.

Jack Pettinger and Paul Bedard[19] were just finishing a cementing job that morning when they saw the black plume. They had already run a number of plugs at Atlantic No. 3 and knew how serious the lost circulation was. They immediately drove over to see how they could help. They left their trucks spotted out on the road. Little did they realize that nearly all of their waking (and sleeping!) hours would be spent from then until November helping win the fight.

In retrospect, the fact that Viking gas had started to charge the overlying sands (Belly River and surface) from February 17, (the date when the D–3 was contacted and circulation partially lost) suggests that the well may have already passed the point of no return by the time the D–3 lifted off the remaining mud column on March 8.

ENDNOTES:
1. Personal communication.
2. Subsea: elevation above (+) or below (–) sea level.
3. Clause 14 in Drilling Contract and Clause 2 in amending letter to the Contract.
4. Popular expression used when bit becomes stuck in hole.
5. Personal communication.
6. Petroleum Industry Oral History Project interview.
7. Lyle Caspell's signed, undated report.
8. The depth at which the casing shoe is landed.
9. Pettinger, born in Oyen in 1916, moved to Calgary with his family. His father was a founding member of the Alberta Wheat Pool. Jack attended the Provincial Institute of Technology and Art (now known as SAIT). Erle P. Halliburton had come up from Duncan, Oklahoma in 1937. Pettinger was hired that year. He spent his entire working career with Halliburton (Welex) and retired in 1978. He had been on previous blow–outs but had never seen anything like Atlantic No. 3.
10. Pettinger letter of May 1981.
11. Ibid.
12. Leiper taped interview, Gibson and Simpson, 1986. Tape on file at Glenbow.
13. Tape on file at Glenbow.
14. Leiper, as above.
15. Personal communication.
16. Personal communication.
17. Ibid.
18. Stafford, as above.
19. Bedard, native of Edmonton, graduated from the Northern Alberta Technology Institute and then joined the RCAF. He served for five years and upon discharge, he worked a short time for the railway. Jack Pettinger was looking for people; he hired Paul and sent him out to Vermilion. When Leduc broke, Paul moved there as a cementer. He was at Atlantic No. 3 during the blow–out and also helped with the plugging. He retired from Halliburton in 1982.

BLOW-OUT: REACTION AND PERSPECTIVES

8

March 8 marked the watershed between what might have been and the cold reality of what was. Of what significance was this date, the turning point in the well's career, to the parties involved?

First: Rebus. The expressions on the faces of those walking away from the blow-out on that morning speak volumes. They could visualize damage to their lands and future crops but would have no idea of the enormously inflated royalty revenues they would be receiving later in the year. Nor would they have any idea of what reservoir damage might do to the value of their minerals. Even the word reservoir would be new to them.

Secondly: other farmers. Their concerns were, like Rebus', focussed on the surface of the land and they were, no doubt, wondering whether they would be compensated (especially those who did not own mineral rights and were constantly lobbying for some form of revenue in lieu of royalties).

Thirdly: the insurance companies. Not having been exposed to such catastrophes in the past, but ever on guard to protect themselves, they were starting to think of being saddled with substantial claims for surface damage.

Fourthly: McMahon. Denton and Spencer were only agents of Atlantic and, as Owner, Frank had full responsibility and liability for the well. But had he been warned of this? As promoter, McMahon may have started to think of thousands of barrels of uncontrolled production and the revenue from that rather than the thousands of dollars in potential law suits. Subsurface damage to the reservoir and migration of offsetting oil onto the Rebus quarter were not of immediate concern to him. Having no technical staff, there was no one in Atlantic to advise Frank, but even so, would he have listened to them?

Fifth: General Petroleums. Cody, in a way, had imperilled G.P.'s position by "being on the brake" although if one questioned Cody's presence in those days, one would have been told where to go, both by Cody himself and other interested parties. One has to keep in mind that there were very few written orders or memos and most communication was by word of mouth. Furthermore, organization charts were the thing of the future as far as the oil patch was concerned.

G.P.'s blow-out prevention equipment had proven not to be

"adequate and efficient" as required by Clause 5 of the contract. It turned out to be more of a hazard than a help because of the primitive well head set-up.

Sixth: Imperial Oil. The hectic pace of drilling activity by this company precluded it from becoming very involved in other people's troubles. The blow-out was certainly noted by Imperial's staff in Leduc but was not of too much concern mainly because, up until March 8, only the Viking had been blowing out and although this was a nuisance, it wasn't a dangerous hazard. When the D-3 began unloading, Imperial's attention became acute.

Seventh: the Conservation Board. Nate Goodman was thoroughly familiar with what had been going on at Atlantic No. 3 and had been reporting to Calgary Headquarters. His diaries do not indicate what input he had but because of his rapport with industry and his practical know-how combined with his technical training, his views were very likely considered. Apart from the Viking blow-out at Leduc Consolidated the summer before, Nate had little exposure to wild wells. And No. 3 was no ordinary wild well.

One must keep in mind that the Board had been very recently reconstituted, with two of the members unprepared for this situation. Nevertheless, the Board's preoccupation with "waste", as practised at Turner Valley, must have been a factor in their concern. In one sense, Turner Valley was a blow-out (albeit controlled) and the Board knew that irreparable damage had been done to that reservoir, leaving millions of barrels of oil locked up forever. The D-3 reservoir had much different characteristics. For one thing, it had an active water drive which would maintain reservoir pressure. However, coning from uncontrolled production would ultimately ruin the relatively thin 38 ft. pay sandwich.

So it was, after March 8, 1948 that new directions had to be undertaken; those breaking trail were to discover that it was a trial and error process.

BLOW-OUT: TRIALS AND ERRORS

9

I: TO THE BIG CEMENT JOB

When McMahon was getting ready to drill, the northwest extremity of the quarter section was occupied by a water storage pit, an integral part of Hector's water system.

Shortly after March 8, because of the natural slope to the northwest, bulldozers constructed a drainage system toward this pond which then became the nucleus of a holding facility for the run–away crude production. Its capacity was increased by bull-dozers blading up mud and snow dykes. But as the snow melted during break–up, leaks developed and some oil ran down the north–south road allowance and got into the North Saskatchewan River. Bill McKellar recalls warning Lyle that oil was leaking out but Caspell was reported to have not paid attention to him. Don Whitney, previously mentioned in Chapter 9, recalls repairing the dyke walls, especially after complaints were heard of an oily taste in Edmonton's drinking water.

Bill McKellar, now retired at Blind Bay, British Columbia, had just arrived in town and noted: "Turner Valley was in Leduc", because all his friends had come there for the boom. He ran into Cody Spencer, who took him on as lease foreman. His crew's job was to prepare well sites, and dig cellars. When the well blew out on March 8, Al Wright, field superintendent, called him to arrange the containment of the oil.

The second day after the blow–out, heavy mud quieted the well down enough to re–install the Hosmer, after several attempts. The Viking was still kicking. The cold weather (–25°F.) slowed down clean–up operations and kept the crew busy thawing out lines. Once again, let Hughie Leiper pick up the story:

> ...It was 10 o'clock the night after and we were using the two steam pumps and Cody Spencer came up to me and from a reading of the Cameron mud gauge and pumping down into the well, the pressure was decreasing considerably and Cody was all smiles and I can remember him yelling in my ear: "Hughie, we got this thing licked". A few minutes later, Dave Gray drove up and said "I just drove by some shot holes about a quarter of a mile away and there is mud and gas blowing up out of

them". Imperial Leduc No. 32, diagonal offset to No. 3 also had to shut down because of gas escaping up into the boiler house.[1]

On March 11, when the 7 in. flow line was opened to bleed off the gas, chunks of shale battered the assembly until the 2 in. fill-up line elbow was knocked off. Dave Gray comments: "This was all done under Cody Spencer, the rest of us were having fits (and) Cody was always grabbing the brake"![2] Over the next week it was a repetition of cement jobs, mud pressure on the drill pipe and leaks on the 7 in. flow line.

On March 15, Bill Kinghorn set up his wire line unit and ran in with an impression block. Kinghorn states he was up to his waist in oil at the time. Upon retrieval, according to Kinghorn, the impression block indicated that it had hit the Totco ring at the top of the bit. Dave Gray tends to dispute this because he thinks there should have been cement there. The lubricator was then replaced with a Halliburton circulating head.

At about this time the decision was taken to shoot off the now stuck drill pipe as near to the bit as possible, pull it out and then go in and side-track. The first step in this operation was to pump a rubber wiper plug down to the bit and check its depth with the Halliburton wire line unit. However, the sinker bar stuck. Barber Machine made up a special cutter actuated by a go-devil to be run on the wire to sever it. This was accomplished at 2,000 ft., not at total depth as was hoped.

Cal Bohme recalls the meeting that was held around the 16th or 17th of March wherein it was decided to try to shoot off the drill pipe to enable more fluid to be pumped down. K.C. "Casey" Ball came over from Lloydminster with nitroglycerin. It was in a carrier, merely a galvanized tube that looked very similar to a down spout or drain pipe. The idea of the rubber plug was to ensure that the drill pipe was clear so that the nitro shots could be run to total depth. But the first rubber wiper plug only got to 2,700 ft. The next day they pumped in several more of these plugs and chased them down to 5,290 ft. At that time the measuring line stuck in the hole. March 19 was spent trying to free this. Then the line cutter stuck. Casey was then told he wouldn't be running his nitro because of the fish in the hole. He packed up his equipment with his torpedoes and disappeared down the road.

Now that the wire and fish were inside the drill pipe below 2,000 ft., a possible alternative was to perforate the drill pipe using a McCullough perforating gun small enough to go inside the drill pipe. This was on its way from California on March 20. Unfortunately, it could only get down as far as 1,965 ft. and it was fired there.

Heavy mud was then pumped down to kill the well, but this only disappeared into the D–3 where other mud and cement plugs had gone. If the plugs had been calculated to just balance the D–3 bottom hole pressure, it might have been possible to plug off the annulus above the D–3 without blocking the perforations at 1,965 ft. in the drill pipe.

The craters developing around the well bore had now created such a fire hazard that the Atlantic No. 3 boilers had to be shut down. Steam lines were then hooked up to the boilers at the GP steam rig drilling Imperial Leduc No. 48. (This rig was later skidded a short distance east to West Relief.) Imperial Oil had already consented to the use of both the rig and the well bore for the struggle at Atlantic No. 3.

Paul Bedard tells the story of Dave Gray helping him to test a tubing line laid from Imperial Leduc No. 48 to Atlantic No. 3. This line was intended to be used for water or mud. Because it would be operating at high pressures, Halliburton was to start up the pumps and Gray was to gradually open up the well. When Gray cocked the well open, the line began to snake and lift under the pressure. Paul accused Dave of trying to kill him!

There was a severe shortage of tubular goods. In order to lay one of the lines from No. 48 to No. 3 for cement slurry and/or mud, 5 in. drill pipe was brought up from the Valley. This turned out to be in 45 ft. lengths and required "the biggest set of chain tongs that were ever seen". Bill McKellar had them brought out from town and it took two men just to pick them up. Hugh Leiper and Jack Emslie thought that they could speed up the process by hiring a team of horses to pull the pipe into place. Unfortunately, this scheme didn't work; the team bolted and they were out all of $2! Back to hand–hauling the drill pipe!

Several versions of comic/tragic events have emerged over the years, invariably embellished and invariably incorrect as to the people involved and the times. As recently as 1985, Ralph Horley (more of him later) was contacted by a person who said he had the real story of the out–house. It was a tool push nicknamed "Sailor" who had gone out to the privy for a smoke.

To set the record straight on this event, here is what really happened. By March 27, smoking was strictly forbidden; those who really needed a drag were told to go over to the No. 48 boiler house. Cliff Covey was reluctant to ask his driller Bill Murray for time off for a cigarette, partly because they didn't get along too well. So he decided to sneak a smoke in the privy, which by now was also bubbling gas and oil. The results: an explosion, with Covey making a hasty departure from the premises. A desperate battle to put the fire out ensued. This was successful by spreading large quantities of dry aquagel "mud", some of the men carrying a 100 lb. sack under each arm. The steam line was hooked up and it also helped douse the flames. Hugh Leiper, who helped put the fire out by swatting at it with wet gunny sacks, states: "I don't know how we did it".[3] Two people vie for the "honour" of taking Covey to Wetaskiwin: Dave Gray and Bill McKellar. Another person said an ambulance was used!

Bedard recalls having a Halliburton Waukesha gasoline engine–powered wagon on the No. 3 lease. This had an added hazard in that the exhaust pipe pointed directly downward and melted the frozen ground beneath the wagon. The boys would move the truck from spot to spot around the rig so as to try and stay on frozen ground which did not crater. Shortly after the Covey incident, Cody appeared, "How are you doing?" "Well we are moving the truck around to avoid the gas." When he found out that Covey had been scorched, he ordered Pettinger to shut the Waukesha motor down immediately. "We'll winch you out", Cody roared, despite the protests of Bedard and Pettinger, who said they could drive the wagon out. Pettinger went on: "You didn't know who you were taking orders from". Cody would change his mind and, as the well became harder to handle, he became more difficult to get along with.

When the well blew out, spraying oil over several farmers' lands, the press coverage alerted the insurers to the potential for heavy surface loss claims. The following exchange of correspondence is particularly informative.

E.A. (Ed) Cote, manager of Halifax Insurance Company's Edmonton office, was personally acquainted with Dr. J.O.G. (Pete) Sanderson, consulting geologist in Calgary. On March 29, he wrote Pete:

> ...We are interested in this oil well which went out of control some time ago and I am wondering if you could advise me in what way an occurrence of this nature would happen – is it a case of the well being too powerful for the equipment or would it be a situation where there was not the proper care or supervision taken. We are interested from the negligence viewpoint and I would appreciate any information you would furnish us with...[4]

Sanderson showed the letter to Gene Denton, General

Petroleums/Denton and Spencer head who obviously was pleased to be made aware of the problem from an insurance standpoint.[5]

Pete replied:

> ...I told him (Mr. Mirtle of Middleton and Tait) it is a petroleum engineer's problem and one upon which I would not care to express a formal opinion, except possibly very specifically on the geological aspects of the case. I informed him also that I do a great deal of my work in co-operation with General Petroleums, the contractor on that job, and would not care to be involved in any way except possibly in their interests. Sorry I cannot be of assistance to you this time...[6]

Meanwhile, back at the well, the 7 in. flow line had come loose and required repairs. This was accomplished by a lead sheathing. Bohme describes the patch fabricated by Earl Griffith, mastermind fabricator, welder and owner of Barber Machine shop in Edmonton, and installed on April 1:

> Quite ingenious, made in two sections so it fitted around the 7 in. flow line in one part and also around the bottom of the Hosmer head so that when it was bolted together it would fit snugly. The patch had a lead gasket in it that was placed up against the leaking portion. When the bolts were tightened up, it very effectively shut off the leak. This was the only possible solution because leaking oil and gas precluded the use of a welding torch.

The next decision was reached: to pump massive amounts of cement slurry down No. 3, using Imperial No. 48 as the base of operations. Bill Cummer recalls ordering out the cement, but because of the road ban and the fact that the roads were in terrible condition (no gravel, let alone asphalt, west of Leduc), only half loads were permitted. This slowed down the mobilization at No. 48. However, 10,000 sacks were stacked on hastily constructed mats, along with 2,000 sacks of lime. (See Appendix E.)

Bohme recalls the "big cement job" in that they spent many days packing the cement through the mud and along 3 in. plank walkways. The trucks could not get to the planked area so the hands carried it on their backs.

At that time, there were just two oil field service companies in Canada: Halliburton and Dowell. The former had seven cement trucks; one of these was an old FWD (four wheel drive) with three horizontal steam pumps, a veteran of Turner Valley days. It was hoped to use all seven but an emergency at Lloydminster required

Set up for the Big Cement Job. Stockpiled cement (10,000 sacks) at Imperial No. 48. Photo taken from fourble board, No. 48.

Photo furnished by Nate Goodman.

two wagons there. Dowell was talked into loaning two of their trucks (both power).

R.H. (Dick) Gibbons, Halliburton's Canadian manager, was approached by Denton and Spencer regarding the proposed cement job. Dick had originally come up from the States and was an admirer of "Cyclone" O'Donnell (a sentiment not shared by other Halliburton hands at Leduc). When O'Donnell arrived from Duncan, Oklahoma headquarters, Pettinger said that "Cyclone" had every-thing figured out in fifteen minutes as to what to do. O'Donnell's theory was cement was just as cheap as mud and if the cement set up in the Atlantic No. 3 surface casing or drill pipe, so much the better.

In preparation for the big cement job, another perforating gun was brought in on April 2, but it got stuck in the drill pipe. An echometer was run on April 5 to try to locate fluid levels in the drill pipe and annulus but nothing definite was obtained. The line on which the gun had been run was pulled out at the socket; this line had to be got out of the way so that a manifold could be installed on the top of the drill pipe at No. 3 to take the slurry from No. 48.

Spencer was on hand that day, wearing his Denton and Spencer hat. He must have been very anxious to see the cement

The Big Cement Job, April 7, 1948. Percy Davis and Earl Altizer on the Halliburton cement wagon. Atlantic No. 3 in background.

Photo furnished by Nate Goodman.

Manhandling cement for the Big Cement Job, April 7, 1948.

Photo furnished by Lyle Caspell.

set up. There was one person in the Halliburton organization that could (and did) stand up to Cody: Lyall Thorne, field superintendent. When an impasse developed, it was Lyall who would move in (not without some pleasure) and force his hard–nosed opinions on Spencer. Pettinger and Thorne were put in charge of the trucks and saw to the hooking up of the manifolds at No. 3 and where the trucks were to be spotted at No. 48.

Prior to staging in the cement slurry, the 2,000 lb. of lime were mixed and pumped down the Atlantic No. 3 well bore. Its purpose was to wash and clean the hole with the hope of getting a good cement bond.

A small army of men (about 75) had been mobilized because the cement (all in 87½ lb. bags) had to be man–handled off the stock pile, carried to the seven cutting tables, slit open and dumped into the hoppers. The cement was then jetted with water into the mixing tank, mixed with water and pumped as a slurry through the lines to Atlantic No. 3.

After many delays in thawing out lines, the trucks started up and all were supposed to be on line at the same time. Paul Bedard's main motor on his truck failed and was pulled off. The two Dowell wagons didn't have enough "pump" and virtually did not contribute. They also came off the line.

The champion was the steamer on the FWD chassis which used steam from No. 48 boilers. It saved the day by processing up to 30 sacks a minute. This required two cutting tables and at least 30 men. The pressure of the work was getting to some of them. One of them told Cody: "I'd rather go to jail than throw cement into that SOB" and he took off.

Initial pumping pressure at the Atlantic No. 3 well had built up to about 2,200 psi, some of it termed "friction", at the commencement of the job at about 3 p.m. It dropped off when the slurry started to move through the lines. The cement was pumped over in seven batches and all of it was away by 7:30 p.m. Everybody was hoping the pressure would build up at some time during the cementing but it kept dropping off because the cement over–balanced all of the formation pressures in the hole. The D–3 formation "just sucked that cement in". The cement went into the well on vacuum. At 11 p.m., there were again 1,000 psi showing on the gauge at No. 3, indicating failure. As Pettinger said, "You might as well have pumped it into the North Saskatchewan River for all the good it did".[7] Tom Wark, who was there all day, echoed Pettinger's comment, "...all that did was make her produce better...never felt it afterwards or anything..."

Because Cyclone thought he knew 50% more than he did, and

to show their "affection" for him, the Halliburton hands organized a going–away party for him. Needless to say, Cyclone was not invited.[8]

ENDNOTES:
1. Taped interview (March 1986). No. 32 problem corroborated by Gibby Gibson.
2. Personal communication.
3. Taped interview (March 1986).
4. J.O.G. Sanderson papers (Glenbow Archives).
5. Ibid.
6. Ibid.
7. Taped interview (January 1986).
8. O'Donnell hung around for a while (see next chapter) but the failed cement job did not enhance his reputation and he left shortly after.

II: KINLEY

"Dare–Devil Kinley inherited his trade".[1] According to Myron's son, J.C. (J. C. Kinley Co., Houston), his grandfather Karl had been one of the first "shooters" in California. He used dynamite down hole as a primitive method of stimulating wells. An oil well blow–out at Santa Fe Springs caught fire and he was able to blow the fire out with his dynamite. Years later, in 1929, Myron and his brother repeated the exercise on the occasion of a wild well fire in the Oklahoma City field. Using an asbestos shield and having water sprayed on them, they snuffed out the blaze with 30 quarts of jellied dynamite. From then on, his career was set and his world–wide reputation as a "shooter"/fire fighter established. After Myron lost his brother in an accident at a wild well, he forbade J.C. to work on them but J.C.'s son carries on the family tradition.

M.M. Kinley at an earlier well fire in the U.S.
Photo furnished by J.C. Kinley.

Ralph Will recalls one well that bested Kinley. This was a burning gas well in Wyoming that had been blowing wild for two years. Ralph had to kill it with two directional holes, pumping water from a nearby river; his account of this struggle would make a book by itself. It is the same tactic that Tip Moroney was later to employ at Atlantic No. 3.

Kinley was brought up to Alberta by the Conservation Board. The arrangement is confirmed by the fact that his $10,000 invoice was paid by that tribunal. Although McMahon indicated it was he who arranged for Kinley, it is probably more accurate to state that Frank and the Board discussed the matter prior to actually calling him in. We know that Frank later consulted with Myron because Frank recalls, in a taped interview, a night meeting when Kinley took off his shirt to show him the shrapnel wounds which he had suffered at previous wild wells.

There is no record of any terms of reference or letter of authorization but it is apparent that Kinley was to "take over" and be in charge on the lease, with Dave Gray as his helper. Operations were then limited to one crew working 12 hours and a night watchman.[2]

In all fairness to Kinley, this was not the kind of wild well he could possibly control with the methods he normally used. There was no need for dynamite because the well was not on fire. The craters had proliferated to such an extent that even if someone had been sufficiently demented to set it on fire, merely dynamiting the fire out would not have solved the problem of controlling the flow. Such usual practice of Kinley's, where a well was blowing out through the well head or casing, was completely inappropriate at Atlantic No. 3.

So far as the well bore was concerned, Myron was faced with a string of drill pipe stuck in the hole and the "only idea he had was to get everything out of the hole".

Kinley visited the well site on April 9 and the first thing he did was order the drill pipe to be cleaned out to as near bottom as possible. This required killing the well (which could only be quieted down for minutes at a time).[3] This was to be followed by lowering a large charge of explosives down the drill pipe, with the intention of shooting it off and bridging the hole. Once this was accomplished, the drill pipe could be pulled out of the hole and the oil and gas would move more freely up through the 10¾ in. surface casing, with less of it being diverted into the craters. From there it would be siphoned off into tanks. Perhaps Kinley hoped that he would be able to go back into the hole, clean it out, sidetrack and run a long string down below the drill pipe into the D-3.

Kinley was a tough, no nonsense hand who gave orders and expected them to be obeyed, but on one occasion, he told the crew to "get out there" and they answered back: "do it yourself, you're getting the big money". On another occasion, Paul Bedard had installed a manifold in readiness to use Halliburton equipment to pump down the hole. Kinley wanted it moved and Paul refused, saying it wasn't his job. Later in the day Myron came up to Bedard: "That's a good attitude...you'll live a long time around these wild wells!"

The next step was to bring an Otis wire-line specialist from Denver to fish out the McCullough perforating gun which had been left down the hole on April 2, along with a go-devil and a quantity of tangled wire–line. It was on this hotshop trip from Denver that Red Adair[4] is believed to have accompanied the Otis representative. By this time, the annular space between the top of the surface casing and the drill pipe had become plugged with shale that was being carried up in the oil flow.

While waiting for Otis, Pettinger remembers chauffeuring Kinley and Cyclone O'Donnell (still around) in a Ford "red and silver"[5] back and forth between the Macdonald Hotel and the well. What with O'Donnell's arrogance and short temper and Kinley's gimpy leg, Pettinger was getting fed up. The driving job, now with Kinley and Red Adair[6] (seated in the back), was taken over by Dave Gray and his jeep. Dave recalls Myron's bad leg hanging out over the edge of the jeep and the compulsory stop at the ice cream parlour on Whyte Avenue (82 Avenue) upon the conclusion of the day's work.

Otis arrived on the 13th of April and rigged up a lubricator and valve. A wire scraper tool was run, followed by an impression block which got to about 1,867 ft. After several fishing attempts, a slip over–shot latched onto the gun. When pulled out, it was found that the gun had not fired.

By the 17th, the bottom had really started to drop out of the roads because of spring break–up. "Adair's boss (Kinley) walked with some difficulty as a result of wounds from previous wild well jobs. He asked that a wooden plank–way be built from the well: 'If that thing goes off, I want to get out of there and I don't want anything in my way'."[6]

The next day, April 18, 1¼ in. macaroni tubing was brought over from Imperial No. 48. This was to have a bit on the end and be run inside the drill pipe, with the hope that whatever was in there could be cleaned out. By this time, oil and gas were erupting to the north of the rig and creating the need for more ditching and dyking. The mess around that northwest corner was unbelievable, yet somehow the oil haulers managed to work their way in to get loaded from the oil–filled pits.

More batches of mud were mixed at No. 48 and pumped over to No. 3. Several of these lots included the very heavy mud weighting material, Baroid.[7] Not only the tank in which they were mixed burst due to the very high specific gravity but that heavy mud disappeared even faster down the hole.

On the 22nd, the rotary table was skidded over and a shop–built circulating assembly installed on the drill pipe. The well was killed long enough to get the macaroni tubing in and 32 ft. of hole (using water) was made, to about 800 ft. After drilling 3 ft., the bit encountered iron.

Rig operations on or about May 13, 1948. Myron Kinley at left; Dave Gray (in sunglasses); behind Dave are Leo Schauer, Cal Bohme and Howard Blanchard; coming out of cellar is Carl Moore.

Photo furnished by Provincial Archives.

At this point, Kinley decided that a Hinderliter head was needed, it being easier to circulate and drill through this device. It arrived on the 27th of April and was installed the following day, replacing the shop–built set–up. The macaroni tubing was then run in and 10 ft. were reamed. They then went in with a spear and an overshot after having run an impression block several times to try to find out just what was inside the drill pipe.

By April 30, it appeared as if the macaroni string had run *outside* the drill pipe and encountered a bridge at 845 ft. Impression blocks suggested that the drill pipe had parted at about 470 ft.

By May 4, working inside the drill pipe either by trying to drill or by trying to fish appeared fruitless. It was then decided to mix roughage at No. 48 and see if that would block the No. 3 well bore. That day, a significant increase in the flow of oil to the dykes was recorded which increased the anxiety of the Board.

After many delays (pump breakdowns and shortages of water)

the roughage was ready for disposal on May 11. The "slurry" was mixed at No. 48, pumped to No. 3, and then down the hole. The following items were run:

Palcoseal (redwood fibre)	16 tons
Cottonseed hulls	43 tons
Sawdust	21 tons
Feathers	¼ tons
Mud	490 sacks
Lime	10 sacks

Tom Wark (tool push on No. 48) graphically describes that procedure:

> ...They told you about the feathers that we pumped down that hole did they? We pumped a ton and a half of feathers down there one day[8]...We threw them into the pit and gunned them up with the mud guns...we got them up into the pumps but sometimes they quit pumping and you would have to take the cap off and pull them feathers out of there and you would swear the chicken had been dead for years! Then we pumped tons of Zonolite and grain and stuff down that hole...just the way it was.[9]

As Wark stated, the pumps weren't used to such mixtures, especially the chicken feathers. The caps on the pumps had to be removed and the valves cleaned out frequently by Murray Varty, now semi-retired in Edmonton, and then pumper/cementer with Halliburton. He confirmed the problem: "I'll never forget the smell of the feathers", (together with some pieces of chicken) which had been obtained from Superstein's mattress factory in Edmonton.

Although there is no written record of it, sugar beet pulp from the Raymond sugar factory was used to try to regain circulation. This also plugged the pumps and resulted in frequent stoppages. The pulp had a vile smell, almost as bad as the feathers.

After the roughage was pumped (with no results whatever), the Board was once more forced to review its options. In retrospect, it is simplistic to criticize the Board for a perceived reluctance to take over the operation. There were so many factors militating against such a move: the legal implications; lack of an operational staff; yet the Board had the mandate to make such a move!

Here was a chairman, new to the job, no doubt being influenced by overly-optimistic reports coming in from the field. A Canadian Press release of May 17 is a case in point: "We hope to stop the cratering in a week if everything goes well". There must have been a period of disillusionment and soul searching at the

Board as it realized that now the situation was becoming desperate and Draconian measures were required.

It has been impossible to fully reconcile some of the statements with the events. We know that the Board, with Moroney in charge of operations, did take over on May 14 by invoking its statutory powers (see Chapter 10, Board Bites the Bullet). The tour sheets show that Kinley was present at No. 3 for some time after that date. Kinley's final act may have been carried out on May 13 when the crew "reefed" on the stuck drill pipe with 110,000 lb. It only moved 11 in. but Kinley said in his later report, he had gained 5 ft.; this could be accounted for by stretch in the pipe. He thought they should go back the next morning and pull on it some more. On May 18, unquestionably under Moroney, they reefed on it again with 110,000 lb., but still nothing moved.

On May 17, the drill pipe at No. 3 was re-entered with the 1¼ in. macaroni string to which a bit was attached. A bridge was encountered about 900 ft. The inside was drilled out to 1,800 ft. with water. The annulus was pressured up with oil to see if it was possible to break the shale bridge, but nothing budged.

In this rather disjointed chain of events, we return to Kinley, who recalls in one of his reports:

> I was informed that Imperial Oil Co. had taken the well over and they did not want to have the 4 in. pipe pulled out of the hole. Dr. Govier informed me that they wanted me to stay until the pumping of water into the offset well had been tried (No. 48). This I did, until after several days of pumping had been tried. It was then obvious no further work was to be done at Atlantic No. 3. I made preparations to return to Houston.[10]

Moroney's version goes like this: "...The first thing I did was to tell Myron Kinley to finish up what he was doing because we were going to make a different approach..."

According to Dave Gray, Kinley was on the derrick floor when he saw a short man walking up the plank road to the rig. He is quoted as saying "I'm long gone...that little SOB ran me off in Louisiana and he's about to do it again." This could not have been Moroney because Tip was quite a tall person. Could this have either been Delaney or Cannon? We will never know.

With Kinley gone, Denton and Spencer's job was also at an end, and Dave Gray returned to Lloydminster.

Reports show that a Hydril BOP was flown in from Los Angeles and installed by May 16. It is probable that the Hydril was ordered by Tip Moroney. Don Wilkin, then "Oilwell Supply" salesman, described a 3 a.m. meeting with Tip and Charlie Visser at the Wales Hotel in Calgary. Don said he had signed an order for 13 BOP's with Imperial at that time, which got him well on his way in the world of "pig–iron".

Because there was insufficient clearance beneath the rig, the installation of the Hydril at No. 3 first required cleaning out the cellar and digging down 4 ft. below the 10¾ in. casing bowl to make room for a cut–off oil drum which was to be filled with dry ice. The only way that the well could be made safe enough to tear out the Hosmer and put on the Hydril was by freezing the top of it solid.

Wilkin and Merv Odham, a Hydril man from California, took the BOP out to the field. Wilkin's taped interview describes the struggle. They hired a democrat (a four–wheeled buggy) and took the steel rims off the wheels to avoid sparks. Because of the bottomless mud on the lease, one of the wheels came off and they had to "piss–ant" (a Ralph Will word for hand haul) the iron in. This was on May 15. A new 12 in. master valve with a "T" to a new 7 in. flowline valve and pipe were also installed. When the casing bowl was removed, it was seen that the shale plugging the annulus had frozen solid. This marked the end of the Hosmer, a device that had outlived its usefulness, to be relegated to the status of the buggy whip.

Campbell Aird (Imperial Oil's pro–duction superintendent) inspecting well head at Atlantic No. 3 shortly after take–over, May 19, 1948.
  Photo furnished by Paul Diemert.

On May 19, the rig was stripped and a 4 in. master valve and Christmas tree was installed by the Imperial Oil crew under Campbell Aird, production superintendent. This was to assist the flow of crude through a hastily constructed 10¾ in. flow line to separators about 1,000 ft. to the east. But there was so much shale coming through the pipe that the separator lines were being blocked as well as the separator.[11] At the same time, other crews were starting on a water line from the river to Imperial's Battery No. 12 to carry on with the next stage, pumping water down Imperial Leduc No. 48, which would only indirectly involve Atlantic No. 3.

A press release that the Conservation Board issued on May 19, a week after it had seized the well, refers to Kinley having succeeded in "practically freeing the drill pipe". The reader will, of course, realize that this was *not* the case. Continuing, "although excellent progress was being made in this operation, it is considered that certain hazards can be eliminated until attempts to flood Atlantic No. 3 by injecting water into Imperial No. 48 can be made". No mention of the two directional holes was made, although plans were well under way. One therefore wonders at the utility or purpose of this release.

Two final notes on the Kinley episode are contained in his two letters from him to the Chairman of the Conservation Board, the first dated June 10:

> I still insist I can control the well as I explained, by pulling the drill pipe and re–cementing the 10 in. casing if not interfered with. I am prepared to make you this proposition: I will complete the job of controlling and killing the well within two weeks. If I do not do so, the only charge will be personal expenses. The fee for successfully killing the well will be $15,000. This is a very small charge compared to the expensive program that is now being followed (drilling the directional holes).

In the second, dated July 22nd:

> The directional wells must be close to completion by now (South Relief should have been!) and I note in the reports from up there that the well is still making over 7,000 barrels per day so apparently it has not weakened any. If the directional wells are not successful, the proposition made to you in my last letter is cancelled.
>
> I still contend that the well can be controlled and killed and will make this second proposition: I will furnish my own crew...I will guarantee to kill the well, if not interfered with. If I do not succeed, there will be no fee other

than expenses. The amount of the fee can only be established after examining the changed conditions.

ENDNOTES:
1. *The Kiwanis Magazine,* April 1953. Kinley was born in Taft, California, 1898; died 1978.
2. Carl Moore, driller; Howard Blanchard, derrick; Leo Schauer, cat
   head; Reg and Cal Bohme, roughhands. See also photo of crew in
   action.
3. Dave Gray said that one of his jobs was to ensure that sufficient mud
   was being mixed to kill the well and that he had to move very rapidly
   because the well was always starting to get away on them again.
4. Mrs. M.M. Kinley, Chickasa, Oklahoma, confirms that Red Adair was
   a McCullough hand and that he started with Kinley in 1948.
   Red Adair, replying to the author, June 11, 1985: "I am sorry to inform
   you that I do not keep records from that far back so I am unable to help
   you with your questions".
   To explain Adair's presence in the Leduc area, the author has had to
   rely on others' recollections. In fact, Adair is mentioned several times
   to the exclusion of Kinley! Some people have even mistaken Kinley for
   Adair in a picture of the former on the rig floor with Dave Gray and
   others.
   Dave Gray recalls Adair's presence, quoting Kinley, "I've sent Red
   out onto an itty bitty gas well" (someplace else).
   Tom Wark's comments, "...so we sent down to Denver to McCullough
   Tool Company to get the tools which were brought up to fish. Red
   Adair was working for McCullough. He brought the tools up. He
   worked with Myron there for two weeks...liked him so he hired him
   away from McCullough to go fire fighting with him. That was Red
   Adair's first time to work on the fire fighting side of it".
5. Halliburton's vehicle colours. Dowell's were orange and black.
6. Pettinger taped interview, January 1986.
7. Barium carbonate used as weighting material. "Bayroyd" is the usual
   pronounciation.
8. Wark's estimate does not tally; he may have thought it looked like one
   and a half tons!
9. Taped interview, March 1986.
10. Kinley wrote the Board in June 1948 asking for his cheque which was
    eventually sent to him. The Board also had to pay $1,060.83 to the
    Receiver General for Canada to cover Myron's non-resident income
    tax.
11. Roger Couture recalls breaking out the separator lines frequently to
    clean out the shale.

III: NO. 48

How on earth did an Imperial Oil well figure in all this?

Firstly, as we have already seen in Part I, Imperial No. 48 was to be used as the staging point for the April 8 big cement job at Atlantic No. 3. Secondly, it was to be temporarily converted to a water injection well. Thirdly, it was finally to be recompleted in 1949 as a D–3 oil well.

The Provincial Department of Lands and Mines had warned Imperial to maintain a balance between the number of freehold wells and those on Crown lands.[1] The purpose of this was to ensure that the Crown got its fair share of royalty, and to limit drainage of Crown lands. The development well, No. 48, located on Crown lands in lsd. 9–22–50–26 was, therefore, "a diagonal offset to Atlantic No. 1". The Drilling Recommendation was approved in February 1948 by Mike Haider, who was now in charge of Imperial operations. Walker Taylor, a Canadian, was now "2i/c". Interestingly enough, No. 48 was originally slated to be drilled by Young Drilling Company for an estimated cost of $70,000. Payout, at 100 barrels per day at $3.00 was forecast to be 230 days.

Once again, Dame Fortune looked kindly upon the future Atlantic No. 3 problem (Leduc field). Instead of the Young rig, General Petroleums' steam rig No. 4, pushed by Tom Wark, was brought in from Bragg Creek. The fact that steam was its source of power was a tremendous plus factor later on.

No. 48 was spudded in on March 20; 314 ft. of 10¾ in. casing were run and cemented with 155 sacks. Drilling was suspended on April 7 to prepare for the massive cement job at Atlantic No. 3, which took place on April 8. The details of this are recorded in Part I of this chapter.

Once the cement job was completed and pronounced a complete failure, drilling at No. 48 was resumed and on May 2 a depth of 5,229 ft. was reached, just above the D–3.

The hole was then logged by Schlumberger. The operator was Frank Black, now head of Caldraft; he recalls the job vividly:

> The whole quarter section was what Hell must look like – a field of surging, bubbling oil, water and mud. Because of the muddy conditions we used a D–8 Cat to bulldoze our unit down the road. It spotted us sideways on the road allowance because the lease was inaccessible. We did the job from 660 ft. since to get closer was impractical. I remember my nervousness over the fact that natu-

PAUL MOSESON

Store clerk, latter day Paul Bunyan, honorary Indian Chief, would–be member of Parliament, head of a drilling company and oil entrepreneur — all of these are wrapped up into one person larger than life: Paul Moseson. Born in Massachusetts of Swedish par–ents, Paul detoured to Malmo at an early age instead of going to California and started his business life selling groceries from his father's store in nearby Wetaskiwin. His entrepreneurial ability resulted in his owning and operating timber limits and sawmills in the Breton area by the 1930's.

Following World War II there was a very heavy demand for lumber. This was accelerated by the discovery of oil at Leduc in 1947, brought on by building construction and the need for lost circulation material. Sawdust suddenly took on an entirely new importance because it was easily obtainable and was well known for its efficacy as a plugging material but it was No. 3 that would really tax the capacity of the saw mills!

Moseson's first direct contact with Atlantic No. 3 came in the form of a call from Imperial Oil's Bill Twaits in the Macdonald Hotel, Edmonton. Twaits was then on a training program on his way to the presidency, thus his assignment at Devon was temporary with the purpose of acquainting him first hand with field operations, and poker game strategy! Paul's recollection of Twait's enquiries is as follows: "Where can I meet you and what kind of a car are you driving?" "How soon can you get the stuff up here?" Moseson relates his search for gunny sacks in which to ship the sawdust. "I got $1 a sack from Imperial Oil for each gunny sack". Later, when the roads went out, Moseson said he was the sole supplier of planking "to make a corduroy about 7 ft. *in depth* with the finest lumber I had...".

As for Moseson's recollection of Red Adair, he says: "half ways out there (to Devon?), we (Twaits? and Moseson) met Red Adair...and of course Red had his ideas which were perfect". Paul quotes Red's concern: "We've got to get in there, we can't let this oil flow all over the country". Thus the need for Moseson to provide planking in order for the men to gain access to the wild well.

In addition to sawdust and planking, Paul also supplied chicken feathers. He explains: ..."I had connections in everything, even then, everywhere because I was involved in politics and I was down east. I bought carloads and nails and anything, you name it. I competed with the major companies. I had no trouble at all...". When asked where he got the chicken feathers, the answer was: "In Montreal. A big wholesale". With all this activity, Moseson got the idea of forming a drilling company using Emsco rigs. He needed a drilling superintendent. Atlantic No. 3, in an indirect way, supplied Paul's requirements in the person of Lloyd Stafford, who by this time had been thoroughly disenchanted with the events at the wild well. Paul hired him away in August of 1948 to run Devon Drilling, which was later rolled into Ponder Oils.

In return for Paul helping to kill Atlantic No. 3 "Imperial Oil gave me one well and four locations, the latter drilled with Model Oil. All of these were producing wells." Compare that reward with what the production hands got in the way of danger pay!

During his 1982 taped interview, Moseson summed up his philosophy of why there are failures in the business world: ..."It's damn simple, you do your job and wait for your pay cheque at the end of the month. You don't know how to take a chance, you don't know how to organize a business, if you haven't got the imagination to figure it out, you'll never get out on your own...".

Moseson, in an expansive mood, talked at length about his friends in high places: C.D. Howe, Louis St. Laurent, A.G.L. McNaughton, Bob Winters, Ed Loughney, their fishing trips and their parties in the Palliser. What a marvellous recollection! What an experience to know this type of risk–taking person and to have re–lived his adventures, the stuff that dreams are made of!

ral gas was bubbling up an old seismic shot hole in the ditch beside the truck when we made the recording".[2]

Moroney must have already had preliminary discussions with the Board and been re–thinking his production casing program at No. 48. It could easily have been just as risky in the D–3 at No. 48 as at Atlantic No. 3, which had now been blowing wild for nearly two months. Caution was the key note.

It was at this point in the operations where Moroney made his next move: "expropriating" one of his own wells to be used as a water injection facility.

A string of 7 in. casing was run and cemented at 5,225 ft. with 200 sacks. A multiplex collar[3] was run at 3,659 ft. on the 7 in. and a second stage of 100 sacks of cement was run. This was to ensure good bonding. On May 11, as has already been noted, Halliburton pumped roughage from No. 48 down Atlantic No. 3. Drilling was resumed, with a 6⅛ in. bit inside the 7 in. pipe and the D–3 was encountered at 5,230 ft. The hole was bottomed at 5,363 ft., just five feet above the oil–water interface, with no lost circulation difficulties. Schlumberger ran a second log on May 22, presumably for comparison purposes with Atlantic No. 3 and other wells nearby.

Next was run 179 ft. of 5 in. liner, cemented on bottom ("tacked") with 35 sacks. The liner was perforated from 5,341 ft. to 5,346 ft. This readied the well bore for water injection, in accordance with Delaney and Cannon's recommendation.[4]

To prepare the well for water injection, the D–3 zone had to be acidized with 5,000 gallons of HCl which went on vacuum after 3,500 gallons had been put away. The drilling rig was released on May 24; by that time, the decision to skid it over to West Relief well site had been made.

Imperial production crews had been called in to lay pipelines and install pumps to bring water from the North Saskatchewan River to Battery No. 12 and thence down Imperial Leduc No. 48. This facility was later used in pumping water over to West Relief for the killing of Atlantic No. 3 itself.

After several delays, one resulting from the sudden flooding of the river, injection of water down No. 48 was commenced on May 28 at about 30,000 barrels per day. According to one report, a total of 691,000 barrels was put away; according to another, 544,000 barrels, from May 28 to mid–June.

Harry Simpson remembers mixing sodium hypochlorite into the No. 48 injection water as a tracer. Jimmy Young, Imperial's scientific guru, had suggested that the substance could be detected using a platinum wire. While there were traces showing in the produced fluids at Atlantic No. 3, the exercise was ineffectual. As Harry explains it, the very high permeability of the D–3 resulted in an initial pressure response over the entire pool area but hindered the anticipated horizontal movement to No. 3.

Some years passed before the framework of the reef systems running from Rimbey to Big Lake was more clearly understood. After much deep drilling both on and off reef along this trend, it was found that the Cooking Lake Formation constitutes an enormous aquifer underlying the D–3 reef chain. This aquifer exerts active pressure on all of the D–3 reservoirs. The massive amounts of water injected into No. 48, merely disappeared into this watery void.

Delaney and Cannon must have been thinking in terms of a layered reservoir bed with little porous rock below the oil/water interface, which would enable lateral movement of the injected water. How could they have known at this time of the virtually bottomless "super aquifer" underlying the thick, porous D–3 reefs.

Another cogent question arises: if this aquifer were so active, why did water not cone up and kill Atlantic No. 3 itself? We must realize that the bottom of the Atlantic No. 3 hole was many feet above the gas/oil contact of the field. What really happened was a D–3 gas blow–out with oil coning up, augmented by the Viking zone gas. The oil/water line was about 45 ft. below TD, too far for the water to cone.

No. 48 was re–worked in the winter of 1948–49. The liner was pulled, a new one run and perforated, and the well put on production as a D–3 oil well.

ENDNOTES:
1. Twp. 50 Rge. 26 W4M is characterized by checkerboarded Crown and freehold, some of the former having been patented out prior to 1887. This required Imperial to drill:
   a. to validate each Crown quarter section as per the 1945 regulations,
   b. freehold leases.
   This set up a Crown–freehold conflict and the Crown wanted to ensure it got its fair share of royalty.
2. Personal communication.
3. Multiplex collar: a device run midway in casing string through which cement is pumped in a second stage.
4. These two were brought up as advisors from The Gulf Coast.

BOARD BITES THE BULLET 10

The Conservation Board was now navigating uncharted waters of hitherto unexperienced responsibilities. And yet it had to steer a course so as to avoid the rocks and thereby carry out its statutory duties. Not an inviting prospect, with nothing but failures to date and the absolute need to "do something".

It had seen Cody Spencer, almost single handedly, try every trick he knew. Red Goodall had been consulted on the decision to drill "dry", and had acquiesced. But the blow-out of March 8 must have sent shock waves through the organization.

Spi Langston recalls Hubert Somerville warning him: "We're going to have to take the thing over".

When oil and gas started to crater up after the frost had gone out of the ground, apprehension must have mounted even more. Along with the Owner and the Contractor, it hoped against hope that the "big cement job" of April 7 would plug the well bore. That massive project having failed, the Board agreed to the hiring of Myron Kinley, wild well fighter. Myron ultimately admitted himself completely stymied: "no fire, no use for dynamite", as was his wont.

The next straw was the "feather job" which achieved no more than the cement had.

As the days and weeks dragged on with no success by Atlantic in controlling the well, Walker Taylor, manager of Imperial Oil, with responsibility for over 80% of the field production, could see nothing but ruin of the field if effective measures were not taken soon. Don Mackenzie, then in Toronto with Imperial Oil, recalls a number of phone calls made by Walker to Oliver B. Hopkins, contact director for "Producing Department" of Imperial Oil. It was Don's understanding that Walker wanted to bring in people and set up an organizational plan to kill the well. His strategy was to maintain discipline and order, hardly possible for unstaffed Atlantic Oil. These conversations may have resulted in Delaney and Cannon being brought up from Houston to look over the problem. Moroney recalls: "McKinnon and I had a number of conversations with respect to what approaches might be made...and McKinnon seemed to think...that Imperial would be (the) most capable of handling this situation".[1]

Gas erupting in the sump at Atlantic No. 3 during the blow–out.
Photo furnished by E.E. Gilbert.

The mud sump at Atlantic No. 3. Note the cratering. John Rebus' farm–stead and Atlantic tank farm in background. Looking northeast.
Photo furnished by Joe Kohlman.

A seething lake of oil.

Photo furnished by N.G. Loudoun.

So a theory of cause and effect that the author has developed appears to have some merit: Taylor pushing on Tanner, John Harvie (Minister and Deputy Minister of Mines) and Ian McKinnon; Moroney being recommended as the man for the job. Records show that McKinnon officially approached Walker Taylor, and in a letter of May 13 sought Moroney's services "...to take charge of operations for us until such time as the well can be brought under control..." He went on to suggest that Imperial keep Tip and his helpers on the Imperial payroll and bill the Board for their services. The following day, Taylor wrote McKinnon that Moroney would be available and "...will act in the capacity of your agent and field manager...and all other loaned personnel will be under his direction..." To protect itself, "...Imperial assumes no responsibility for the conduct of the operations or the control of personnel..."

As Cal Bohme summarized this long period of travail: "It was a pretty loose operation until the Board took over".

The Board had to make up its mind as to a course of action, but was wary of the legal and political consequences of sequestering private property. However, this was the decision taken. Its first step was to cite Section 16 of the Oil and Gas Conservation Act (Chapter 66 of the revised statutes of 1942) which gave the Board the power to "control and regulate the production of petroleum, either by restriction or prohibition or both". It then issued Board Order No. 5L which stated: "...that from 8:00 a.m. on the 13th day of May 1948, and until further notice, no oil may be produced from any well in the

Leduc Area...'' The Order was duly approved by the Executive Council of the government and countersigned by Lieutenant Governor J.C. Bowen.

Although the document has not been found, it is generally acknowledged that Nate Goodman, under instructions, telegraphed the Chairman to the effect that Atlantic No. 3 was *not* complying with Order No. 5L. This opened the way for McKinnon to invoke Section 46(1) under Part IV of the Act:

> ...the Board may take such steps and employ such persons as it considers necessary for the enforcement of any order made by it, and for the purposes thereof may forcibly or otherwise enter upon, seize and take possession of the whole or part of the moveable and immoveable property in, on or about any well or used in connection therewith...and may, until the order has been complied with, either discontinue all production or may take over the management and control thereof.

Subsections 2, 3 and 4 of Section 46 directed:

> ...every officer and employee of the Owner to obey the orders of the Board...and the Board, by taking possession, is empowered to deal with and dispose of all petroleum produced,...as if it were the property of the Board subject to the obligation to account for the net proceeds thereof to the persons entitled thereto...the cost and expenses shall be at the Board's discretion and the Board may direct by whom and to what extent they shall be paid...

This legislation had been passed in 1938, when the Board was formed. It applied perfectly to the Atlantic No. 3 situation.

Moroney had already prepared himself for the task because he, in his letter of May 19 to the Board, had set out his plans:

1. Suspend operations for removal of drill pipe.
2. Connect the drill pipe to pass the oil flow through separators in order to relieve pressure on the well.
3. Continue the drilling of two directional holes.
4. Prepare Imperial No. 48 as a water injection well...in an attempt to flood Atlantic No. 3.
5. Prepare Atlantic No. 1 and 2 as injection wells for excess oil that cannot be handled by pipeline facilities.
6. Take steps to reduce hazard of fire as follows:
   a. restrict movement,
   b. eliminate from the danger zone all gas and gasoline

Atlantic No. 3, shortly after blowing out from the D–3, March 8, 1948.
Photo furnished by Howard Blanchard.

engine operated equipment and boilers as soon as they can be replaced by diesel or steam equipment.

c. install wind signals (sic) in order that operators of the above equipment can be at all times aware of the wind direction so that equipment can be immediately shut down when the winds are unfavourable.

7. Activate safety inspection of personnel and equipment and maintain a first aid and ambulance station near the danger zone.

8. Appoint assistants.

PIPELINES

One of the first considerations, when Imperial realized that the D-3 would produce large amounts of crude, was to plan a pipeline.

But the ever-increasing number of wells resulted in crude backing up at the batteries. This problem was solved by trucking crude to a siding in Leduc town. It was pumped directly from the truck into waiting tank cars. Gibby Gibson supervised the loading. He had to stop pumping oil whenever a train approached because sparks from the passing steam locomotive could easily ignite the heavy fumes evolving from the crude.

This unsatisfactory procedure was eliminated as soon as possible. A subsidiary, Imperial Pipeline Company Limited was recreated by Imperial Oil. There was already a cadre of pipelining hands in existence, plus some ancient equipment in the Valley that had been operated by Valley Pipeline which was a subsidiary of Royalite, also in the Imperial stable.

These crews were moved up to Nisku, the site chosen for the pipeline terminus. At that time, Nisku was merely a siding with a few elevators and nothing else. The hands were forced to live in tents. An 8 in. line, capable of moving about 15,000 barrels per day without an intermediate pumping station, was selected for the short distance from Leduc to Nisku.

Surveying started in early summer. Bill Clark recalls surveying the right-of-way along the north side of the road allowance from Nisku west to the field. Two obstacles lay in his path: a deep coulee and a community hall. The coulee was traversed by a bridge. The hall problem was a lot tougher because it was, at first, impossible to obtain an easement. The farmers who were connected with this hall made their point forcibly with axes and other weapons. Compromise was ultimately reached whereby the line went ahead after promises were made to restore the land. The pipeline was wrapped and tarred by hand and it was put into operation in October 1947.

When Atlantic No. 3's uncontrolled oil production commenced, Atlantic hired trucks to haul the oil away from the pits in the northwest extremity of the Rebus quarter. As the rampage increased, so did concern grow as to how to handle the larger amounts. Don Whitney remembers one of the McMahon brothers coming up to inspect the lease and being unconvinced that the pits held oil rather than water.

The Board finally stepped in and handed the oil transportation problem over to Imperial Oil and Imperial Pipeline. This galvanized crews into action. Mud hogs, destined as back-up pumps for wildcat wells, were diverted to a new use. Two were rigged up on the north side of the road allowance to pump oil from the pits. Storage tanks were hastily erected. A line crossed the road to the Leduc Consolidated lease to the east. Lines were also laid from the tanks to Atlantic No. 1 and 2 well heads. When asked why oil was being pumped back down these two wells, Moroney replied: "Well I can't drink it, it belongs to the lease until it is sold. If we have to recirculate it, that's what we're going to do because I have had all the oil I can drink".

Harry Andruski with the pumps used to move crude from Leduc Consoli-dated lease tanks into Nisku pipeline. Note steam line.

Photo furnished by Bill Bray.

A connecting line crossed over to the north side of the road where there were a series of pumping units that had been re-allocated by Imperial Pipe Line. This equipment had been ordered in to pump crude elsewhere in the field. Harry Andruski, Imperial Pipeline hand, remembers having to assemble the units and later run them. They were powered by gasoline engines which had to be converted with special spark plugs to use natural gas. Five of these units grew to ten. The amount of oil produced was scheduled firstly, back into the No. 1 and No. 2 wells, secondly, into the holding tanks and thirdly, shipped every three hours across the road to the pump-ing units and then to Nisku. All of this in turn had to be co-ordinated with the other oil wells' production which had been allowed to resume.

Despite the enormous uncontrolled flow of oil from Atlantic No. 3, wells had been put back on production as far south as Calmar. It was therefore necessary to erect a 10,000 barrel tank one mile to the west of the Atlantic tank farm. This was masterminded by the late Johnny Lyle, who did the impossible in two days. This facility, indirectly, gave a greater degree of flexibility to the overall scheduling of production. Lyle's recollections were of a 3 in. line running from the pumps across from the Atlantic pits one mile west to his 10,000 barrel tank, from which oil was shipped to Nisku by pipeline.

In the hopes that much of the oil from Atlantic No. 3 could be produced through a hastily constructed production head on the top of the drill pipe, a 10¾ in. line was laid from the well to separators. From there, the oil flowed over to the Leduc Consolidated facilities. However, as Roger Couture explained, "shale fragments lodged in the production head and had to be cleaned out frequently, thus limiting its use".

Part of the oil gathering system. The oil from Atlantic No. 3 (left) was passed through the separators on its way to the collection area and the Nisku pipeline.
Photo furnished by Don Gamble.

Lines for quite a different purpose were hastily laid by Imperial Oil productions crews. According to Bill Clark, rights–of–way were waived by the farmers who by now were sharing fears of a field–wide conflagration. Two 4 in. lines (using drill pipe) were laid from the North Saskatchewan River bottom to Battery No. 12. Down by the river, there were two pumps, one a centrifugal and the other a positive displacement type, to enable the water to be pushed up the hill to Battery No. 12. Just as things were getting into place, the North Saskatchewan River rose very suddenly, on May 24, many feet above its normal level. Ben Owre, one of the production hands

Laying the water line from the North Saskatchewan River to Imperial No.48. Norm Wilkinson is at the centre of the pipe joint being carried. Other workers unidentified.

Photo furnished by Provincial Archives.

recalls frantic all–night efforts to skid the pumps up to higher ground to prevent their being inundated. At Battery No. 12, two Ideal C350 pumps were rigged up to push water up into the rectangular holding tanks. From there, it was pumped down Imperial Leduc No. 48 during May and June. Much later, these lines were extended to West Relief to supply the water to kill Atlantic No. 3.

Mark Blain Sr., Hugh Leiper's uncle, recalls being unable to keep ahead of the oil dykes with the pumps they had. The amount of oil in the dykes was reckoned by daily measurement on yardsticks placed in the pits. (See Appendices F and G.)

When the well caught fire on September 6, these same crews helped in keeping the flaming oil away from the main storage pits, saving large quantities of crude. By late November 1948, all the surface installations had been dismantled; the mud hogs shipped back to the drilling rigs, the gas pumps put on line at the batteries and the crews returned to their normal duties.

Let Tip tell about his arrangement with the Board as he recited it in his 1957 interview with Mr. Carscallen:

> ...As soon as they took it over, I was loaned to the Conservation Board and the well was put in my charge. This was done with the consent of the company and my consent and I was asked if I would take the job; I said I'd take the job if I was in charge — that is, absolutely in charge. I wasn't going to bother going to people asking if it was alright to do this or that, I was just going to go ahead and fix it, if I could. And when they got tired of the way I was doing it, all they had to do was say goodbye and I'd leave. That way, while I had it, I'd really have it. And that was just what they wanted.

ENDNOTE:
1. There is no record of either the Board or Imperial signing a contract for the two relief holes to be drilled by General Petroleums.

MORONEY, VISSER AND TOD

11

"We used a lot of luck".

This masterpiece of understatement underscores Moroney's main attributes: his tough, effective leadership, his ability to identify people he had only known for a few months who would become his trusted working companions, and his ability to seize opportunities and act on them. As Jim Tod, veteran mud man, stated: "He had a mind of his own, you had to convince him but he wasn't stubborn...calm and cool...didn't fly off the handle".[1]

When Moroney was given the job of subduing Atlantic No. 3, he had no one to fall back on, but he combined his previous experience with the harnessing up of everyone and anyone who could assist him. So his laconic comment was, in a sense, a subliminal way of expressing his success in killing Atlantic No. 3.

Vincent John (Tip) Moroney was born in Findlay, Ohio, the son of a tank strapper. His father moved out to Okmulgee, Oklahoma to set up a newspaper. Tip recalled standing in the shade of horses as a boy in 1907, watching a treaty being signed between Indian tribes and the white man. It was the year that Oklahoma entered the union.

Although there had been some small discoveries made before the turn of the century, the first big find was the Glenn field in 1904, about 25 miles north of Tip's home. As the boom extended, other fields were found and the entire area around Okmulgee was dotted with oil wells. Tip's uncles had been involved in the oil business as land men so it was not surprising that Tip would also be attracted.

Moroney attended Georgetown University (Washington, D.C.), graduating from there in science and physics in 1926. It was there that he met his first wife, whom he married in 1927. She passed away in 1964, and Tip later re-married. Many years later, Tip confided to Gibby Gibson that he had seriously considered professional football because he had excelled in sports while attending university. Fortunately for many people, and the oil patch in particular, he opted for petroleum.

Upon graduation, Tip started a life-long career with Standard Oil Company of New Jersey (now Exxon), living in a company house with his bride in the Seminole field. In those days, supervisors were graduates of the "school of hard knocks" which meant minimum formal education. Moroney recalled that as a young engineer, he kept a low profile, "it was thought best not to let on one knew too much".

Rotary rigs were just then coming into use. At Seminole, the derricks were insecure because they were guyed down with turn-buckles and were subject to collapse in high winds. One can sur-mise that, when Tip watched the collapsing Atlantic No. 3 rig on Labour Day, 1948, he harked back to those days in Seminole. One experience, of value in future blow-outs, was when he moved quickly and decisively to kill a well that had a blown out valve gasket and had caught fire.

In those days it was an unwritten law that Jersey junior profes-sionals take a foreign assignment. Moroney learned much of inter-nal politics when various postings were considered by his seniors. He turned down Indonesia and Romania for Peru.

In 1930, he, his wife and young family sailed from New York City, arriving at Talara ten days later. The Brea–Parinas fields had been producing for a number of years and steps were being taken to re–work the wells. Re–drilling with rotary tools was carried out and liners were run through the gas cap. When killing the first well, a slug of mud and oil kicked back and blew off the 10 in. valve, killing two men. Moroney moved quickly in this crisis and brought the well under control. Having been promoted after this unfortunate inci-dent, he introduced new ideas in secondary recovery. When he left in 1946, both production and reserves had increased over what was originally expected back in 1930 when he first arrived.

Two interesting extra–curricular activities of his must be men-tioned: his study of and proficiency in the Spanish language, and Peruvian Indian dialects. Tip later theorized, noting the kinship of the Athapaskan tongues of the Northwest Territories in Canada with those of South America, that the native inhabitants of Peru had also migrated across the land bridge from Siberia at the end of the Ice Age.

Tip's ability to handle emergencies was put to the test in World War II when he was asked to keep an eye on the very strong German colony at Negritos. Security leaks enabled these Germans to relay perfect information on military movements to Berlin. Moroney "arranged" for the pro–German Peruvian general sta-tioned in the area to be replaced by one with Indian blood who was friendly to the U.S. cause. A top German who had escaped from an Ontario prisoner of war camp was spotted in Negritos by Moroney and picked up shortly thereafter. Tip used Chinese to sort out the Japanese in the area while any "aliens" who were regarded as threats were gathered up and shipped to Texas for internment.

Tip was transferred to Venezuela in 1946, but this was a short–lived assignment. A well blew out while he was there but as he said, "there were about 15 people interfering, so I kept away from it". This occurrence would also stand him in good stead when laying out his program for taking over Atlantic No. 3.

Late in 1947, Tip received a phone call from New York asking him how soon he could be in Calgary. By that time, Jersey had realized that Leduc was no flash in the pan and was moving experienced people in to help the modest Canadian operation. Moroney and his family picked up a car in New York, drove to Okmulgee and, after a short holiday, crossed the border at Coutts on January 3, 1948.

It did not take Tip long to get settled in. When word came to Tip that there was something amiss in Atlantic No. 3, he stated: "I don't remember whether it was daylight or dark at the time, but the day that the thing got loose, I was made aware of it...it was, of course, a very great shock to the Imperial people..."[2]

Tip Moroney (left) and Charlie Visser (right) at South Relief, July, 1948, standing in front of Moroney's "company" Packard.

Photo furnished by Jerry Moroney and Chris Wood.

THE COMMISSIONAIRES AND REBUS

One of the priorities on Moroney's list when he took over May 14, was to secure the area as soon as possible. In a 1957 taped interview, he recalled confronting Tanner (Minister of Lands and Mines) and McKinnon:

> ...The first thing we were going to do was close the area off to traffic...there was altogether too much running around in there...we'd set up guards and anybody in there would have to have a pass. We could scrutinize the people and the purpose of their being there...we had to have workmen in the area all the time, on the rig(s), on the oil–saving program and the risk of having traffic and uncontrolled entry was just too great if it could be avoided and it could be. So when I mentioned that we were going to do this, they said..."we have no law to allow us to do this". So I said, "well, you just get busy and make a quick law, because we're going to close it off"...they just shook their heads. I said "well, that's what we're going to do because we're going to be having a lot of men running around in there and I'm going to be running around in there with them"...Ian MacKinnon after a little while said they'd decided that they could close the area off all right under the Forestries Act. I said "OK. I don't care what act you use, just close the gate"...

The Prevention of Prairie and Forest Fires Act was invoked and ads were run in the newspapers as if to legalize the restrictions which were already in place. McKinnon was a stickler for the law, following procedures which Moroney was more at home in cutting through.

How to man these check points? McKinnon immediately thought of the Canadian Corps of Commissionaires, mostly World War I veterans who had seen security work during World War II. They were given little huts to stay in and posted at strategic corners. Passes were issued to those who had to enter the area under the provisions of the Campers and Travellers' regulations.

Because the Commissionaires were being paid by the Board, the Board had to feed them. Thus Bill Kinghorn recalls one of his jobs being to supply the guards with groceries.

Matches, cigarettes and other inflammable substances were to be removed from the workers as they entered the danger zone.

It is particularly instructive to keep the following excerpt from Section 13 (1) of the Act in mind when reading the Moroney and

McMahon accounts of their visits to John Rebus: "...and to shut out therefrom all persons except such as are specifically authorized..."

Moroney, despite his ability to delegate, still had one item he (and Charlie Visser) had to attend to personally. Here is Tip describing his visit to the Rebus house:

> ...one of the conditions we made for taking over the lease that he (Rebus) would move. He was living too close to this thing...I didn't think I was going to have to talk to him because I thought that was up to the government people. But they had sent representatives...one of the Ministers came out to see him and he told him he wouldn't move...So I finally went over to see him. Charlie (Visser) and I...told him he was...going to move whether he liked it or not.
>
> He said: "Oh I go. If Imperial Oil wants to send me to California, I go and pay my expenses."
>
> "You're going to get off here."
>
> "Noooo."
>
> "Yeah, you're going John, there's no doubt about it...You're just being plain hardheaded. Are you going to sit here and burn yourself up? Fine, but I don't want you to burn anybody else up, which is what you're apt to do."
>
> His wife wanted to butt in on the conversation. She was a school teacher. I decided after talking to him and hearing words come out of the kitchen, I said to him: "John, is this your farm or not?"
>
> "Yes", he said, "it's my farm."
>
> "Well John, we're going to move you."
>
> Across the road from the Rebus farm, in another field was...General Pete's camp.
>
> "Well, what about that cookshack?"
>
> "You just keep your eye on that cookshack for another ten minutes."
>
> Just as I was talking, a truck backed up and they threw a winch line onto the shack and up she goes onto the truck. That whole camp was moved while I was talking to him.
>
> "You mean there isn't going to be anything going on in here at all?"
>
> "Nope, not a thing.
>
> "Well, I'll go maybe on Wednesday."
>
> "You're going now. Right now. No more cooking in this house."
>
> "Well, where are we going to eat?"

"John, I don't know where you're going to eat...But you're going to get out so I can put these fellows to work over here. We've got lots of things to do and we haven't got time to sit around here talking to an iron–headed Dutchman."

"Well, OK, nobody ever talked to me like that before."

"Everybody's been out here talking to you. Now I'm talking to you and you're going to move."

"Well, you talk to me like a man. I like that. I'll move."

He was gone in 30 minutes...We had no more prob-lems. He came out a few times and he wanted to talk to me, for example about people leaving his gates open...He was always friendly though. He came out a number of times while we were working there and he always tried to find Charlie or me and we'd sit down and talk to him...and he was friendly enough.

Frank McMahon, on one of his visits to Leduc, recorded in a "Daily Field Report" dated June 1, a somewhat different version which showed the close rapport between lessee and lessor.

John Rebus came over to the tank farm and asked me to come over to his home, as he wanted to see me and talk over a situation. I went over to Rebus' for dinner and evidently on May 21st, Mr. Moroney of the Imperial Oil came out to the Rebus farm and told Rebus to move off. Evidently Rebus told him where to go so on Saturday morning, May 22nd, Moroney, McKinnon, Huestis and two R.C.M.P. officers came out to the Rebus farm again and considerable discussion was held. At any rate, John told them he would not move off the farm unless they gave him a letter to the effect that they would substan-tially reimburse him. They also informed him that he was not to use any tractors around his farm. Evidently these instructions were also issued to farmers to adjoining property, but Rebus said nobody is paying any attention to it. He was pretty riled up at the Government's attitude. I told Rebus to just sit tight and everything would probably turn out all right in the end. At least, Atlantic Oil would take care of him concerning the damage done to his property. Rebus has been very good with our boys on the Atlantic lease and has co–operated in every way with us all along and from his attitude I am sure he will continue to do so. He is very anxious to buy a new car in the low–price class so I assured him I would try to locate one for him somehow.

A lot of the locals and some other inquisitive types bypassed the check points and would walk across the field into the danger zone.

Jim Rennie, retired, (public affairs officer with Imperial at the time) was asked by Ross Beesley, Associated Screen News as to the best way to get near the well. Rennie told him but the vigilant Moroney caught up with Ross, though not before he had taken some photos.

Major Lowrey, head of Home Oil at that time, told Jimmy Stafford, field manager, (no relation to Lloyd) not to apply for passes. He sternly warned him to drive around the check–points. Then in case the well caught fire, there would be no question of laying any responsibility at Home Oil's door–step. Jimmy became friends with the commissionaires – what Lowery didn't know wouldn't hurt him!

This pass was issued to those peo–ple assigned to controlling Atlantic No. 3 (lsd. 12–23–50–26 W4M) wild well, and permitted them to enter the danger area.

Tom Hallett, mechanic with Barber Machine, did not have a pass. He was required to accompany Griff (Earl Griffith, owner) out to the well one night to do some work. In order to save time, Griff covered him with a blanket in the back seat and told him to lay quietly while he was smuggled in and out of the area.

We now turn to Charlie (The Dutchman) Visser who, in early 1948, was drilling superintendent for Imperial Oil/Royalite operations. Visser was born in Rotterdam, The Netherlands and emigrated with his parents to Okotoks in 1913. His father was one of the first rig builders in the west. This was a special art which required the skilful shaping of timbers and spiking them together to end up with a structure capable of withstanding live multi-ton weights, continual vibration and wind loads. These have long been replaced, first by steel bolted derricks and, later, by portable jack-knife masts that are raised in one piece.

Visser's career with Imperial began at Dead Horse Coulee in 1924 but he had worked as a tool dresser, sharpening and tempering fish-tail bits in earlier years. At Dead Horse Coulee, he had his first, but not his last, exposure to a blow-out. He recalls that he, along with a burly blacksmith, fought it with homemade tools.[3]

During the depression, when Royalite's activities declined, he was forced to go out on his own to earn a few dollars. He recalls getting half of his wages during the drilling of a typical well and the other half only if the well were successful.

When Royalite was revitalized as a result of the 1936 oil "discovery" at Turner Valley, he rejoined it and advanced to tool push in 1938. From there on, a lot of experience in drilling deep tests in Saskatchewan resulted in his ultimately becoming drilling superintendent. Charlie could be best remembered for his steady unflappable demeanour. His favorite advice in times of crisis was: "Do *something,* even if it's wrong".

One of the more fascinating aspects of this story is that Moroney immediately identified Visser as a drilling expert. Indeed, when Moroney was given the job of bringing Atlantic No. 3 under control, one of his stipulations was that Visser be his right-hand man.

We now come to the third man of the trio: Jim Tod. Like Charlie, Jim started off in the Valley roughnecking on the rigs. Having a bent for improving conditions, he set about developing better drilling muds. Up to that time, the practice was to boil up local mud in boxes at the rig and use it. No one was particularly interested in mud, let alone its technology. Nevertheless, Jim persevered, becoming Canada's pioneer mud man. His experience was put to a real test in southern Saskatchewan where Imperial drilled a series of deep stratigraphic tests which intersected great thicknesses of salt and anhydrite. Both of these minerals were instant death to bentonite mud, flocculating it and turning it into unpumpable "porridge".

At the time of Leduc, Tod's responsibility was to look after the

Jim Tod, Royalite–Imperial pioneer mud man.

Photo furnished by Jim Tod

mud for all Imperial Oil holes drilled, making sure the drilling fluid was in shape to run drillstem tests and casing. "It was the hardest job I ever had in my life." Visser and Tod had worked closely together in Saskatchewan, so Tod was appointed to look after the mud at the directional relief holes and act as a back–up to Visser on drilling matters.

Thus the fates combined in bringing these three experts together. They proved to be the team that ultimately brought Atlantic No. 3 under control.

ENDNOTES:
1. Personal communication.
2. Taped interview, 1981, on file at Glenbow.
3. *Imperial Oil Review,* December–January 1949–1950 issue p. 30 by Jim Rennie.

MORONEY'S GAME PLAN

I: DIRECTIONAL DRILLING

12

Why had General Petroleums not converted its obsolescent steam rigs to power like other contractors had? The answer was that they may have been rented (from Snyder and Head or some other firm?) Al Wright, then Field Superintendent, recalls G.P. buying the Newell and Chandler rigs for $75,000. Furthermore, G.P. was in a financial bind and did not have the money to switch over.

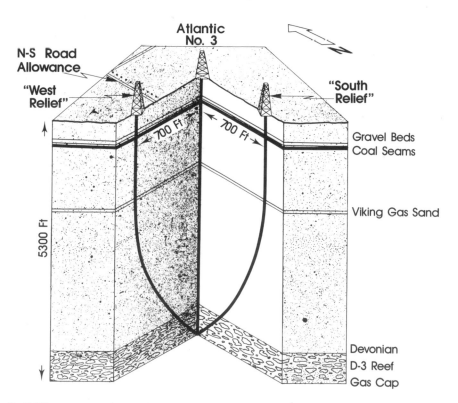

3–D Diagram to show wild well bore and traces of two reliefs.
Illustration furnished by Petro Canada Reprographics

Because the key to the successful killing of Atlantic No. 3 lay in drilling *two* directional holes, Moroney in his 1957 interview cited his reasons:

> The justification...was this: we knew very little about the characteristic drift of rotary holes in the area...and what it took to control directional drilling. We did know, however, from experience here and everywhere else that directional drilling was tricky. You could get into a lot of hole trouble, particularly if it wouldn't stand up over a long period...so I looked at it this way; it took normally 45 to 55 days to drill a hole if you didn't have lost circulation...so if it took twice that long, maybe four months, and if you had trouble, you had to look at more time ...if we spent a whole summer drilling one directional hole and then got into trouble and lost it, which was something that *could* happen...then we would be into winter and have to start drilling another...so the chances of getting one of them down were much better...so we just ordered the two rigs out and started them to work.

It was obvious that power rigs could not be used because of the sparks and heat from the diesel engines' exhausts. And here was G.P. with these two steam rigs, a 100% day work contract in its hand, payment guaranteed by the Conservation Board. What a windfall!

The Viking gas sand, the villainous Mr. Hyde, initially responsible for the blow–out and continuing to cause problems, was at one and the same time the benevolent Dr. Jekyll, supplying boiler fuel for the two rigs.

The Board accordingly issued licences to itself as both Owner and Operator. South Relief was designated as No. 1 on the application form and West Relief was known as No. 2. Locations for these were made 700 ft. south and west respectively, of Atlantic No. 3. Bill Clark obtained the surface rights from the farmers. Locations were surveyed in by Doug Stevenson and Gordon Turnock (both Esso retirees). The G.P. rig that had drilled Imperial Leduc No. 48 was to be skidded a short distance east to the West Relief location. The boilers used at No. 48 were left where they were in an up–wind position and longer steam lines were laid. The other set of boilers was placed to the west of South Relief, also up–wind. Super–heaters on the steam lines boosted temperatures to 400°F and the steam was so hot that it burned the sawdust insulation from time to time. A wind sock (rented from the RCAF for $22) plus a phone system would alert the crews and firemen to unfavourable wind

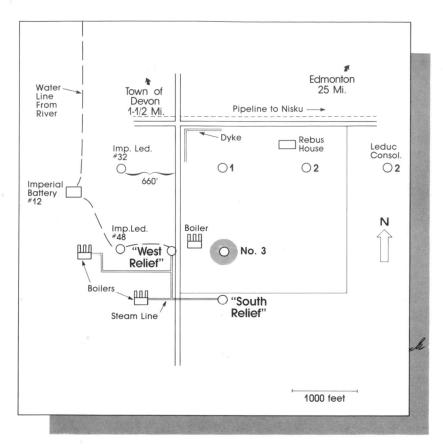

Atlantic "quarter" (160 acres), summer, 1948.
Illustration furnished by Petro–Canada Reprographics.

shifts so their boilers could be shut down without leaving the drill bit on bottom with no mud pump available.

Tom Wark was given the job of tool pusher at West Relief. He had, as drillers: Bill Murray, Jack Emslie (who was killed at the Bonnie Glen blow–out and fire) and Carl Moore. Tom had come from Gladys Ridge, one of a family of 12. He started off in Turner Valley digging ditches and rig cellars and loading sacks of cement. He went roughnecking in 1936 for Snyder and Head. Woodrow Wilson, who helped supervise the two relief holes, was his first boss. Tom was no stranger to the perils of the Turner Valley oil patch. He had been gassed on several occasions with H_2S. He had also helped badly injured fellow workers in not infrequent accidents (no hard hats!).

One of the boiler installations supplying the relief drilling rigs. Note super–heater in right background.

Photo furnished by G.P. ''Rig–n–Dig'', Johnny Yeo.

At West Relief. Standing left to right: Hic Kern, HOMCO; Nurse (unidentified); Intern (unidentified). Seated: Tom Wark, G.P. push; Lloyd Stafford, G.P. push.
Photo furnished by W.J. Gibson and L. Stafford.

Prior to coming to Leduc, Tom spent some time at Norman Wells. He was pushing tools at Bragg Creek when the call came to move his No. 4 rig up to Imperial Leduc No. 48. Tom is still active doing some consulting and also working out at the old cable tool rig at Heritage Park.

The push on South Relief (G.P. Rig No.19) was quite a different cat: B.W.L. (Ben) Quarti, a native of Australia. His drillers were Johnny McDonald, Wilf Boyer and Alf Addison plus Messrs. Gareau, Gobin and Witting. Quarti was not your average drilling hand. He had spent much time in the jungles of the Far East, his only reading material being the Composite Catalogue which he said he had memorized. He was of an inventive nature and actually filed on several patents related to drilling. Unpredictable but innovative, Quarti knew the art of drilling as few others did.

Ben Quarti (left) explaining author's correlation charts to ?.
Photo furnished by Provincial Archives

Ben kept a close eye on his rig from his tool pusher's shack through the telescopic sight of his rifle. His partying exploits brought him wide-spread notoriety: a wall climbing exhibition in which he would wet his stocking feet in beer, proceed to go up the wall and even a step or two on the ceiling before coming back down. His driving exploits were equally spectacular. On one occasion, he left the road, took out a couple of telephone poles and wrapped the truck up in the wires upside down. In those days, the battery was under the floor. Acid dripped on the trapped man, inflicting painful burns.

Under Tip's and Charlie's command, the two rigs spudded in the latter part of May. The Board licence on South Relief had specified 300 ft. of surface casing. Tip was taking no chances: 13⅜ in. casing was set at about 500 ft. with nearly 300 sacks assuring returns. There was no shortage of blow-out prevention equipment, two of the hydraulic type plus adequate relief valves being installed. The BOP's were tested regularly to ensure that they were fully operative. Tip's plan called for straight hole drilling to about 2,800 ft. at South Relief and 2,000 ft. at West Relief. The reason for the shallower depth was that West Relief had more horizontal ground to cover to reach its target. Despite this precaution, it fell short by 400 ft. or so.

Two directional drilling experts were called in: Hickman (Hick) Kern of HOMCO on West Relief and Charlie Smith of Eastman on South Relief. Both crews were in awe of those chaps! Hick had the advantage of a new Monel metal (non-magnetic) drill collar which permitted surveying (angle and azimuth) without coming out of the hole. This was accomplished by a camera that was run to bottom on a wire-line and retrieved after photographing the compass. Both rigs used the Stokenbury method of setting whipstocks.

Al Phillips, then cat-head man, remembers Charlie Smith, a 20-year veteran and a dedicated expert as having taken him under his wing. Phillips left G.P. early in 1949 to go with Smith at Eastman and has recently retired from Computalog Gearhart. "If it hadn't of been for Atlantic No. 3 (and Charlie Smith), I doubt very much that I would have ended up in the directional business. I didn't know anything about it then but it still is a sort of romantic occupation."

Paraphrasing Al's description of the tedious method of setting whipstocks, the drill pipe with the whipstock was oriented into the hole so that the face of its chisel was pointed in the desired direction. It was absolutely necessary to maintain this setting and this was insured by the telescopic sighting, by an extra hand above the derrick man, of alignment clamps on the drill pipe. These were attached and removed as the pipe was lowered in the hole, maintaining the same orientation. When the pipe reached the bottom of the hole, the whipstock was facing in the desired direction. The tool was then spudded on bottom to shear the pin and allow the pilot bit to be rotated. This bit (6⅛ in.) then drilled down the face of the whipstock and made about 12–15 ft. of new hole. The whipstock and pilot bit were then retrieved. A 9 in. bit was run and the pilot hole reamed out. A survey was taken to check the drift and azimuth. If satisfactory, drilling resumed as nearly to normal as could be expected given the difficult hole conditions. Compare this all–day job with present steering devices which are controlled during drill–ing from a control cab at the surface!

When directional drilling, there is a tendency for the bit to "walk" to the right. Therefore, whipstocks were deliberately set a little to the left of the desired directions to compensate for this, thus achieving a more accurate approach. Because only Totco surveys had been run at Atlantic No. 3 (some even in the dog house!), the precise bottom hole position was impossible to ascertain because that tool gave the angle of the hole only. Moroney studied the other holes in the vicinity, especially No. 48, which had been "steered" and surveyed for a short interval (to assist Tip?). He concluded correctly that No. 3 might have drifted a short distance to the northeast.

Once whipstocking had started, the drill pipe scraped the hole sideways. These extra amounts of rock, along with normal bit cuttings, had to be removed so as to keep the hole as clean as possible and try to prevent fishing jobs. In order to handle this demanding task, Jim Tod set up requirements for high viscosity mud. What was advocated was not always carried out.

Even at the best of times, directional drilling takes its toll of draw works and drill pipe. This is because there are many round trips, hole conditions are much more severe and hazards such as key–seats, dog–legs and shoulders lie in wait for the driller. To quote Al Phillips when he referred to the excessive wear on the drill pipe, "The box ends (of the drill pipe) on these particular wells were so thin that you could shave with them". Because of the shortage of tubular goods, most of the drill pipe was old to start with.

The brakes on the draw works suffered most abuse because of the frequent trips and even though there was supposed to be a spare brake band as a replacement at all times, accidents did happen. On one occasion at West Relief, when Jack Emslie was spudding the whipstock, the brakes failed completely. The travell–ing block came crashing down, bending the kelly 90° out through the V–door. Emslie was having his picture taken standing on the bent kelly when Lloyd Stafford happened along. Jack was set back to roughnecking for awhile.

Quarti predictably reached casing point sooner than West Relief because he had more straight hole and he did not "mud up" as soon as he should have. This created problems at 2,800 ft., where he was to start steering. At a depth of 5,220 ft. (5,110 ft. true vertical depth), the hole showed an angle of about 17° at an azimuth of N 07° E. It was also well known that there was a shoulder at about 3,700 ft. so an extra precaution was taken in preparation for running casing. This consisted of identifying the joint of casing that would be going through the table when the shoe joint reached this bad spot. It was marked with yellow chalk which would alert the driller to take it easy. But they did not reckon with Cody Spencer. As Al recalls: "Cody Spencer had a history of speed up everytime he ran casing. Didn't matter how long it took to drill a hole, but you had to get that casing in right now". So instead of delegating the job to the driller as he should have, he simply had to have his hand on the brake and, as it turned out, with dire consequences. When they reached the joint with the chalk mark, that's when Cody cocked the brake back and wham! Cody picked up the casing a couple of times and eased it down trying to get it around and said, "OK, let's pick up the kelly and we'll pump it around", but the damage had been done. There is conflicting evidence about Tip's and Charlie's where-abouts during this period. According to Moroney's note pad, he and Charlie had gone to lunch. Phillips recalls that Charlie was in the door of the dog house when Cody hit the tight spot. "I never thought it would happen, we must be hung up in the BOP". Charlie's reply was: "No, Cody, you're on bottom" (meaning that Cody had hit the shoulder at 3,700 ft.). Cody tried to break circulation with his mud pumps. When he found he couldn't, he switched to the Halliburton wagon that was standing by for the expected cement job and it couldn't either. So it was out of the hole, laying down the casing. The shoe joint had been totally collapsed, testifying to the speed.

When the drillers went back in with drill pipe to clean out, they could not find the original hole below 3,700 ft. Charlie Smith made several attempts to locate it using stinger bits, but to no avail. This was to set South Relief back nearly two months in its schedule. Jim Tod noted wryly: "It done (sic) two month's worth of delay".

Charlie Visser wasn't going to make the same mistake twice because he suggested to Cody that, with the number of rigs G.P. was running for Imperial Oil, Cody never put his foot on the derrick floor of either of the relief holes. And Cody never did. He would just sit in his big white car on the edge of the lease and watch what was going on. It must have been a great trial to him.

The running of the casing also was the occasion of a very serious accident in which the lead tong man, Bozo Lazslo had his hand taken off. Both cat–heads are used when running casing, one for spinning it in and the other for snapping up. The latter man–oeuvre requires a number of wraps around the cat head. There was a mix–up in the number of wraps Al was putting on. Bozo's hand was inside the latch of the tongs when Al applied the strain on the snapping–up line. Phillips recalls that when Bozo had recovered, he came out one night looking for him. Fortunately cooler heads prevailed and Bozo was calmed down. Howard Stafford, Lloyd's son (now Assistant Manager, Geology at the Conservation Board), was roustabout that summer and helped out running casing that fateful day. After witnessing the accident and resultant confusion, he made the big decision not to follow in his father's footsteps!

During the countless hours spent drilling off the face of the whipstocks, the crews were not that busy. Quarti put them to work helping to cannibalize what was left of the Atlantic No. 3 rig. As Al Phillips recalls:

> It was his suggestion (Ben's) that we latch onto one of the boilers at the wild well...we had a steam driven sand line that we used for down hole surveys...so we rigged up the snatch block, built ourselves a stone boat totally out of wood, took a line and dragged it from South Relief to the wild well with the unit. When we got the stone boat full of fittings and valves, we would pull it back.

Bill Cummer, then Leduc office manager for General Petroleums, recalls an inventory being made of their rig No. 19 at the West Relief well site.[1] The purpose of this was to establish the value of a fully equipped rig which would serve as a yardstick from which to base an ultimate settlement on the equipment at Atlantic No. 3. Ralph Peacock, retired partner of the insurance adjuster, Crosland and Peacock, visited rig No. 19 to check over the inventory. He was struck by the devastation that was being caused by the blow–out. He made a telling comment: "It was never the same after Atlantic No. 3; the whole face of insurance was changed". But neither Cummer nor Peacock would know that part of the doomed rig had been "liberated". The final settlement, even though only a fraction of the claimed $138,000 or more, was not that unfair, especially since other observers considered the equipment to be second hand, obsolescent and old.

One of the more frequent visitors to the relief holes was Mike Rebus (Administrator and one of the beneficiaries). By this time Mike had received his share of the McMahon bonus plus royalties from No. 1 and 2. It did not take much complicated arithmetic to figure out that the uncontrolled 15,000 barrels a day would generate a total of over $6,000 a day in royalties. And the longer this well produced at that rate, the more royalties would accrue to the Rebus family. Mike was reported, by reliable authorities, to have quite a good stock of alcoholic beverages in the trunk of his newly purchased Cadillac and he is said to have plied the roughnecks with liquor. There is no indication that he really did influence the progress of the two directional holes. but he is said to have tried. Mike was later reported to have gotten into the oil business trading in leases and royalties but was not particularly successful.

West Relief fared better than South Relief but it had its share of difficulties. By August 5, it was apparent that the hole was not drifting in the desired direction and there were a lot of tight spots. So it was plugged back to 4,670 ft. Despite every precaution, the bit kept working back into the old hole but finally, at about 5,000 ft., new hole was commenced.

Home was always in the forefront of trying to keep adequate supplies of tubular goods. In order that there be minimum difficulty in running the casing, Tip Moroney "traded" the West Relief string for Home's "extreme line" which had more clearance. Gordon Webster, then Chief Engineer with Home Oil recalls that Red Goodall told him that they were going to pick up the casing. Gordon said he would have to obtain permission to release it because the last time he loaned pipe, he got into serious trouble. Red was reported to have warned him: "If we don't get permission, we'll pass an order–in–council and take it anyway". The 7 in. extreme-line casing acquired from Home Oil was run on August 23 using 800 sacks. There is no report of returns but there is sufficient evidence that they got a good bond.

Paul Bedard has a story about Cody Spencer coming into the dog house when Red McKitrick and Tom Wark were having a snooze during the running of a drill stem test in the D-2 at West Relief. He woke them up rather violently and told them that a one-armed school marm would do better than what they were doing. McKitrick lashed back and said, "Go ahead and get one of them and then maybe we can get this job done and we can all go home!"

Another anecdote on the same subject is typical. Charlie Visser came in one morning early to use the telephone at West Relief and found Murray and his crew sprawled all over the floor. Charlie with his usual sarcasm apologized: "Oh I'm sorry Bill, I just wanted to come in and use the telephone". Murray was equally nonchalant: "That's all right Charlie, we were just about to get up anyway".

Joe Streeter, then well site geologist and now senior officer at

One of the drilling crews at the West Relief well. From left to right: H. Pidgeon, steam engineer; S. Donaldson, rough hand; Packnoski, rough hand; O. Puzzi, cathead; W.R. Murray, driller; G.E. Wilson, derrickman.

Photo furnished by George Wilson.

a Los Angeles bank recalls being sent out to pick the D–3 top at West Relief, laboriously catching samples every foot. He had to stay on the lease for over 24 hours. Drilling was continued to 5,340 ft. (still too far west and in shale). At this time the mud was displaced with water and the pipe pulled out of the hole so as to run in with a retrievable retainer. This enabled pressure on the open hole to be built up so as to try to force water to the Atlantic No. 3 well bore. It took 2,100 psi to put away 40–90 barrels of water an hour, which was not nearly enough. Tip knew that they had to increase the rate so on September 3, a 1,600 gallon acid job was run. This didn't do the job either. As a matter of fact, when the well was opened up after being pressured up, it started to bleed back fluid because it was still bottomed in green shale. More hole had to be drilled. This meant pulling out the retainer and going to 5,370 ft. But, unlike the D–3 at No. 3, the porosity at West Relief was limited.

As it turned out, Hic was not the expert Charlie Smith was and had missed his target by 500 ft.

On the morning of September 6, the day the wild well caught fire, a 2,000 gallon acid job finally succeeded in breaking through to the No. 3 well bore and injection of 500 barrels of water an hour at

750 psi was achieved. This was increased to 1,500 barrels an hour at 1,000 psi, a total of 36,000 barrels a day, nearly three times the volume of oil that was flowing to the surface. It created a massive hydrostatic head in the Atlantic No. 3 well bore that started to hold back the oil. Two more acid jobs further reduced the back pressure. On September 10, the flow of oil ceased and the rogue well was dead.

West Relief's job was done on October 20 when pumping of water ceased; the drill pipe was pulled out and a Christmas tree rigged up to take the tubing string and tubing landing bowl. At 10 a.m. October 21, the rig was released after having pumped over 600,000 barrels of water, or nearly half of the oil that had been produced out of the wild well.

South Relief continued to have serious hole troubles, being stuck in the hole and twisting off on several occasions. On August 7, 75 barrels of Lloydminster crude were spotted to try to get the drill pipe loose. The pressure in the drill pipe caused another accident, not nearly as serious, but distressing to Tom Wark who happened to be over on South Relief helping to free the pipe. As luck would have it, he was sporting a new summer suit. The strain on the drill pipe was too much for it and it parted below the table. Tom Wark's stetson and his suit were soaked – "well I got some of it free anyway!"

There were to be several more fishing jobs and twist–offs, but finally, on the 10th of September, 5,230 ft. of 7 in. casing were run using 1,200 sacks of cement. The hole was still in green shale. Control heads were installed along with the blow–out preventers. 3½ in. drill pipe was picked up and drilling resumed. As they neared the D-3, on all trips they broke circulation every 500 ft., going in the hole and coming out, to ensure that the hole was full of mud. Finally, on September 15, at 5,344 ft., circulation was suddenly lost when the bit dropped into a cavern. Let R.H.J. (Bob) Elliott, retired oil executive, but then a Camrose farm boy who had never seen an oil field before, tell the story:

> I was on the South Relief hole to pick the top of the D–3...As I recall, we were about 15 ft. above the prog-nosticated depth when I arrived on the hole after check-ing a couple of samples showing green shale. I was getting ready to settle down for a long boring night...All of a sudden the kelly dropped, I think 10 or 12 ft. which meant the bit had either run into the old hole or a horrendous cavern (later consensus was that it had hit the Atlantic 3 hole). This caused great excitement on the derrick floor.

Tremendous activity immediately....start the auxiliary mud pumps...douse the derrick lights...start mixing more mud, etc. There was a check list in the doghouse and after looking after the immediate essentials, the driller came into the dog house where I was standing. After checking the list he came to Item 9 or 10 which was: "Notify the tool push". The driller turned to me and said, "Come on with me, I need a witness for this". So away we went over to the tool pusher's trailer. When we got there, the driller banged on the door several times. There was no response but from the noise inside, there was quite a party going on. Finally the driller opened the door and hollered, "Ben, we ran into the old hole and the drill string dropped but everything is OK". With that he slammed the door, said "That takes care of that" and referred to the next item on the list. Everything went like clockwork so I guess it was just an example of delegation of authority by the pusher and no harm was done.

ENDNOTE:
1. Inventory took up fifteen pages and totalled $138,417.19, listing hundreds of items ranging from a Regan 8–sheave crown block valued at $3,180; a 150–ton Wiggle Ideal hook – $1,500; a 60" Ridgid wrench – $36.90; one garden rake – $3.30; and the smallest item, a 60–amp fuse at 15 cents. Complete inventory list at Glenbow.

RED CROSS

The safety record of the men who worked on Atlantic No. 3 during its violent and uncontrolled life is one that continues to amaze people even today. The very fact that danger pay was offered to the Imperial Oil production hands is indicative of the level of risk that was assumed by all who came within the well's ambit. One must also remember that this was prior to the days of the Workmen's Compensation Board. Nonetheless, in spite of the high level of danger and the low level of safety regulations, very few casualties were reported.

Undoubtedly, one institution that, by its mere presence, offered assurance to the workers was the Canadian Red Cross. In its annual report for 1948, the Red Cross's Disaster Drive Committee submitted the following information: "The final major disaster call came from Leduc on May 20, when the famous Atlantic No. 3 oil well went out of control. For four months Red Cross stood on guard with a well-equipped emergency station, ambulance and staff. During this time eight girls from the Red Cross Blood Transfusion Service Depot were loaned for eleven days on twenty-four hour duty, in eight-hour shifts.

...The Provincial Oil Control Board (sic), at whose request the station was installed, expressed its warm appreciation of the speedy, and what they called 'comforting', co-operation given by Red Cross."

In addition to the Conservation Board's increased recognition of the need to improve safety standards in the oil patch, there was also evidence to show that the oil industry itself was prepared to take more responsibility. In a press release that appeared in the Western Oil Examiner on May 15, 1948 (one day following the Board's announcement that it would take over Atlantic No. 3), the following statement was made:

Leduc Oil Field May Get Ambulance
The T.V. Ambulance Committee will meet next week to consider an application from operators in the Leduc field for a similar service to that developed in the Valley. The committee consists of King Houston, W.S. Herron and W.H. Jones.

Although both the Board and industry were cognizant of their responsibility for a safety policy, it is significant to realize that neither took any action in this until after Atlantic No. 3's uncontrolled condition was brought to world attention. Undoubtedly, as in many other accidents, Atlantic No. 3 proved to be the catalyst for bringing about unprecedented changes!

Some time after the Red Cross set up their emergency station at the wild well site, its personnel was increased by an intern and a small team of nurses. As well, a number of beds were set aside at the University Hospital. Fortunately, to the best of the writer's knowledge, these beds were never needed. Regrettably, few of the hands interviewed for this book recall the names of of the medical personnel, let alone their presence at the site. This, in itself, is indicative of the amazing safety record that prevailed during the Atlantic No. 3 blow–out.

D. Maw

DANGER PAY

When Roly Horsfield was sent out from Toronto by Imperial Oil Limited as a summer student, little did he know of the windfall he was to share in. Roly, who would later assume senior positions in the company, was assigned to Maurice Paulson, Leduc District Engineer. When Campbell Aird, Production Superintendent, issued the call for Atlantic No. 3 "volunteers", Roly grabbed at the chance. He would make double and even treble over the normal hourly wages. "Just fine for a young student" who needed tuition fee money. The fact that this was "danger pay" didn't bother him until he broke his arm handling line pipe. The other two labourers had forgotten to hang on to it and there was Roly trying to hold the whole thing up. Roly was on the point of being run off, through no fault of his own, but Maury Paulson took him back into the office where he completed his summer stint (but no more danger pay).

Sye Ellert recalled working on the water line from the river. "...most of those crews got time and a half and double time, plus danger pay and could work as long as they could stand up."

Don Gamble, an R.C.A.F. veteran, was also an Imperial Oil roustabout helping lay boardwalk. He also had the job of "tonging up" 10 in. pipe to be used as a flow line from No. 3 to the temporary battery to the east (no welding was allowed).

Paul Diemert (VIP) recalls his crew of 12 using brass shovels. He was also occupied with feeding "the hungry pumps" with oats, feathers and cement, and remembers having to clean out batteries when these materials came back at him.

Howard Wagar, still with Esso at Devon, also qualified for extra pay: "I was only 18 years old at the time...a lot of nerve and seeing no danger...once this 1,600 lb. pressure worked its way up to the surface...the game was over and the real tough grind [was] just beginning''.

Roger Couture, retired in Vernon, was close to the perils. He recalls the fittings on Atlantic No. 3 well head lasting only a short time because of the abrasive action of the sand and shale being produced with the oil. He was under Jack Wurzer's direction and was one of those that had to go in to try to right the derrick amidst the oil spray and gas vapour. One spark and that crew would have been incinerated.

Our oldest informant, Norm Wilkinson, still alert at the age of 92 at Leduc, remembers his danger pay and taxi transportation to the field. He took samples at the pressure gauge on the well, looking for lost circulation material, but none showed up. Norm also recalls his last visit to the well head prior to the derrick falling over: ''It had started to shake and the surface casing was whipping''; a prelude to the final debacle.

Other Imperial Oil hands weren't rewarded even though they felt they should have been because they were also exposed to perils. One of these was Doug Stevenson, surveyor, who had to go in close to the well. Arnold Johnson was exposed to many dangers but did not get anything extra. His excellent report, written shortly afterward for course credits at the University of Alberta, has an illustrative passage. This was when he had to try to measure the gas flow: ''This flow of gas fairly shrieked and it was considered important to know what the rate of flow really was. I would work my way along this line by holding onto it for support although it was bouncing like a bronco. When I reached the end, I would hold a pitot tube in the stream with one hand, while hanging on for dear life to the line. I recall that each time I did this, there was a flow of approximately 29 MMcf per day roaring down the line. It was scary!''

Imperial Pipelines ran their own affairs. When management met with employees, one of the latter's representatives, according to Harry Andruski, also an Imperial Pipeline person, had had too much to drink. In a belligerent mood, he told the management to stuff it. They did, and those men did *not* get danger pay.

When the General Petroleums drilling crews found out about this fringe benefit, they tried to get it also. One of the chief instigators: Harry (Turkey) Knight tried to organize the men. Al Phillips recalls Harry going in to the Board of Industrial Relations in Edmonton but coming away empty–handed. Even G.A. (Al) Wright, though he was ''management'', felt strongly about the discrimina– tion and spoke up for the hands on the two rigs because they were equally exposed to the fire hazard. But he got nowhere with his superiors.

Andruski also tells a story of heroism on the night of the fire. A Lithuanian, Joe Purych (sp?), was an Atlantic roustabout ("true blue and a top worker"). He worked for Don Whitney at the tank farm. He took a shovel, running ahead of the fire, closing the ditches. His labours were helped by Don alongside, "wading in our rubber boots through the muck of bubbling oil and gas around us". Bulldozers also helped to prevent the fire from reaching the main pits. Whitney asked for danger pay for himself and Joe but remembers that he was turned down by Lyle Caspell.

One of three unsolicited letters received by the author in 1985 is reproduced here without comment. The others came from a Bill Craig (Enderby, B.C.) and an Alister McCallum (Taber). . Attempts to track all three down failed.

Aubrey Kerr

Hope you can get the right information on Atlantic 3, I was one of the firemen.

Yes sir the hell was scared out of us many times and the absence of the drilling company officials was very noticeable. Seemed Lyle was doing everything, night and day and the crews really respected him 100%. If the contractor had put a blow-out preventor on it would have been so easy to control the well. Langston toddled around without one doing

much, there sure were 8 or 10 men
that _really_ were important.

I was on shift the day Ramsey
blew the toilet shack up, he
was a lucky man. - I watched Caspell
and his few willing helpers in HELL
under the derrick floor in a sea of
mad oil gas many times - Who
climbed the derrick in blowing
oil and gas to tie guy-lines Caspell.
Griffith was a great help at
one of our worst hours.
   I'm an old man now but
remember # 3 very well
   I often wonder what happened
to Caspell and others
              Good luck
                   JC Rose
                        Comox B.C.

   One final comment: the danger of thunderstorms was an unmentionable threat. Despite all precautions, such a force of nature could have ignited the wild well. Mere man could not have stopped it as he had done in the Covey incident!

II: FIRE AND WATER

"At or about 6:18 p.m., Monday, September 6, 1948, Atlantic No. 3 caught fire, the exact cause is unknown." So spoke Harry Howard, chartered accountant and secretary of General Petroleums, both with precision and ambiguity. (See Appendix H.)

With the approach of Labour Day (the 6th), cratering became more concentrated around the rig itself. Howard Blanchard recalls how "a small round hill formed under the derrick...the guy lines became very tight." This had forced the dog house down onto the ground, which was was becoming very unstable. The Kerber brothers, working for Hislop, were on the lease daily, trying to keep the derrick from tipping over. Production hands from Imperial's danger pay gang helped them in shoring up the corners. This was done by bringing in "Japan squares" (16 in. x 16 in. timbers) and jacking up each corner.

Ever mindful of the safety of his men, Tip was dividing his time between the tottering derrick and the two directional holes. To quote him:

> We had a whole bunch of rig builders in and out of that thing all day trying to level it up which by this time was swaying around and...the pattern of the blow-out was getting closer to the hole all the time...and I finally decided it was long past time that we should have any-body under that in that situation so I called all the people and said, "No more monkeying around that hole by that derrick". We knew it would fall over and it fell over during the night.

Rocks and loose pieces of iron were now being tossed around by the force of the oil and gas, presenting more than ever a deadly fire hazard. One spark and the workers would have been burnt.

Ian McKinnon was present at the death struggle of the Atlantic No. 3 rig, staying up all Sunday night at the lease with Moroney. McKinnon: "We expected the derrick to fall, it was standing shortly after midnight when we knocked off for a spot of coffee. A couple of minutes later at 12:45 a.m., the derrick was down." And later, "...We thought we had somehow luckily avoided it...I was just asleep at home when I got the alarm."

"Look!" Hick Kern's cry heralded the conflagration which was to attract world-wide attention. Kern, Charlie Smith and Al Phillips had gone over to the churning crater where the kelly and swivel were sticking up in the air, the only remaining evidence of a rig and

*Atlantic No. 3 on September 5. Note heaved–up ground caused by inten-
sified cratering which caused derrick to topple early morning September
6.*

Photo furnished by Jim Tod.

*September 6, 1948, just before the fire. About all that remained standing
was the kelly and swivel. Note build–up of ejecta.*

Photo furnished by Bill McKellar.

The fire at Atlantic No. 3. The oil sumps in the northwest extremity of the quarter section, from which the oil was pipelined, were saved from burning by the heroic all–night efforts of the "hands".

Photo furnished by Norm Bullivant.

Raging inferno.

Photo furnished by N.G. Loudoun.

derrick, all else having fallen that morning when the derrick collapsed. They were there to take snapshots when Kern yelled out.
Smith described: "Over the crater hung a ball of fire...it just hung
there quite still for what seemed a long time...actually I suppose it
was a fraction of a second...then there was a big whoosh and up
she went."[1]

Charlie Smith was reported to have run over the back of Hick
because his footprints were in Kern's back...but this couldn't be
true because Charlie had left his boots where he had been standing
by the crater! "As it turned out, we could have walked because the
fire spread so slowly over the ground...(Al Phillips' recollection)[2]

Word of the fire travelled around the world. The London Illustrated News, not noted for its sensationalism, printed a centre-fold
picture of the fire. Newspaper accounts are noted for many inac-
curacies but some of them attained new heights of dramatic rhetoric:

> *Financial Post* – September 18: Normalcy was
> restored by Alberta's Oil Conservation Board Sept. 10
> following ending of one of the most lurid chapters in
> Canadian oil through death of the wildest oil well in the
> industry.
>
> Death came to Atlantic No. 3 in a blazing 59 hour
> funeral pyre that marked a spectacular end to a six month
> rampage that focussed world-wide attention on Alberta's
> 200 million barrel Leduc Woodbend field.

"Quick reflexes and fast running help Texans". So read the
heading in the Calgary Albertan (predecessor of the Sun). Kern was
quoted as saying, "In about a second there was a small explosion...we started to run...when I looked around after doing a couple
of hundred yards in near record time...the flames and smoke were
shooting 700 ft. up into the air..."

Tom Wark, pushing tools at West Relief, observed: "A ball of
fire danced over the derrick floor about fifteen to thirty seconds and
then the flame crawled down the side, into the main crater around
the well. It never really exploded. It then just seemed to start
everything on fire at once."

The most valuable eyewitness account is that of Ralph Horley,
then fledgling CBC reporter, whose words are immortalized on a
primitive recording device. CBC had not yet officially started broadcasting from the Macdonald Hotel but an opening celebration was
going on when someone looked out the window of the hotel and
spotted the smoke and flames. To quote Ralph in his interview on
CBC AM, September 7, 1985, (Ted Barris' radio show):

We had all the brass there and they said, "Go get it", and so our engineer said, "Well the only portable recorder is in pieces on the work bench and it will take us a half an hour to get it put together"...The tape recorders weren't very good and we had what was called a 'wire-rec' recorder, a stainless steel wire and if anything went wrong, the wire broke and you had wire all over the room.

Knowing that Ralph Horley had made the broadcast on the fateful evening, the author was determined to locate the interview. Thanks to the good offices of Iqbal I. Rahemtulla in CBC headquarters in Ottawa, he obtained a copy. The recording is doubly historical because it opens with the voice of John Fisher, Mister Canada, who was at the celebration. Quoting Ralph's words: "It's the worst oil fire I have ever seen...we'll have to wait until it burns out on top and try to control it from below..." Ralph even recorded the roar of the fire and the bulldozers as they rushed to push up the dykes to contain the fire. "To make the picture complete, we took our CBC microphone with technician Gordon Shillabeer who recorded a description of what we saw, the flames rolling almost to our eye level as we flew along at 3,600 ft." (See Appendix I for full text.)

Thirty-eight years later, memories are vivid but vary as to details.

Lois Snyder, Devon resident and widow of Rollin, recalls her experience: "It had been particularly active...huge amounts of oil and gas and rocks were being flung out...as we watched, a collision of two rocks high above the well created a spark and the well flared." Lois recalled Rollin's reaction as running over to save the pumps that were pumping oil from a dyked area.

Ruth Welch, also a long-time resident of Devon and Vern Hunter's secretary at the very first of the operations in 1947, recalls the event: "Dean Hunter (Vern's wife) and I were driving home (to Devon) from Leduc when it happened. Quite frightening...such an inferno and such tremendous force behind it...and the fire followed along the ditches which had been dug to contain the surface oil". Ruth's son Larry was roughnecking for Commonwealth near Atlantic No. 3 and recalls seeing pictures being taken.

Out on the firing line, the weary workers re-grouped along with their Cats – no need to worry about smoking anymore – with the objective of containing the fire and keeping it from jumping to the main pit. And they were successful!

When asked how the well caught fire, Moroney gives the most logical explanation:

My theory is that the fire was ignited statically

because we subsequently established the fact that you could set up a static cloud while it was producing water and you get a potential to create a considerable spark gap and we later proved this in the field by deliberately experimenting on a well up north of Edmonton.

Some workers attributed the fire to rocks hitting against iron and setting off sparks. A couple of hands thought that it was deliberately set! With all the precautions and the desperate fire hazard, no one in his right mind could believe that.

Recently unearthed reports give another first–hand account by Don Whitney:

Sept. 4 Contacted farmer [Rebus?] about plowing fire guard around Atlantic #3 lease.

Sept. 6 Derrick collapsed at approximately 1:30 this morning at Atlantic #3. To Atlantic #3 well head (?) to inspect the damage caused...

Atlantic #3 caught fire. Got tractors, plows, men, etc., to plow fire guard. Filled in trenches between pits to keep fire from spreading. Extinguished fires around Atlantic Battery. Helped Rebus move his furniture. Acted as night watchman, etc. This happened shortly after 6:00 p.m.

Atlantic No. 3 on fire, September 7, 1948. Note the cratering at left and the build–up of ejecta around the well bore and the board walk. The boilers at lower right powered G.P. Rig No. 10 that drilled the well.

Photo furnished by George Wilson.

Sept. 7 Atlantic Battery to check safety measures, fire guards, etc.

And what of John Rebus and his family? If we are to believe that he had stayed on at his home despite warnings and the reported eviction by Tip Moroney, we are left with a dilemma. According to Blair Fraser's article, Moroney is reported to have sent word to the Rebus family that they had better not sleep at home that night. Quoting Fraser:

John Rebus moved all his furniture out of the farm house and loaded it on his truck and spent the night on his tractor, ploughing up fire guards around the house and buildings. By morning, the danger was past: Rebus put his furniture back in the house without having had to move it out of his front yard.

ENDNOTES:
1. Blair Fraser's article in *Macleans* magazine, November 1, 1948. Fraser interviewed Charlie Smith in his rented quarters in Edmonton in September.
2. Al Phillips recollection.

To the Manager of
the Run - A- Way Well.
Calmer,
Alberta, Canada.

St. Paul, Minn.
Sept. 6 - 1948.

Dear Sir:
    I was in Edmonton
on August 26th. and my
brother Dr. R. B. Sandin
of the University told me
you had a run-a-way
well.
    Since then I have
formed a plan to stop
the flow. You dont use

140

cement or dynamite to ruin your casing. My plan is simple and I think it will work.

If you wish to know of my plan I could meet your agent here or in Edmonton with all my expenses paid.

Please let me know if you will consider my plan.

Yours truly,
John Sandin.
790 E. Hyacinth Ave.
St. Paul 6, Minn.

III: CALSEAL AND THE BAZOOKA

Red Goodall, in his March 1981 interview, describes the dying moments of the fire "...after it (the water) hit bottom, you could see the flame turning red and then steam started to come with it and it just died out".

Grey smoke with the flames had started to appear on the second day of the fire (September 7), a sure sign that the massive injections of water down West Relief well bore were mixing with the oil. This enormous influx of water created a hydrostatic head in the No. 3 well bore sufficient to stop, once and for all, the crude flow (and, thereby, the fire). Water had to be continually pumped to ensure maintenance of that control. An article in the September 10, Edmonton Bulletin, eloquently expressed the government's gratitude and great relief:

> Government officials on Thursday were highly elated at the success of the fire fighters at Atlantic No. 3. Honourable N.E. Tanner, Minister of Lands and Mines said, "The men at the well have done a splendid job. They have been working night and day and have accomplished a great feat. There is a lot of work still to be done but the main thing is, the fire has been put out. (See Appendix J.)

Plans were now made to plug the cavern at the bottom of Atlantic No. 3 through South Relief. The perhaps unexpected drop of South Relief's bit directly into the Atlantic No. 3 well bore confirmed the presence of a void space of very large but unknown dimensions. It also marked the beginning of a new struggle that would last for more than two months. Moroney knew what he was up against when he stated: "Our work has just begun".

In his 1957 interview:

> I drew a picture of the way I visualized it (the bottom of No. 3 hole)...shaped like a big church with a steeple on it, the steeple being the well which was blowing out. The problem was to cement up that steeple without filling the church full of cement. When I decided that was the problem, that's what we did...it didn't take too long to make up my mind...
> The first thing we had to do was put a bridge in that would hold...we tried lots of tricks. We made all sorts of mixes of plugging material and none of them worked...we would just lose stuff in there as big as that door knob, just

tons of it and you never could find it and it wasn't just going through little tiny holes.

Various combinations of Calseal,[1] cement, common salt, calgon and mud were tried. As Paul Bedard described the procedure:

> If we mixed cement with Calseal, we could get about a thirty minute set...just had one truck mixing a light cement slurry and another mixing Calseal and we would "Y" them on the discharge line and pump down the drill pipe...we had the right amount of water (to chase the mix) and we would blast 'er down and try to get 'er out...a lot of times we never made it...it would expand on setting and even set when moving...

None of these plugs held, circulation being lost almost immediately. The touchy nature of the Calseal was demonstrated when one of the plugging operations came to an abrupt (although temporary) halt when one job set up too soon, solidly cementing up 34 stands of drill pipe. George Wilson, roughneck on South Relief:

> I can still see the line of Dixie cups set out as samples while being mixed and pumped down...however, something went wrong, whether Calseal Andy (Hamilton) hadn't calculated the bottom hole temperature or what, but he left the job with a tag to his name, "Can't Seal Andy" as 5,000 ft. of cemented up drill pipe were hauled away to be drilled out.[2]

Tom Wark, tool push on both West and South Relief, recalls:

> ...We were pumping cement with "lime quick set" (Calseal); you could dip a paper cup out of the box, set it down and in fifteen minutes, you could stand on it, it set up that fast. We found out sadly that we didn't get it all out of the drill pipe one time. We cemented 105 joints solid, just couldn't pump it out fast enough. It set up before it went out the bottom of the drill pipe. We had to slow down a little on that. We were mixing it with the steam pumping unit.[3]

On September 21, an incident was recorded in Tip's notepad which showed that he would not stand for any unnecessary delays. After all, he and Visser had been fighting the well constantly since May. Here are his scathing remarks, taken directly from his notepad:

> Start circulating at 1:10 p.m. Left with instructions to pull out and go in with bit at 1:45 p.m. Returned from lunch

to find General Petroleums safety man had rig shut down and holding safety meeting. Both Charlie and I poured it on him.

1. If rig can operate without a tool push, it certainly can do without such sham.

2. We have been working day and night to get this job done and this iron head shuts us down to waste daylight while Halliburton stands by.

3. If GP were really safety conscious, they would not let men work on such a pile of junk as this rig.

4. This safety knuckle brain wears a safety hat to drive a Chev coupe while the tool pusher walks.

5. If GP thought the tool pusher was worthwhile as such, they wouldn't have left him without transportation for days at a time.[4]

Casting about for answers that might assist Moroney, the author requested R.D. Sluzar (now with Saskoil in Regina), one of his geologists, to examine the crater(s). By measuring the rock types and volume of rock thrown out during the uncontrolled production, there was a possibility that clues might be unearthed to get an idea of how much void space was present down hole.

The crater. Rebus house in distance.

Photo furnished by Harvey Maloney.

Sluzar went out to the well site on October 5, 1948 with Messrs. Doug Stevenson and Gordon Turnock (then Imperial Oil surveyors, now retired). He wrote a geological report to which was attached a plan and elevation drafted by Norman C. Gill. Norm was noted for his meticulous penmanship, long before Leroys and Letrasets!

Sluzar observed no carbonate rocks in the ejecta, noting that shale was the dominant rock type. Much of it was sintered due to the fire and it appeared to have come from shallow beds of the Upper Cretaceous. Fragments of coal were observed: "reddish, burnt, sintered". Sluzar also reported "pseudo–layering" involving incompetent slabs which had flaked off due to the heat.

The main crater at the well bore was 90 ft. in diameter at the top of the cone of ejecta. The bottom of the crater measured about 30 ft. across. The build–up of ejecta from grade was about 12 ft., resulting in an annular ring of material having an estimated volume of 5,160 cubic yards (24,800 barrels U.S.).

Halliburton tables were used to compare hole capacities with the crater volume. A normal 9 in. hole drilled to 5,300 ft. has a capacity of 417 barrels or a little over 1% of the 24,800 barrels. But the tables only go to a 36 in. diameter hole. For the same depth of 5,300 ft., a 36 in. hole has a capacity of 6,700 barrels (U.S.), still only accounting for one–quarter of the estimated volume of the rock pile. This means that enormous cavities had been created, most of them presumably in the shaly sections of the Cretaceous.

Sluzar also reported on the subsidiary craters which had formed earlier around the mud pits but made no estimates of rock volume since these craters were only present in the shallow beds above the bottom of the surface casing in the well.

Although no direct help was given Tip, "the survey did show the enormous forces at work during the summer, the large volume of rock blasted out and the effects of the fire on the sediments".[5]

Somebody then thought of using Turner Valley shale to create the bridge. This rock does not disintegrate as other shales normally do. Quoting Tom Wark again:

> We hauled two loads of shale from the rock cut...on the road between Black Diamond and Turner Valley where all that rock was (quite a uniform size – ½ in. to 1 in.)...we just dropped it down the hole (through a big funnel on top of the open 7 in. casing) as it was, using wheelbarrows...it took quite a little while. We didn't want to drop it fast enough to bridge it off but after those two truck loads went in, we just ran in with the pipe and never touched a damn thing.

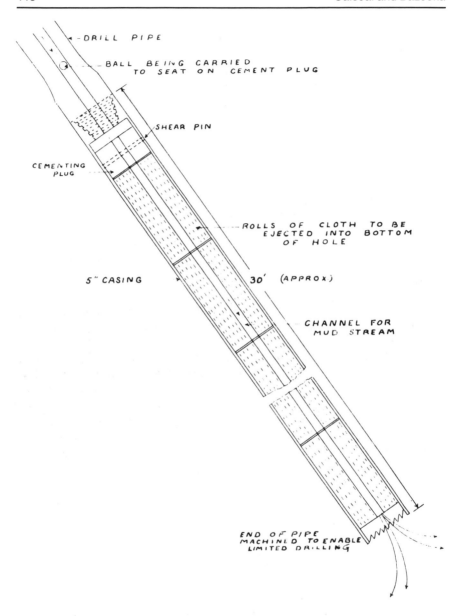

Bazooka: tool used to aid in cementing off Atlantic No. 3 from the D–3 zone.

Illustrated from Arnold Johnson (Appendix K).

Shortly thereafter, according to Tip's notepad, bridges were starting to show up and some of the plugs were taking a little weight. Nevertheless, by October 23, it was realized something other than cement/Calseal plugs would have to be tried.

Who hit on the idea of a "bazooka"? Don Mackenzie believes it was Charlie Visser. Earl Griffith[6] was enlisted to help fabricate a piece of 5 in. casing so as to accommodate a shear pin and a cementing plug near the top and a cutting edge at the bottom end (see Arnold Johnson's diagram below).

Moroney describes the invention:

> ...5 in. diameter light–weight pipe with a tool joint on the top and a milling shoe with teeth so that we could treat it a little bit rough on bottom and turn it. I got some 3 ft. wide by 6 ft. wide 1 in. mesh chicken wire and made rolls of it and we'd roll this up with burlap from gel–flake bags...very large bags ending up in a long tube almost as big as the top of that desk. The purpose of the tube was to enable mud to be circulated down the inside...we would shove a series of these up into the bazooka.

Inside was a top roll held to a cementing plug through which a hole had been drilled about 1⅛ in. and that was fastened with shear pins to the top part of this device. Down the centre of the casing was a piece of tubing. Moroney would:

> ...be sure we had this thing down exactly where we wanted it, then I'd unscrew the kelly and drop a bridging ball...it's drillable and it would go down when we started to pump and when it hit this plug, it would close off the opening in the plug and the tube and the bare pump pressure would just push the chicken wire and welcome mats out...you'd have a series of wire mesh falling like link sausage tumbling and unwrapping.

The first run was on October 23 and Tip refers to it as a "barrel" with a roll of screened wire and gel–flake and a 5 in. rubber plug.

On October 24, 75 sacks of Zonolite, 40 of cotton seed hulls and 160 of sawdust were run. Returns started to come around while pumping this but did not hold. Hopes were building that the circulation was improving and, prior to trying another cement plug, they added sawdust, but then returns stopped completely.

The next time the "gadget" was run, full returns were obtained for about ten minutes. On the following run, there were mixtures of sawdust, cotton seed hulls and Zonolite in the mud with 6 ft. rolls of

DALE SIMMONS LETTER

"...I have decided to go into petroleum engineering as I have more interest in drilling a well than I've had in anything else up here..." So wrote Dale Simmons in a 1948 letter, obviously having been influenced by Tip Moroney's address to him and his fellow students in first year engineering at the University of Alberta.

Thanks to Sandra Leblanc for bringing this letter to the author's attention and to Dale Simmons for permission to publish excerpts from it.

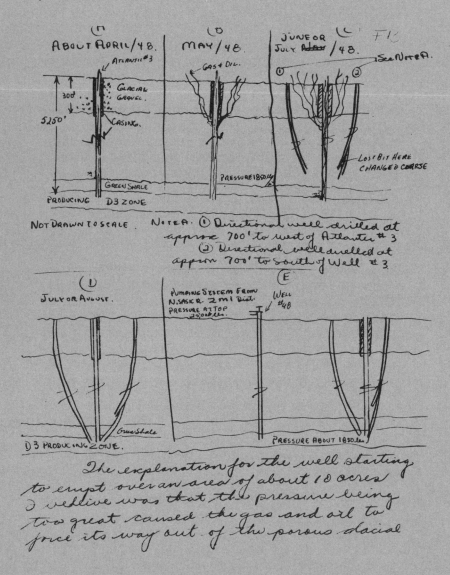

ABOUT APRIL/48.   MAY/48.   JUNE OR JULY/48.   F13

ATLANTIC #3   GAS + OIL.   See Note A.

300'   GLACIAL GRAVEL.

5250'   CASING.

LOST BIT HERE CHANGED COURSE

PRESSURE 1850 #

GREEN SHALE

PRODUCING   D3 ZONE

NOT DRAWN TO SCALE

Note A. ① Directional well drilled at approx. 700' to west of Atlantic #3
② Directional well drilled at approx. 700' to south of Well #3

JULY OR AUGUST.   PUMPING SYSTEM FROM N. SASK R. 2 mi Dist. PRESSURE AT TOP 2500#/#.   WELL #48

D3 PRODUCING ZONE.   Green Shale   PRESSURE ABOUT 1850#/#

The explanation for the well starting to erupt over an area of about 10 acres I believe was that the pressure being too great caused the gas and oil to force its way out of the porous glacial

148

gravel and thence to the surface. As
this condition was noticed the
production of the well was stopped.
At first the unusual proceedure of trying to
pump water down the well at
sufficient pressure to overcome the
pressure of the gas cap (which was about
1850 lbs per sq in.) and thus stop the
flow at the bottom, failed. The two
directional wells indicated in Ⓒ were
then started. The reason for drilling
two such wells was two-fold. In the
first place directional wells are quite
tricky to drill and an ordinary well
can be completed (at hedue) in about 55
days. So they figured that it would take
at least 50% to 150% longer to drill
a directional well and if anything
should go wrong with one of the
wells they would be so out the time
lost and would have to start over
again. The second reason was that
they were not exactly sure of the
position vertically below them of the
place where Atlantic #3 entered the
U3 Zone. From the records of deviation
of the gyro-compass they knew that
it would lie in an area of radius
25' from the top of the well vertically
below. For a while this had them
stumped until they thought of looking
at the records of the wells in the
field with regard to the deviation.
They found that in general all the
wells in the field sloped to the
North-West. So with this fairly
scant information drilling of the

149

directional wells was commenced. In the meantime after having tried to force water down #3 they thought of trying to pump water down well #4C which was about to enter pay zone. Drilling was completed and the well was closed down in the usual manner (see Fig. E) Then a pipe line was constructed to the N Saskatchewan River at distance 2 miles. The water was pumped in and applied down the well at a p surface pressure at the top of about 2500 # (I'd not sure of that figure) It was hoped that that water would create enough pressure at the bottom of at #3 to subdue the oil & gas. This however proved fruitless. In the meantime drilling was continuing on the Directional Wells. At about 5800 ft the Southerly well encountered difficulties of one kind or another so the course was altered slightly (This proved to be a very lucky occurence, as I will explain later) While this was going on sumps were prepared over the area of 10 acres and the oil was pumped away to storage tanks. This oil was not simply seeping out it was spurting out in large guysers, some of which may have been 20-30 feet high. At one time the oil was coming so fast that it was pumped back down the adjacent well. (There is a technicality here involving Specific Gravities of the oil which I was unable to completely decipher or understand) Finally the Westerly Directional #① well was completed and water was pumped down it in hopes of stopping up #3. The Directional #① well was only down to the Green shale and it was hoped that the pressure (as) if applied close enough would stop #3. However this failed as the water was not close enough to the #3 bottom. Next Hydrochloric acid was applied, as tests showed that this shale was slightly soluble in Hydrochloric acid. At First 5,000 gallons were applied. This did not seem to help much so several more shots of 5,000 gals each were tried. At this point the well caught on fire and the derrick collapsed. During the time of the fire an experiment was tried. It is known that certain salts give off different colors when burned. They believed that some of the water they were pumping into Directional well #① was comming up out of the at #3. So they added salts of one type or another to the water being pumped into the well and examined the flames with a spectroscope and found the

desired results. Some of their water was
comming thru. About this time
Directional Well #2 from the south
was completed and luck of all
luck they hit the bottom of #3
right on the button. Had they not
had the supposed missfortune of
having to change course they would
have missed it. By this time they had
managed to get enough water thru
Directional Well #1 and with #2 to
put out the fire. Now their problem
was to plug the bottom of the well.
The first try was to get shale from
the banks of the N Sask river and
poured it down Directional #2. However
this proved fruitless, after dumping
45 cu, yards of it down the hole #2
as it was fairly soluble in water, that
is it turned into mud. All this
time they were amazed at the seemingly
bottomless cavern with which they
were working - at the bottom.
Their next try was to put ordinary
wood shavings, together with mud
aquajell and some type of cement
down in hopes that it would
float up into the well and form a
plug. Appearently their main
objective was to get some kind of
a foundation formed across the
bottom of the well. This too failed,
I'm not just sure why but nonetheless

152

it failed. With nearly all hope abandoned they were about to send for a trainload of some type of pummice from Mexico when an idea was hit upon. They built a drum out of a section of 5" pipe 30' long. A sort of Drill was employed at one end. It was fitted so mud could circulate down thru the centre. The top was fixed so that it could collapse when necessary. Then they obtained some ordinary building ~~paper~~. They cut it in strips 10' long and 36" wide. They then joined these together in this manner so they could be rolled up and placed in the drum.

This entire rig with drums, building paper etc. was then lowered into the Southerly directional well and when at the bottom the top collapsed as per schedule, the mud pushed the building paper out and it floated into place. Quick drying Plaster of Paris (or some such compound) was then sent to the bottom. It formed, together with the building paper, a bridge which they had so desired. They had no method of working at the Atlantic # 3 well from the doubled ¼ in. mesh wire plus burlap with additional 3 ft. x 6 ft. wrapping of ½ in. mesh in the bazooka.

Moroney continues in his notepad to refer to the "gadget" as "socket, barrel and even shotgun". By October 29, partial returns were being obtained after having run the "shotgun" with ten rolls of chicken wire. The next day, October 30, a 50–sack cement plug was drilled out and circulation was "good", losing about six barrels in fifteen minutes. They then ran 50 sacks of cement and 200 lb. of calcium chloride, pumping a total of 37 barrels following the cement. This may have been the job that finally did the trick. On November 2, the crew ran the drill pipe in after a cement job and found hard cement at 5,340 ft.

The hole was still taking mud but it now looked as if Moroney and Visser were gaining. On November 4, two more plugs were run. These were pressured up to 1,250 psi which bled off slowly. More lost circulation material achieved its goal on November 8 when returns were obtained.

With the onset of cold weather, there were again intermittent shortages of gas as fuel for the boilers and this interfered seriously with the work. Fortunately the fire hazard had disappeared.

On November 9, there was another squeeze job at 1,400 psi, the cement was drilled out to 5,340 ft. and two more plugs run. Now it was a succession of running plugs, setting the Hydril blow–out preventer and squeezing. It was no longer necessary to use the bazooka.

Success was coming closer and closer with hard cement being drilled on November 12 and squeezed to 1,400 psi. November 14 was the final wrap–up where "pressure reported very high...started running in, found plug at 5,095 ft., started to lay down drill pipe but decided to drill out cement to 5,341 ft. in order to leave for observation purposes...If Atlantic No. 3 should become active, it should be apparent first at this well..." The cement was very hard when drilled out to 5,341 ft. On the following day, the pressure held at 1,600 psi and the well was shut in.

On the 15th, all of the drill pipe was laid down and the wellhead swedged up so that pressures could be observed. The South Relief rig was released, five and a half months after it had spudded.

At West Relief water continued to be injected from September 6 to October 20 at rates gradually declining from about 1,200 barrels per hour (30,000 barrels per day) to 400 barrels per hour. The men were still on duty there during all this time. They were kept busy mixing large quantities of mud and pumping it over to South Relief and helping out during cement jobs.

On October 19, the drill pipe was pulled and a 5½ in. liner run.

On the 20th, a Christmas tree was rigged up to take the tubing string. The West Relief rig was released October 21.

When the job of killing was complete, the tubing pressure on South Relief was zero. West Relief pressure stood at 1,500 psi because the bottom of that hole was in communication with the D–3 below the plugs run from South Relief. "This indicated a permanent solid seal between the producing zone and Atlantic No. 3 (well bore)". (See Appendix K for Johnson's report.)

The absolute necessity for *two* relief holes should now be apparent to the reader. To recapitulate, if only one relief well bore had been drilled, it would have been impossible to keep the No. 3 well bore killed with water, and at the same time attempt to plug it with cement. In the event, West Relief did kill Atlantic No. 3 with massive amounts of water. However, pumping had to be continued there to ensure that No. 3 did not get away again. South Relief inherited the job of cementing and plugging the No. 3 well bore, a daunting task in itself. Had South Relief only been drilled, Moroney would have been faced with *two* live well bores, lost circulation, and the real possibility that he could not have contained No. 3 without drilling that indispensible second hole.

No doubt about it, Tip's game plan was absolutely sound! Alternatives only make one shudder at what might have been.

ENDNOTES
1. A patented dehydrated (residual 2% water) sulphate of lime ($CaSO_4$) manufactured by Andy Hamilton at Ardmore, Pa. The initial setting time was 30 minutes and this could be accelerated by mixing in common salt or Portland Cement.
2. The drill pipe was taken to the Tuboscope yard in Edmonton where an electric drill would clean out the cement and get it ready for re-use.
3. Halliburton's old steam wagon was the most powerful unit in the field but, as Paul Bedard stated, it came to a screaming halt with 3,500 psi on the drill pipe.
4. Paragraph 4: Was the tool push Quarti? Was the reason for the "push" (Quarti) being on foot because he had smashed up his truck? As a matter of fact, Tom Wark had effectively taken over as "push" long before, trying to manage both West Relief and South Relief.
5. Original complete report and drawing on file at Glenbow.
6. Earl Griffith, proprietor of Barber Machine Shop in Edmonton, one of the most skilled welders and fabricators in the trade.

BOARD AS TRUSTEE, MEDIATOR AND PAYMASTER

13

The reader is now asked to go back in time, from the successful completion of the Atlantic No. 3 project in November, to May 14, 1948, the day the Board seized No. 3. This is necessary to more clearly set forth, in chronological sequence, the Board's new function as trustee.

Its first task, which it had to address immediately, was to set up the mechanism for keeping track of *its* production and sales of crude from the NW quarter of Section 23. As George Warne[1] recently indicated, this was the first (and the last, he hoped!) time this tribunal would wear these new hats.

At the time of the take–over, there was fierce competition for crude. Imperial Oil owned by far the largest number of wells. British American Oil Company[2] needed crude for its Calgary and Moose Jaw refineries, but had failed to find production in the Leduc field. It had to rely on the smaller independent producers, and, in order to sign them up, it had to pay bonuses. Even the Co–op refineries situated in socialist Saskatchewan became hairy chested free enterprisers and aggressively identified and drilled up productive lands. They were really in better shape than British American. Regardless of who had what, the only outlet for Leduc crude was via the tank cars. An oil pipeline to Edmonton was proposed to supply the Canol refinery which had been moved there from Whitehorse. It had only 4,000 barrels a day capacity.[3] The Board therefore had to resolve this dilemma and they did so by requiring each of the purchasing companies to take the same proportionate amount of crude that they would have purchased were the field producing normally. Imperial Oil agreed to take on the task of invoicing for oil sold and Imperial Pipeline would bill the Board for shipping costs to Nisku. By early June, Moroney had make–shift oil transportation facilities in place. They consisted of two mud hogs[4] just north of the dykes on the north side of the road allowance that moved crude over to the Leduc Consolidated quarter to the east, where storage tanks had been set up. Smaller engines fired with natural gas pumped the oil from these tanks into the Nisku pipeline. The facilities also were rigged up to re–inject oil down Atlantic No. 1 and 2 well bores when the uncontrolled production couldn't be handled through the pipeline.

Considerable pressure was exerted on the Board to get the

shut–in wells back on stream. The independents needed cash flow urgently to pay their drilling and completion expenses. Imperial Oil was also in dire need of funds to pay for its enormous development costs. It had made a 180–degree about turn from its 1946 posture and was aggressively spending large amounts on geophysical exploration and wildcatting.[5]

Moroney, in his role as czar had, as his ultimate priority, the killing of Atlantic No. 3. A large part of the exercise was to handle the oil in as orderly a manner as possible. However, he was also fully aware that such facilities would enable Imperial (and other producers) to get wells back on stream. The Conservation Board now considered that the producers could be given some relief and at the same time it could accommodate the Atlantic No. 3 produc-tion. It therefore issued Order No. 6L, dated June 3. It permitted D–2 wells to produce 800 barrels each over a ten day period. D–3 wells were limited to 1,200 barrels of "combined oil and water" for the same period. The Board reserved the right to rescind the Order at any time without notice. The Order also required the two com-pleted oil wells on the Atlantic quarter to remain shut–in (except for Atlantic No. 3!).

With growing confidence in Tip's success in handling the uncontrolled production, the Board issued on June 11, Order No. 7L, which extended the period of permitted production to June 30 and increased the allowables. Further orders modified production throughout the remainder of 1948 and into 1949. It was not until April 1, 1949 that the Board finally allowed Atlantic No. 1 and 2 to resume production at 100 barrels per day of combined oil and water from the D–3. (The D–2 was not productive on this lease.)

A matter of urgency for the Board was the handling of liability. Regardless of who (if anyone) was to blame, the government must have felt that it had to shield Atlantic Oil Company Limited from hawkish predators. It therefore met with its department people and the Attorney–General's office. It also had the benefit of input from some of the Calgary legal profession in formulating legislation to forestall law–suits.

The Contractor sought payment:

    a. from the Board, for its rig rental on the Atlantic No. 3 location from May 14 to September 6 (this was disallowed),

    b. from the insurer, for the value of the rig lost on September 6, the value of which was to be based on an inventory taken at a nearby G.P. steam rig of equivalent size.

The farmers sought satisfaction from both the Owner and Contractor for damage to crops and surface. They were later compensated by the Conservation Board from the Trust Fund.

McKinnon was assured by George McMahon that Atlantic had settled or had reached a basis of settlement for all the claims of surface damages except with one Harysh, "who is claiming an unreasonable amount". McKinnon said he was sending Mr. Meldrum of the Arbitration Board to see if he could break the impasse.

There is no evidence that the Board took out insurance on behalf of its own liability when it sequestered the operation nor is there any evidence that the Contractor for the two relief holes took out insurance (although they both must have had some sort of protection). The insurers later agreed not to sue Atlantic for the amount payable to General Petroleums for the loss of the rig.

When the Conservation Board took over the well, was the drilling contract abrogated, thereby relieving the Owner of responsibilty and preventing the Contractor from carrying out work under the terms of the day work contract clause?

What portion of the rig was really destroyed by falling into the crater prior to the fire? It was reported that the draw-works caught fire then fell in the crater.

To better understand some of the ramifications of the incident that could affect insurers and the insured, one must look back to Turner Valley days. D.P. McDonald, Q.C. is retired after a long career in all phases of the oil patch. He was a classmate of Red Goodall's at the University of Alberta and played as a star forward in university hockey. D.P. articled with Rae Fisher, and in the early thirties, acted for more than twenty small producers in the Valley. He was thoroughly familiar with surface hazards such as plant fires and explosions. McDonald studied U.S. cases involving wild wells. In so doing, he identified, in 1943, another, quite different, type of hazard. He accordingly drafted up a clause protecting insurers from any subsurface loss to adjacent property occasioned by any operations of the insured. This meant that negligent action on the part of the insured whereby subsurface flooding could damage productive capabilities on an adjacent parcel would not be the liability of the insurer. This took on a new importance in 1948.

From much of the evidence brought out, it seems that the lawyers were not insisting on moving into the courtroom on the basis of negligence. Actually, the loss due to "underground drainage'' because of the enormity of the blow–out became of far more importance.

To carry this scenario to its "worst case", if the operations had been left as they were without Moroney in charge, there might have been a fire much sooner and more crude would have gone up in flames. Atlantic's gain would then have been greatly reduced; the loss of crude plus the costs incurred by the Conservation Board might even have exceeded the amount in the trust fund. Then what would have been left for the insurance companies and/or the other operators to sue Atlantic for?

Atlantic might have considered G.P. negligent but Atlantic's contract with G.P. may have legally terminated the day the Conservation Board took over. What was the Board's responsibility when it took over on that day? Did it act with the consent and approval of Atlantic, i.e., as agent? Did the Board take out its *own* insurance? Just what risk did it assume?

Although Section 46 of the Conservation Board Act gave the Board the power to seize the well, it made no provisions for the paying out of monies. Some invoices had already been paid out of the trust fund but without legal authorization. To remedy this situation, a stop–gap Order–in–Council, OC1495/48, was passed on December 21, 1948. Clause 2 of the Order–in–Council enabled the Board to pay out claims against Atlantic that were limited to surface matters.

For the Rebus family Clause 3 was a heartbreaker, in a sort of way. It was just a few days before Christmas and visions of sugar plums might have been dancing in front of their eyes as they mentally calculated their royalty due. For the moment, they had to be satisfied with $16,934.52, payable to National Trust (trustee for the Rebus family). This was calculated from May 14 to November 30, using a deemed production of 45,625 barrels.[6]

The Order–in–Council also referred to over–production of 565,195 barrels: this was to guide the Board in scheduling the restricted production of Atlantic No. 1 and 2.

As the year drew to a close, Bill No. 70 "an Act to determine all Claims Arising from the Atlantic No. 3 oil well Disaster" was being drafted.

The Board brought all the producers together to explain the legislation. A meeting was called for 10 a.m. January 26, 1949 to discuss the final form of the new Act. As the minutes stated: "To consider a proposal submitted by Atlantic Oils (sic) to the producers in the Leduc field". (See Appendix L.)

The purpose of the meeting was to obtain the agreement of all the working interest owners to this proposal and forestall legal action against Atlantic. Royalty interest owners (e.g. Rebus and Harysh) could also claim that they were aggrieved. As they were not producers or working interest owners, they were not invited.

The meeting opened with Moroney reciting the chain of events culminating in the plugging of the well, and the installation of three small pumps on shallow wells that had been drilled near Atlantic No. 3 to drain the oil–charged surface beds. He also reported on a deep ditch cut on the north and west sides of the crater to prevent oil from draining toward the North Saskatchewan River as it had done in the earlier part of the year. Always thinking ahead, he had left the two relief well heads in a state of readiness.

We now pause to examine the case of one of the chief dissidents: Leduc Consolidated. This company was incorporated on May 15, 1947. Its landman, J. (Red) Phillips had just acquired the east half of 23, Twp. 50, Rge. 26, W4M (the east offset to Rebus) from Harysh.

According to Garnet Edwards, then drilling superintendent for Union Drilling, an affiliated company and contractor to Leduc Consolidated, Phillips had tried to obtain the Rebus quarter. "He (John) was much too hard to deal with despite the fact Red offered him a substantial (unstated) bonus". The company, without evidence one way or another, decided that their parcel was well within the limits of the D–3 reservoir. By July, they had moved *three* rigs into drill *simultaneously,* lsd 7, 10 and 15, numbered 3, 1 and 2 respectively. Their world came to an end with the bad news that both No. 3 and 1 were off reef (D–3) and without D–2 production. No. 2, the northernmost, caught just a few feet of D–3 above the oil water interface. Thus four step outs (the three Leduc Consolidateds plus BA Pyrcz) had sharply defined the east edge of the D–3 reservoir.

No. 2 was plugged back and whipstocked to be completed 100 ft. higher in the D–3. This took place just before the above meeting. But it was Leduc Consolidated that bore the brunt of the reservoir damage inflicted on the area by the many attempts to kill Atlantic No. 3. Garnet Edwards recalls feathers, oats and sawdust coming up with the oil.

It was therefore not unexpected to have four directors of the Leduc Consolidated Oil Company show up at the Board meeting. Two of these, Bill Kemp and Bill Jeffries, also represented the extra costs which had been incurred to whipstock No. 2. The other directors: Red Phillips and Bill Maughan (misspelled Mahon in the minutes) were also outspoken in their insistence on receiving redress for damage to their one producer. Quoting D.P. McDonald,

"Bill Maughan told the meeting 'I didn't drill my well just to get feathers out of it'". Leduc Consolidated ultimately received over $100,000 in damages from the Board Trust Fund.

When Peter Harysh, the mineral owner and lessor to Leduc Consolidated, learned of this compensation, he filed a statement of claim seeking 12½% royalty on the $100,000 ($12,500) plus $2,500 damages. The outcome is not completely known in this instance but Harysh did receive compensation for damage to the surface.

Gordon H. Allen[7] had been very diligent on behalf of Atlantic Oil, his client, in drafting the "proposal". This document, Appendix "M", deserves the close attention of the reader because of the pleadings by Atlantic. (The best defence is an offence!) It maintained that there was no negligence on anyone's part. Atlantic referred to *assumed* over-production and argued that the apparent surplus of $316,849.50 was "small recompense" for "...its loss of more than 1,000,000 barrels of oil". It failed to mention that drainage of offset oil could have occurred. Frank McMahon would have found great comfort in Harry Simpson's 1986 report which mentions a 2,500,000 barrel loss, but he would not have wanted to be reminded that Atlantic's portion of the pool-wide loss was only a fraction of his claimed 1,000,000 barrels!

After the "proposal" had been reviewed, Don Mackenzie judged the deemed over-production (565,195 barrels) to be "fair and reasonable" (this is 72% of the actual 784,686 barrels). He recommended:

a. that this over-production be in terms of barrels rather than dollars,

b. that Atlantic's make-up for four deemed locations be 33⅓% of the existing allowable until the over-production had been made up.

Gordon Webster represented Home Oil. He remembers Major Jim Lowery chewing him out upon his return to the office for not objecting. Lowery's argument was "We don't know how much damage it's done to the reservoir". Lowery, dead for over thirty years, and other attendees, would also liked to have had Simpson's report to back up their claims.

The Deputy Attorney General, W.J. Wilson, spoke on behalf of the proposed Bill.

Moroney supported the entire concept of settlement for two very practical reasons: "It could easily happen to us (Imperial Oil), so let's not set a precedent, especially since we don't really know whether it was negligence..." Further, "...this case could drag on in the courts for years". His views were not shared by some others in the Imperial Oil organization, but his well–respected, well–reasoned position carried the day. Now Atlantic could be really grateful that the same no–nonsense person that had killed their well was running interference for them.

The meeting closed with "the majority of the producers being in favour of the proposed legislation". The approval obviously could not be unanimous, with the strong feelings and the realization that the McMahons had come out far ahead!

The way was now clear for the Attorney General's office and the Department to complete the Bill. It was tabled in the legislature and promulgated March 29, 1949. Payments were to be formalized (amounts unspecified in the Act) to claimants; said payments "as the Board may consider to be just and equitable" (with no appeal!). (See Appendix N.)

The Atlantic No. 1 and 2 wells were to be restricted to 66⅔% of the allowable as set from time to time (this would be equivalent to one–third of the allowable of four deemed wells, as proposed by Don Mackenzie at the January 26 meeting). The Act also forbade the drilling of either lsd 11 or 12. The Board was empowered to hold trust funds for two more years (to 1951) and this was later extended because by mid–1951, there were still some funds held. The lease had not yet been cleaned up to the Board's satisfaction.

Imperial, of course, was the major recipient of trust funds; it was reimbursed for:

a. the drilling and supervision of the directional drilling and the costs of laying pipelines;

b. loss of production at No. 48. This well was being readied for production at the time of the January meeting,

c. monies owing Imperial for the 100,000 barrel production payment agreed to by Atlantic Oils at the time of signing the lease.

The following is a break–out of the rounded–out total receipts and expenditures:

Board's receipts from sale of crude	$2,800,000
Total expenses	1,800,000
Royalties to National Trust	360,000
Paid to Atlantic by July 31, 1951	1,000,000
To be paid after Board satisfied	50,000[8]

But all these problems were as nothing compared to the long term possibilities for Atlantic Oil: Frank McMahon, the now rich entrepreneur, saw above and beyond all the niggling legal "trivia" to the real value to him of this near disaster.

ENDNOTES:
1. Technical Assistant to the Board and member of working committee.
2. Before it was taken over by Gulf of Pittsburg.
3. On stream July 17, 1948. Throughput: 4,000 barrels a day. Nisku–Edmonton pipeline opened in September 1948.
4. Pumps used to circulate mud at drilling wells.
5. Imperial Oil eventually sold its 100% Royalite interest to the Bronfmans and its International Petroleum subsidiary back to its parent "Jersey".
6. 45,625 barrels, arrived at by calculating what the wells would have produced under normal conditions. Royalty revenue for the period: April–May 14 already reported in Chapter 6 "McMahon". The Rebus family ultimately received the royalty due them as the parcel worked its way out of its over–production.
7. Then partner, Porter, Allen, Millard (now McKimmie Matthews).
8. Prospectus dated November 14, 1951 re Canadian Atlantic stock offering.

THE CLEAN-UP

14

Three small pumps had been installed in shallow holes to extract oil from the shallow beds near the Atlantic No. 3 well bore. Lyle Caspell comments that later only water, with a rainbow of oil, was being pumped but in the early days immediately after they were installed, there was some oil "produced".

Mention has already been made of Leduc Consolidated producing feathers, oats and sawdust along with small amounts of oil. Several other leases in the vicinity also reported producing lost circulation material. It kept reappearing in their separators and tanks for several years, pointing up the excellent communication in the D–3 reservoir of the area.

Another problem resulting from the Atlantic No. 3 blow–out was experienced in 1949. Ralph Will, who drilled some of the infill wells near Atlantic No. 3, encountered gas at about 2,200 ft. (in Belly River sands) which blew the mud out of the hole. Will would close his BOP and let the gas blow itself out before drilling ahead. This sometimes took as much as three days. When the Viking gas blow–out at Atlantic No. 3 was temporarily "under control" and the well "shut in", in late February and early March 1948, the 2,200 ft. zone and the shallow near–surface sands were being gas charged. Will's experience further suggests that Atlantic No. 3 may have already passed the "point of no return" prior to the D–3 unloading that morning of March 8.

The January 26, 1949 Conservation Board meeting could be said to be the end of the Imperial "occupation". This was the signal for Atlantic to start remedial operations on the surface to restore it to a condition that would meet with the Board's approval. There was a degree of urgency in this insofar as Atlantic was concerned because the final release of all the monies said to be owing to it would not take place until a final OK had been obtained from the Board's field personnel.

The summers of 1949 and 1950 saw Frank Ronaghan and Al McIntosh, then junior employees of Pacific, out at the lease. Their jobs were to rehabilitate the ground under the ultimate supervision of the Board. This activity continued until 1951. Exchanges of letters as to details indicated that the land would soon be ready for cultivation.

Lyle Caspell noted, in his letter of October 25, 1950 to D.P.

Goodall, that General Petroleums had not cleaned up the lease. (Why G.P. should be responsible escapes the author!) Caspell promises to "make an effort to remove materials strewn on this acreage", but his next sentences are contradictory:

> The general area north of the main crater has been worked on, but due to the undermi(n)ing we will be limited on complete renovation for some time (sic). We have worked much of this area over a number of times with great success and are pleased to say that grain will be grown within a few feet of the crater this coming year. Further work is still planned on the portion showing mud and oil.

His letter then turns to the relief wells. "The south well situation is very satisfactory". The west relief well showed gas escaping into the cellar and it was the company's proposal to set a bridging plug near the bottom of the 7 in. casing using 100 sacks of cement, then perforate the production casing below the surface casing and run a cement squeeze job to prevent any communication between the Viking and the cellar. This cement would also go into the shallow beds.

The next record of interest is a meeting of the Board and Atlantic, held on February 13, 1951. The following items were reported:

1. Main crater had been filled.
2. Scrap iron removed from surface.
3. Area north of main crater: 1 ft. of dirt added to the soft portion.
4. Problem of disposing of sediment and water from the north-west pit.

It was reckoned that between $30,000–35,000 would have to be spent to clean up the gas leak at West Relief.

Because the two year period as set down in the 1949 Act was now drawing to a close, and since the Board was determined to ensure a proper clean-up, an extension to this arrangement was agreed to whereupon there would be $50,000 held back by the Board until such time as the entire lease was in satisfactory condition.

There were two other vague communications from Caspell referring to undermining and the uselessness of trying to fill in the crater. Robert H. Teskey of Imperial Oil reported in a hand-written note on the Caspell memo that: "Many of the major components of the rig were never encountered in the restoration operations and no doubt fell in the crater".

The final memo that can be found in the files is dated January 8, 1953, written by Murray Blackadar to D.P. Goodall. He reports that he and McIntosh inspected the lease. Blackadar concluded by saying, "The surface of this area is now in good condition and almost entirely free of debris".

By far the major portion of the quarter section was again under cultivation.

The following is the final disposition of the funds:

Total – $1,051,092.68 to Atlantic, of which over $51,000 were released on February 27, 1953.

Of the total revenue from the sale of crude oil: $2,831,860.49, expenditures were $1,780,767.81, resulting in the above total payable to Atlantic.

As mentioned above, Leduc Consolidated received $100,000 while Imperial Oil was awarded $100,000 for inconvenience and loss of production at their No.48 well, which was used as a water injection facility in May and June of 1948.

The terms of the over–production had been met by 1957 and it was in that year that the two remaining undrilled locations in the NW quarter of Section 23 were completed as oil wells. It is interesting to note that the well bore in lsd 12 of 23 was located only 150 ft. away from the original No. 3. Extreme cautionary measures were taken and the well was drilled and casing run without incident.

Paul Diemert (VIP) has a somewhat different story from Caspell's which would indicate Imperial still had some input into cleaning up the lease:

> ...I was on I.O.L. Construction as Utilityman and a year later we levelled the ground around the (wild well) site and planted grass and grain. Three years later the farmer (Rebus heirs) planted his crop over the 'wild well' location and drew a damn good crop – contrary to the predictions of environmentalists...

If one were to visit the Leduc oilfield to look for any marker pointing to the Atlantic No. 3 wild well, he or she would find none. Even if one stood on the exact spot, a wellhead marked "Pacific Unit 12–23", drilled in 1957 150 ft. to the east, would be the only visible object.

There is only one vague link: a sign on the way from Leduc to Calmar noting "Atlantic 3 Road". And the choice of this name is due to Reg Bara, who, as a school boy, watched the seething oil and gas craters that later caught fire. In searching for an alternative to a nearby fertilizer plant's request for a highway sign, Reg harked back to those early days when in 1982 he, as Councillor, proposed that name to the Leduc County Council.

Let Johnny Lyle (deceased), then a student engineer with Imperial Pipeline, end this chapter with his comments to Gibby Gibson in 1977:

> To the best of my knowledge, no one was killed or seriously injured in all the danger and excitement of the Atlantic No. 3 episode. Present day conservationists and ecologists would have gone stark raving mad had they been there to see it. Believe it or not, good crops of grain have been grown these last 25 years on the field that was so thoroughly oil soaked and ripped up during 1948. I would recommend that a historic marker be placed to point out the site of the disaster and to commemorate the heroic efforts made to control that amazing flow of oil and gas.

The Imperial Leduc discovery well of February 1947, one mile to the west of Atlantic No. 3, is appropriately designated and that is as it should be. But it is equally important that this near disaster, so well remembered in people's minds, should have a much more tangible form of recognition than a mere highway sign which was put up for quite another purpose.

MEASURING THE LOSS 15

In a totally unprecedented chain of events linked to Atlantic No. 3, the Conservation Board had thrust on it many new responsibilities. One task, with which it fortunately had some familiarity and competence, involved studies of reserves, both gas and oil. The work included investigating the pool reservoir pressures before and after the blow–out. Matching these values to the amount of controlled and uncontrolled production during the six months of

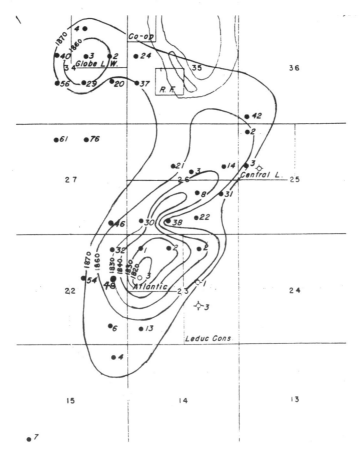

Pressure contours of D–3 zone around Atlantic No. 3 blow–out. Contour interval 10 psi. Datum –2,980 ft. subsea. May 13–May 20, 1948.
Adapted from Conservation Board Publication.

1948 would then yield an estimate of reservoir damage, including a calculation of the vertical movement of the gas/oil and oil/water interfaces. The Board needed these studies when it was deciding what course of action it should take as Trustee of the crude oil rampage.

The Leduc D–3A reservoir is a dolomite–type rock with a multitude of pores of every size ranging from pin holes to room size. The voids are interconnected so as to provide excellent permeability; this enables fluids to move readily from one part of the reservoir to another. Even so, a pressure sink had developed in the vicinity of Atlantic No. 3 by May 1948 as a result of the uncontrolled production. (See isobaric map.[1])

J.E. (Ted) Baugh,[3] had just rejoined the Board early in 1948 after an absence of two years. He had been a fellow graduate of Harry S. Simpson[4] in Chemical Engineering at the University of Alberta. As engineer, he was asked to estimate total D–3 pool reserves in 1948 by both volumetric[5] and material balance[6] methods. He estimated initial oil in place (volumetric) to be 230,550,000 barrels. The material balance method yielded 28,300,000 barrels, obviously too low (insufficient reliable data because of the early stage of depletion of the pool). Baugh also estimated gas cap gas in place at 393 Bcf.

Simpson, using his own experience and knowledge and applying the Esso and Conservation Board D–3A estimates from data available as of December 31, 1985 calculates that 386 million barrels of oil and 412 Bcf of original gas cap gas were originally in place. Original solution gas[7] in place amounted to 185 Bcf, for a total original gas in place of 597 Bcf.

Considering the paucity of 1948 reservoir data and the fact that the pool limits had not been defined, Baugh is to be commended for his pioneer efforts.

In his report to the Board, Baugh attempted to relate bottom hole pressure declines to oil production and arrived at 22,300 barrels withdrawal for every one pound drop. This was temporarily reversed during the water injection into No. 48. Quoting from Baugh's report..."There is indication of the effect of the water injection (in)to Imperial No. 48 during June, on the July 1 contour map where the (pressure in the) central portion of the field was definitely raised...leaving various low areas in the outlying sections...it appears that there was a definite (low) pressure area surrounding Atlantic No. 3 but drainage would appear to be from most of the field. During the latter part of the blow–out, maximum pressure differential was in the neighbourhood of 15 psi which indicates rapid establishment of equilibrium and excellent horizontal permeability."[8] Thus while Imperial Leduc No. 48 water injection failed to drown out Atlantic No. 3, Baugh showed that it was an effective form of pressure maintenance.

He also estimated crude production from Atlantic No. 3 and the rest of the field during the six month rampage to have been 2,800,000 barrels of crude and 20–25 Bcf[9] of gas cap gas. Arnold Johnson, then a summer engineering student, reported[10] measuring 29 MMcf per day with a pitot tube at the wild well. This works out for six months' production at only 5.4 Bcf. But the measurement was at only one of many places where gas was escaping as cratering progressed in the vicinity of the well bore.

The tally on Atlantic No. 3 cumulated to 1,407,979 barrels (how could they get that accurate?). The virgin bottom hole pressure of 1,894 psig dropped to 1,837 on May 1, then rose to 1,862 on May 15 due to water injection at No. 48. Thereafter it declined to 1,822 by September 1. Bottom hole pressures for all surveyed wells are recorded in Table 3 of Baugh's Conservation Board report.

Baugh went into considerable detail in his findings [11] in the "calculation of oil encroachment into the gas cap". He concluded that the volume of oil encroached which cannot be recovered would be in the order of 619,000 barrels. He also reckoned the height that the oil moved up into the gas cap at 0.365 ft..."Since the loss of gas represents 5.95% of the total gas cap, this gas is no longer available for production of oil". Accordingly, the loss of oil production due to the gas waste was 1,510,000 barrels.

The Table in Simpson's informal 1986 report entitled "Summary of Oil and Gas Reserves Losses Resulting From Atlantic No. 3 Blowout"[12] shows total oil produced at 1,407,000 barrels, of which 1,242,000 were saved. The balance, 165,000, was lost either by migration into thief horizons, spraying into the atmosphere, seeping into the ground or being burned during those last few days in September 1948.

Simpson goes on to say the oil zone moved up 1.5 ft. into the gas cap between March 8 and September 10, 1948 (the period of uncontrolled flow of Atlantic No. 3) due to the production of gas cap gas.[13] Current Esso computer reservoir simulation runs, taking into account all production and pressure history to the present, suggest that 2,500,000 barrels were irretrievably lost to the gas cap despite later downward sweeping of gas cap.

To put it in perspective, the estimated total loss of over 2.5 million barrels represents only about 1% of the total expected oil recovery from the pool. (See Appendix O for full report.)

At the time, Dr. George H. Fancher was a professor of petroleum engineering at the University of Texas, Austin. He was retained by the Conservation Board to submit an independent appraisal of reservoir damage and to comment on the feasibility of secondary recovery in the Leduc D–3 reservoir. His four page letter is a combination of well–known petroleum engineering principles and hypothetical conjecturing. He felt that the reservoir pressure could be restored and maintained by injection of water into the aquifer below the oil zone, or gas into the gas cap, or *both* (which in fact was done later in the efficient depletion of this pool). Thus he unwittingly anticipated future development.

He commented on what was already known: "water sufficient in amount to compensate for about half of the pressure lost was injected successfully into the reservoir. Continued injection of the water can eliminate completely the damage".

His statements on the "proposed settlement of the liability of the Operator for damage" are vague. He does not give reasons for his acceptance, contenting himself with: "I particularly like the feature of considering damage to the reservoir as a whole as I am a firm believer in the principle that sufficient and maximum recovery of oil can be obtained from any reservoir only if the problem be considered from the point of view of the reservoir as a whole". He concludes his letter with the statement that secondary recovery undertaken early in the productive life of the field will increase recovery and will greatly exceed damage incurred...and that "history will record the Atlantic No. 3 blow–out as a blessing in disguise" (philosophical rhetoric!).

For his efforts, Dr. Fancher was sent a bank draft in the amount of $1,126.40 (U.S.) Mr. Moffatt, then accountant at the Board, was meticulous in noting the deduction of $135.00 as non–resident tax payable to the Receiver General for Canada.

The Conservation Board paid Atlantic the residue of the monies it held in trust received from the sale of oil: $1,130,000 (after paying $370,000 to the Rebus family for royalties). In one scenario, the estimated surface loss of 165,000 barrels, and the estimated future oil recovery loss of 2,500,000 barrels, valued at $480,000 and $7,200,000 respectively (at $2.90 per barrel), could have been the responsibility of the lessee. Therefore, if one wanted to stretch one's imagination, Atlantic could have been liable for nearly $7.7 million.

ENDNOTES:
1. Isobars join values of equal pressure. The same plat shows a small sink in the Globe Leduc West quarter[2] nearly two miles to the north.
2. Globe Leduc West had drilled up its quarter and was the first independent producer in Leduc, starting in the summer of 1947.
3. After a distinguished career in industry, Baugh accepted the Chairmanship of the new Canada–Newfoundland Offshore Petroleum Board in St. John's, January 1986.
4. Simpson's equally distinguished career was entirely with Esso, from 1946 in Turner Valley until his retirement in 1985. His specialty is reservoir engineering. He is a member of the working committee of this book.
5. Volumetric estimates: the product of pore space in %, rock volume in acre–feet, 1 minus water saturation, shrinkage factor, recovery factor and a constant (a unit conversion factor).
6. The material balance method utilizes historical reservoir pressures, produced volumes of oil, gas and water, and their respective properties.
7. Solution gas is gas dissolved in the crude oil which may help drive the oil to the surface. The gas comes out of solution with the reduction in pressure and is separated from the oil at the surface. It is then either returned to the reservoir, sold or flared.
8. Report with all the details is on file both at the ERCB and Glenbow Museum.
9. Esso currently estimates, using inverse simulation techniques, that the amount of gas lost in the blow–out was 30 Bcf. Excellent agreement with Baugh.
10. Report to University of Alberta in partial fulfillment of course requirements.
11. Baugh's report.
12. Simpson's Report in its entirety constitutes Appendix 0. It is particularly useful as an account of the pool to 1986. Barry Dawe, Senior Engineer with Esso, is thanked for his assistance in the report's preparation.
13. From 1948 to 1960, there was prorated production as prescribed by the Board. From 1960 to the present, the pool has been operating as a unit, allowing operating flexibility and maximization of recovery. Over the past 38 years, the gas cap has gradually moved down and the oil water contact up, resulting in a 4 ft. oil "sandwich" where there was once a pay thickness of 38 ft.

L'ENVOI 16

As the author takes his leave at the conclusion of this journey, will you, gentle reader, wish to conjecture as to what it all meant?

– if you are or have been a driller, you will be struck by the desperate struggle to kill the well and the many problems at the two relief holes.

– as a production person, you may be concerned about the reservoir damage caused by the uncontrolled rampage.

– if you have a regulatory background, you may well appreciate the Board's problem in taking over the operation and also understand why it appeared to be dilatory.

– if you have a legal bent, you might ponder the intricacies of the lease dispute and the knotty question of responsibility and be surprised that no law suits were launched.

You may also appreciate how that wild well catapulted Alberta oil onto the world stage, and marvel that no fatalities or serious accidents occurred.

One may say that a danger signal was sent out at 5:00 a.m., May 7, 1947 when the first drill stem test of the D–3 at Imperial Leduc No. 2, the discovery well, flowed oil to the surface in only seven minutes. But at that time, no one really knew the forces lurking in the D–3 that could be (and were) unleashed from it where there was almost infinite permeability and enormous producibility, especially when aided and abetted by the Viking gas sand.

From May 1947 on a heady, hectic boom atmosphere of success (a "success syndrome" if you will) permeated the minds of many of the oil companies, promoters and the drilling crews. Well control had not yet become a subject for serious discussion. Government was preoccupied with regulations ensuring the equal drilling of Crown lands and left many significant aspects of safety to industry.

The euphoria came to a shuddering halt the morning of March 8, 1948 when everyone involved realized what they were up against. The operating companies, contractors and the Board were forced to look at an entirely new set of conditions and start setting new courses of action.

Of all the players in this drama, two especially, stand out: Cody Spencer and V.J. "Tip" Moroney.

Cody, with his insatiable desire for speed, running into a situation unlike any he had ever experienced, fighting it in his own way, hanging on like a bulldog, but finally having to let go.

Tip, "Cool Hand Luke", the career professional, with past disasters indelibly printed on his mind, not only providing leadership but being seen to provide leadership, his men instinctively following him through thick and thin. He knew what he needed: absolute control. When the dust had settled in November 1948 he was proven to have been fully justified in his actions. Pettinger summed it up: "Pretty fair for a man whose business was not killing wells".

Looking back on it with 20–20 hindsight, was the near disaster inevitable?

The answer may be "yes", given the unsuspected enormous productive capacity of the D–3 at Atlantic No. 3.

The answer may be "no" if one believes that the fateful doghouse decision of March 6 to make a dash for it, drilling "dry", instead of running production casing, was unwarranted. The risk, taken for whatever reasons, resulted in a nightmare reality.

The amount of surface casing, even with lost circulation, had seemed sufficient for holes previously drilled in the area. If a decision to run long string had been taken as soon as the D–3 had been encountered, the surface casing would not have been a factor.

What good came out of this near–disaster?

- lessons in well control, learned the hard way,
- legislation that would set guidelines for the common good,
- a symbiotic relationship that could and did develop between three disparate organizations; circumstances pushing them together to achieve a common goal – Atlantic, the promoter firm with little staff; Imperial Oil, the largest company, with the most experienced people; and the Board, armed only with its regulatory authority,
- and, finally, the emergence of a greater sense of responsibility towards those whose lives and property continue to be affected by the oil patch.

APPENDICES

APPENDIX A

McMahon, the high roller, the gambler, displays his entrepreneurial style in excerpts from an interview in the *Victoria Daily Colonist* 1969:

> They (Pacific) were happy with the profits they were making, so I went it alone. I bought a lease from a farmer named John Rebus. I had to pay him $200,000 for the 160 acres and I had to get the money myself...That was Atlantic No. 3 and it blew in all over the place. We had oil all over and it flowed for months before it caught fire...Not many people, or big companies, were interested in coming to Alberta at that time, but once this well blew out, it created a lot of enthusiasm. We got $40,000,000 worth of publicity all over the world and oil companies came into Alberta after that.

APPENDIX B

McMahon's version of his successful efforts to sign up Rebus comes from Earle Gray's taped interviews in 1980–1. McMahon fails to acknowledge Bus Lacey nor does he disclose how he discovered the flaw in the title:

> I made the deal with Rebus. I had a hell of a time keeping him quiet. I paid him with money and also bought his wife a kitchen stove or something, washing machine...she'd never had much before, she was looking after the chickens. I told him that you'll never know that we've been here. All of a sudden we got this wild well and we're digging up the whole god damned property, putting these big sumps in. And finally, the rig tipped over...fell down the hole...the boilers and everything else. The boilers were as big as this room. I tried to get Rebus to move out, he was living on the farm close by. I was going to get the police to get him to move out. Finally, I met him when the policeman got hold of him and he was carting his stuff out of his house...mattresses, stoves, and what all so they wouldn't get killed anyway. I had a moral responsibility to look after them, I had to look after their property.

APPENDIX C

Lyle Caspell is quoted from his undated, signed report regarding the Rebus leasing:

Prior to formal agreement of property, (Caspell) visited Mr. and Mrs. John Rebus, who were interested in development of their property but were skeptical of procedures. Rebus, living in an unimproved residence, had real personal dreams of having first, a new stove, a washing machine, refrigerator, new water well and bathroom with hot water. This was their dream. A formal list of requests was made, largely regarding home, with hopes of one day going to the Calgary Stampede in a new car. Thanks to McMahon, this all happened.

APPENDIX D

This version of the dispute between Imperial Oil and McMahon is derived from a phone conversation in 1981 with Art Bessemer, one of Imperial's lawyers at the time. It is somewhat at variance with facts, as the author's bracketed comments point up, but is intensely interesting!

Johnny Jackson (Imperial Oil) had a lease all drawn up for signature by Bronislaw, the father, but when he arrived at the house he was told by John (Rebus) the son, that Bronislaw had been dead for 15 years, (actually 6) and they brought out the old man's will which showed that the widow was entitled to the property as to a life estate, and the sons were to look after the mortgage and come in equally when she died. (There were more than two heirs). The understanding that Johnny had was that the mother had signed over the estate to John, the son, so Johnny agreed to this and got her name and the remaindermen off the lease.

When Johnny returned to Edmonton that day, he got a phone call (presumably from John), to the effect that he (Johnny) had taken a lease from the mother that was no good, because Johnny did not get the executors (Administrators) on the lease. So Johnny tore up the lease and went and got the signatures of the two executors (Administrators). This lease, of course, was no good either, because there was no court consent and the brothers trafficked the thing off to whomever they wanted because many companies were top leasing. One of these was Frank McMahon.

Buster Lacey went out and arranged for a form of a lease,

forcing John to sign the documents or else they (the brothers and sisters?) would beat him (Bus?)(John?) over the head with a neck–yoke. The conveyancing was done by Porter, Allen and Millard (Gordon Allen).

Johnny Jackson (Imperial Oil) had a lease all drawn up for Rebus. Buster put the lease together on behalf of Frank McMahon, and Frank paid a visit to Walker Taylor, then Western Regional Manager for Imperial Oil, and confronted him with the problem by asking Walker: "Where do we stand? It all hangs on an old lady's life. You are sitting pretty if she lives for fifteen or twenty years because she is the one that's controlling it, but if she dies, then tomorrow you have nothing". Both Walker Taylor and Frank McMahon realized that all that would be accomplished by a law–suit would be the drainage of the quarter section by offset production while the case was in the Courts, nobody winning. So Walker wheeled his revolving chair around with his back towards Frank, looked out the window and asked with his back to him, "How much will you pay us?" And that is how the 100,000 barrel oil payment arrangement was made which was kept secret from everyone in the Imperial Oil organization.

APPENDIX E

This unsigned, but dated report is undoubtedly a product of the Imperial Oil District office, then in Leduc town. It would have been prepared to update Calgary headquarters which, by this time, was becoming aware of the growing peril. This memo has a unique value in that it provides a summary of events leading up to the decision to do the big cement job.

ATLANTIC #3 BLOW–OUT

This well experienced extreme difficulty due to lost circulation after encountering the D3 zone at a depth of 5265 ft. (–2909 sub sea) on February 16, 1948. Numerous cement plugs were spotted , but as these were drilled out, circulation would be lost again. Fibrous material and gelflake seemed to have no effect whatsoever.

On March 6th, it was decided to drill the hole "dry", that is, without any returns of circulation, and then spot a large cement plug before reaching the oil contact. This is a recognized practice in some fields if proper blow–out equipment is in place. On March 7th, after reaching a depth of 5331 ft., the well suddenly blew in with an estimated gas flow of thirty million cubic feet per day and an oil flow variously estimated between one hundred and two hundred barrels per hour. It blew so suddenly that the crew was unable to put the "Hosmer" control in place. The "Hosmer" is a rubber packer that can be clamped around the drill pipe above the rotary table and then dropped into a landing bowl on top of the well head. The weight of the drill pipe can then be set on top of it. This is a very inexpensive control and is very useful in conjunction with a ram type blow-out preventer. In this case no ram type preventer was installed and the uncontrolled blow–out can be attributed to this fact.

The well blew wild for thirty–eight hours before being partially killed with large quantities of weighted mud, followed by one hundred and fifty sacks of cement. This procedure apparently shut off the oil zone in the D3 and the crew were able to put the "Hosmer" control in place. Gas from the upper horizons continued to come into the hole and held 1,000 p.s.i. on the casing below the "Hosmer".

It was then decided to plug the bit and perforate the drill pipe below the Viking sand in order to get returns of circulation. The bit was effectively plugged but a measuring line which was following the plug became stuck. In trying to cut this line, a piece of two–inch pipe was dropped and became lodged at 2060 ft. The drill pipe was perforated just above 2000 ft. and on March 21 as mud was being pumped in, a bad leak developed in the flow nipple in the cellar and the well was out of control again. The gas also broke out through the ground all around the lease and as far away as Imperial Leduc #32 and 11.

The next day 500 barrels of weighted mud and 800 sacks of cement were pumped into the hole without any apparent effect. It was then decided to stage cement with approximately 100 sacks of cement every four or five hours and the operators believe that the gas flow is diminishing to some extent. They believe that a cement bridge has been formed in the annulus above the perforations as the gas pressure built up on the drill pipe is 1000 p.s.i. with practically an open flow on the annulus. It is their hope and belief that the gas now coming to the surface is coming from the charged up sands below the shoe on the surface pipe. This, however, is problematical, although the gas flow to the surface seems to be diminishing.

The operators are now waiting for fifty tons of Cal–Seal from The United States and expect to be able to effectively kill the well with this quick–setting material. All hope of saving the hole has been abandoned and the problem now is to abandon the well properly by covering any potentially productive forma-tions with cement.

Present well information known is as follows:

Depth: 5331 ft.

Surface casing (10¾'') set at 300 ft.

Drill pipe is in the hole with bit plugged.

Drill pipe perforated at 2000 ft. with four shots.

Gas escaping through the ground and the leak in the flow nipple carries no oil. It is apparently coming from the Viking or Lower Cretaceous Sand although a possibility exists that it is also coming from the top of the D3 zone.

LEDUC, Alberta.
March 30, 1948

APPENDIX F

Atlantic personnel still had a presence on their own lease. The following excerpts from Lyle Caspell's field report illustrate this point. Caspell does not appear to have been kept up to date, according to his comments.

June 17, 1948

...to the Atlantic lease and looked over the oil pit situation and found that the well was making far more oil than I had ever seen it make before. There was a high wind blowing this day and the oil was squirting up through the craters to a height of about 30 feet and blowing all over the country. There are a lot of fire hazards attached to it under these conditions. There is oil spread on two or three farmers wheat crops in the area and I suppose we will have to do something about it at a later date. The oil was blowing as far as ³/₄ mile away from the rig and could be seen on cars, buildings and road. Even the watchmen on the locations had to be moved. It was really quite a mess. In fact, I understand 2 or 3 wells in the area had to shut down. I checked with the Imperial Oil Pipe Line and found that they had shipped 315,000 bbls. of oil from Atlantic #3 location.

June 18, 1948

Went directly to Atlantic Lease again this morning 8:15. I was very worried about this oil blowing around the country. I was afraid of fire and wanted to talk to one or two of the Imperial Oil men. I also was concerned over the amount of fluid that they were pumping down into Atlantic #1 and #2 wells, as I could not get a record or find anybody that had any records of the amount that had been pumped into the wells. On contacting the Conservation Board representative he told me that they did have an estimate of the amount of oil put back into the pay and I told him that he should be sure that this is done as we want a complete report on that work when this situation is cleared up...

APPENDIX G

In the early stages of assembling data for the book, Doug Hughes approached me with an article and a number of photographs he had taken as a watchman at the Atlantic No. 3 lease. He has kindly agreed to the printing of his reminiscences.

RECOLLECTIONS OF ATLANTIC NO. 3

My introduction to Atlantic No. 3 came in early June 1948, when, as a young University student, I was hired by Pacific Petroleums as a watchman on the afternoon shift.

In keeping with a student's usual mode of transportation in those days, I had hitch–hiked from Edmonton to Leduc to see what I could find in the way of summer employment. By this time Leduc had experienced nearly a year and a half of oil activity, and while there were jobs available, being in the right place at the right time was still the surest way of finding one.

Somewhere along the way I had learned that the most knowledgeable man in a booming oil town is the local bartender, so that was my first stop, followed by the Imperial Cafe across the street. The bartender didn't know of anyone looking for men but wished me luck. Later, as I came out of the Imperial Cafe, a man approached me from the direction of the bar and said "I hear you're looking for work." Never underestimate the influence of a bartender. I was hired in the middle of the street, told to find a place to stay, and the next day I would be taken out to Atlantic No. 3.

I was fortunate to find a room because Leduc was bursting at the seams and accommodations were at a premium. My only prospect was a very small room with two beds and two men to a bed. "Take it or leave it." I took it. My bed–partner, who I was to meet a day or two later, turned out to be a student from U. of A. who was on a different shift. The two guys in the other bed cleaned storage tanks, which was one of the dirtiest jobs in the business. Two things which stand out in my mind about this experience are the repertoire of songs those tank cleaners had, and the lack of washing facilities. The tank cleaners had a guitar and one of their favorite ditties went like this:

"There were two boys from Darby town,
And they were very rich,
One was the son of a millionaire,
The other a son of a ...
Hokey Pokey, Diddley Oakey,
You may think I lie,
But you go down to Darby town,
You'll see the same as I."

That is the mildest version I can think of for publication, but there were endless verses, some of which would make a long–shoreman blush.

The washing facilities left much to be desired. When I would come off shift at midnight, I had to heat enough water to wash by using one of those electric probe–heaters that travellers now use to heat water for coffee. Needless to say, after a few days you had to be considerate enough to stand downwind from your friends. When I got a day off I would hitch–hike to Edmonton, where for 50 cents, hotels such as the Lincoln would let you take a bath. It did feel good.

Being a student at Montana School of Mines, Butte, I had not even seen an oil well, let alone heard of Atlantic No. 3, so was a little unprepared for what I saw on my first day. The rig was still standing but for at least 600 ft. around the well the ground was saturated, and oil was bubbling up through the field in miniature geysers. The well and surrounding ground was estimated to be producing 13,000 barrels per day, which was running down the field as a small creek. The oil was being collected in 3 or 4 sumps said to contain about 50,000 barrels each. Pacific Petroleums, as operator, was pumping about 10,000 barrels per day down Atlantic 1 and 2, in order to minimize the loss in reservoir pressure from Atlantic 3. Two directional relief wells were being drilled, one to the west and one to the south of Atlantic 3, with the objective of bottoming close enough to the bottom of Atlantic 3 to kill it with water.

While I did some general roustabout work, my job was basically that of a watchman to keep visitors off the site because of the high potential fire hazard, and to insure that Pacific's tools and equipment didn't mysteriously disappear. I was ever mindful of the fire hazard as I walked across the oil-saturated lease. I often wondered if it did catch fire whether it would come as one giant "woompf", or if it would spread slow enough that, with such a strong motivator and light running shoes, I could distance myself from the property. Fortunately there was no fire while I was there and the question went unanswered. I left sometime after mid–summer when Pacific decided they no longer needed someone on afternoon shift. Sometime later the rig fell over and in early September the well caught fire. Presumably a rock had been blown from the subsurface, struck the rig and caused a spark to ignite the oil and gas. I was just as glad I was not there. The relief wells bottomed about the same time as the fire occurred and it was soon extinguished by pumping water down the relief wells.

Such was my first encounter with the fascinating oil business. Obviously I liked what I saw because the next summer, 1949, I worked for Sparling Davis Pipe Line Contractors around Leduc, and in 1950 roughnecked for Regent Drilling at Richard and Hafford, Saskatchewan. I graduated with a B.Sc. in Petroleum Engineering from Montana School of Mines in 1951 and received my M.Sc. from the University of Kansas in 1956. After nearly 30 years in the business I retired from Shell Canada in early 1980.

Douglas F. Hughes

APPENDIX H

Blazing Atlantic No. 3 Well Has Had Turbulent History

Here is a history of the Atlantic Oil Company's runaway producer beginning with the commencement of drilling on or about January 15 of this year.

March 8—The well came in with a spectacular 150-foot gusher, pressurized by an estimated 15,000,000-cubic-foot-per-day as flow.

March 9—The well continued to blow great volumes of gas and brought first worries of damage to the entire field through depressurizing.

March 10—After a rampaging 40 hours, the well was brought under control by pumping 100 tons of drill mud into the hole.

FRACTURES AREA

March 21—Efforts to clear a stuck drill pipe in the well resulted in fracturing of the surrounding area and gas began to escape over a wide radius about the drill hole.

March 22—Officials warned of extreme danger of fire in the area of the well and road blocks were set up on approaches to the site.

April 7—Six huge cement pumps forced 11,300 sacks of cement, 1,000 sacks of calseal plus lime and other chemicals into the hole in an unsuccessful attempt to block the flow of gas and oil.

April 19—Danger of Edmonton's water supply being affected by oil being swept into the Saskatchewan River by melting snow was voiced.

April 19—Sludge found in storage tanks of Consolidated Leduc No. 2 was believed to have been calseal which flowed more than a mile underground from the rampant well.

PLANES WARNED AWAY

April 26—An oily taste in Edmonton's water was attributed to oil escaping from the well finding its way into the city's water supply.

May 7—Danger of fire at the still-raging well brought a warning for aircraft to stay away from the area.

May 8—Ten thousand pounds of feathers, 28 tons of redwood fibre,

55 tons of cotton-seed hulls, balsam fibre and mud were pumped into the hole, again without success.

May 12—Plans for complete shutdown of the Leduc field, pending further action against the well, were announced.

May 13—The Leduc field was shut down as clean-up crews endeavored to trap surface oil. Beginning of thunderstorm season caused worry of fire being started by lightning.

May 15—Operation of the errant well was taken over by the Alberta Natural Gas and Oil Conservation Board.

May 17—A crew of welders began piecing together one and one-half miles of pipe to carry off oil collected in surface sumps.

May 20—Plans to cut off the flow from the well by forcing water down nearby Imperial Leduc 48 were announced.

DRILL RELIEF WELLS

May 22—Completion of erection of derricks for two directional relief wells west and south of Atlantic Leduc 3 was announced.

May 25—Attempts to flood out the wild well from Imperial 48 began.

May 26—Rising spring floods of the Saskatchewan River forced temporary abandonment of pump sites and attempts to flood out the Atlantic runaway.

June 2—Flow of oil from the wild well was reported to have dropped from 10,000 to 4,000 barrels per day.

June 3—Run-off of collected oil from the well to date was estimated at 160,000 barrels. No results had been achieved by pumping of water into nearby Imperial Leduc 48.

June 4—Removal of oil to Nisku via pipeline was authorized by conservation board officials.

June 5—Resumption of production of other wells in the Leduc field was authorized by conservation board.

June 7—Average daily production of oil escaping from Atlantic Leduc 3 was set at 11,097 barrels.

June 12—Contrary to expecta-

tions, production of the run-away well remained at over 10,000 barrels per day.

June 15—Atlantic Leduc 1 and 2 were brought into use returning oil from Atlantic 3 to the formation. Injection of water through Imperial 48 continued at the rate of 40,000 barrels daily.

June 17—Injection of water into the formation was halted temporarily.

MAJOR PRODUCER

June 21—Leduc field became Alberta's major crude producer at 13,779 barrels per day.

June 23—Deliveries from the rogue well totalled nearly 400,000 barrels.

June 28—Average daily production of the wild Atlantic well was set at 12,600 barrels.

July 5—Production was believed to be dropping below 10,000 barrels per day.

July 10—Directional relief wells were reported to be below 4,000 feet and attempts to end well's rampage were expected within 10 days.

July 13—Drilling of south relief well was reported nearly complete and west relief well was expected to finish within two or three days of the other.

PRODUCTION DROPS

July 19—Production of the errant well had dropped to an average of 7,772 barrels daily.

July 31—Failure to bring the well under control necessitated continuation of production on restrictions on other Leduc wells.

August 9—Total production of oil from the well was set at 865,732 barrels.

September 6—Derrick toppled in morning. Well ignited accidentally at 6:20 p.m.

APPENDIX I

Ralph Horley, former CBC radio announcer, was first to report the Atlantic No.3 story. He recalls the events leading up to his commentary:

>We were at a party that night at the home of the CBC radio manager Don Cameron and we were entertaining the chairman of the board of governors of the CBC, Davidson Dunton; the general manager of the CBC, Ernie Bushnell; and our regional director John Fisher, who was "Mr. Canada" on radio at that time; we were all here for the opening of CBX. The official opening was Wednesday, September 8.
>
>This was Labour Day Monday, September 6. We had been keeping an eye on this because the well had blown; the oil was coming up from the ground, bubbling around the base of the derrick; aircraft had been routed around because there was a chance of a spark from the gas; and I guess the derrick shifted, a rock fell, it sparked and that was it, it just caught fire and we saw the cloud of smoke going up from that area so we phoned and officials confirmed that, yes, the well was on fire.
>
>We had all the brass there and they said "go get it" and so our engineer said, "well the only portable recorder we have is in pieces on the work bench and it will take us half an hour to get it", so we said, "well go and get it." While there were tape recorders at the time they weren't very good and we had what was state–of–the–art at that time, a "Wire–rec" recorder, a stainless steel wire, and the only problem with it was if anything went wrong the wire broke and you had wire all over the room, and that's what we took with us to do the recording.

Here's that recently discovered CBC radio broadcast saved by the CBC archives people in Ottawa. The news report begins with the voice of John Fisher, Mr. Canada:

> Fisher: Last night the wild oil well in the Leduc field, 20 miles south of Edmonton, caught fire. Thousands of barrels of oil went up in flame and smoke. CBC reporters at the new CBC station in Alberta spotted the black smoke from the studios of the Macdonald Hotel in Edmonton and grabbed microphones and recording equipment. One of the men was Ralph Horley, who reports now from Edmonton.
>
> Horley: "It's the worst oil fire I've ever seen." "This brings back memories of the bombing of Berlin." "We'll have to wait until it burns out on top and then try to control it from below."
> Those are some of the statements we heard from the men who stood helplessly by as Atlantic No. 3 roared and belched huge hanging clouds of black smoke.

After a hectic ride on a highway literally choked with weekend holidayers and hundreds of carloads of the curious who had been drawn to the area by the huge canopy of oil smoke and a wait of almost two hours while permission was being obtained from the Mounties on duty to proceed to the danger area, we arrived at the site of the outlaw Atlantic No. 3 Leduc. 500 feet is not very far away when you find that the temperature at the well was registering 2,000 degrees Fahrenheit. We saw the boiling and the bubbling up from below that sent the flames hundreds of feet into the air; eruptions that sent mud and shale flying in every direction from the centre of the well. To the north of the well a sump or a man-made lake containing 70,000 barrels of the crude that had been recovered as it seeped up through the earth and also caught fire and was adding to the heat, smoke and the flames. This is the roar that was picked up on our CBC microphones: (roaring sound). And in the background we could also hear the bulldozers as they rushed to push up the dyke to contain the fire to keep it from spreading. To make the picture complete, we took our CBC microphone out to the specially chartered plane. Technician Gordon Shillabeer (deceased) recorded a description of what we saw and at one point in our circuit of the flaming pillar the flames rolled almost to our eye level as we flew along at 3,600 feet.

(Voice from aircraft – engine noise)
We're flying at 3,800 feet in the vicinity of Atlantic Well No. 3 in the Leduc oil field. The flames are still burning as high as they were last night and blew over 300 feet into the air, dense clouds of black smoke arising from it, levelling off way above it somewhere around 9,000 feet. It's quite a different sight from the air than it was from the ground where we witnessed this spectacle last night. From the air you can see the dozens and dozens of pools of oil that surround Atlantic No. 3; some of them are burning, some of them have not yet caught fire and perhaps they won't. Precautionary measures have been taken; bulldozers have pushed up the dyke to keep the flames back to keep it from spreading to the other pools of oil which are in the area. We're making a circuit of the field now to get a view of it from all sides. We can see the injection wells that they are using. They have drilled to the base of Atlantic No. 3 to inject hot water, acid and everything

else they can think of, everything known to the science of oil to try and stop the flow of oil from Atlantic Well No. 3...

APPENDIX J

This is one article in the press that analyzed the possibilities intelligently. The three suggested consequences are realistic but none of them materialized, thanks to McMahon's strenuous efforts, the Board's attitude and Imperial's philosophy.

Financial Post – September 11: When Atlantic No. 3 caught fire it caused almost as much furore in the stock market as it did at Leduc. For months two schools of thought existed on the very problematical question of the value of Atlantic shares. The first school holds that, as Atlantic management did everything humanly possible to keep the Atlantic well from going wild in the first place, bulk of the nearly $3 million of production should find a final resting place in the company's coffers. New York buyers are reported to have accumulated a half a million shares on this theory.

The second school points out that the company pays all the costs of bringing the well under control plus all the costs of putting the fire out. These expenses will, perhaps, be surprisingly large. Then it is pointed out that "almost endless" claims for damages are expected to be filed by other operators forced to restrict production or by operators claiming damage. And even if the oil technically does belong to the company (although marketed by the Conservation Board) a sum approaching $500,000 is payable in royalties. Then what about taxes on production?

Cost of the control hasn't been released but an official of Atlantic queried a month ago said that he thought it would probably exceed $400,000. By now, of course, the cost may be greater, $1 million having been guesstimated.

Fears of the layman that the fire might spread underground can apparently be discarded.

APPENDIX K

INTRODUCTION

In this paper the author will attempt to describe the killing and plugging operations carried out at Atlantic #3. Only a sketchy account can be given of events prior to May 13, 1948. It was on this date that the Alberta Government took over control of the wild well. Necessary precautions were instituted to offset the tremendous fire hazard in the area and large scale control measures began to take form.

The methods generally used in all operations of wild well killing were used at Atlantic #3 and in addition to these a number of new operations were tried and proved successful. But for the ingenuity of the men on the job, the operation could have taken a much longer time to complete. This is particularly true of the method used to eject wire netting into the original Atlantic #3 hole and which will undoubtedly prove to be of inestimable value in plugging wild wells of the future.

(Signed)
A. F. Johnson
March 1949

...A few days after the blowout, it was found impossible to get instruments down the drill pipe more than 800 feet. It is believed that the enormous flow of gas, possibly aided by shale carried by the flow, cut the drill string at this point. This discovery brought with it the realization of the hopelessness of killing the well from the well head.

Even after it became apparent that nothing could be done from the well head of Atlantic #3, the derrick and draw works had to be left in position due to the fire hazard, lest sparks struck, during removal operations, might set nearly a quarter section of land on fire. For the same reason, it was too dangerous to move the boilers from the lease, although they were located fully 50 yards from the derrick.

On May 13, 1948 the Alberta Government and the Petroleum and Natural Gas Conservation Board issued a special order closing down the field entirely so that the Imperial pipeline from the oil field to Nisku could be used exclusively to carry away the oil which had been trapped in large pits in the ground. Oil covered the ground over an area of roughly 600 yards by 200 yards. It varied in depth from a few inches to 5 or 6 feet. The soil of the rest of the quarter section was soaked with oil from spray. In some cases this same spray was carried as much as three quarters of a mile by the wind.

Mr. V.J. Moroney, Production Manager for the Western Division of Imperial Oil Limited, was appointed to take over full charge of the field operations.

Two seven inch flow lines were connected to the casing head and the flow through these was opened up wide in an endeavor to reduce the cratering around the well.

Atlantic had, in the same quarter section, two wells already com-

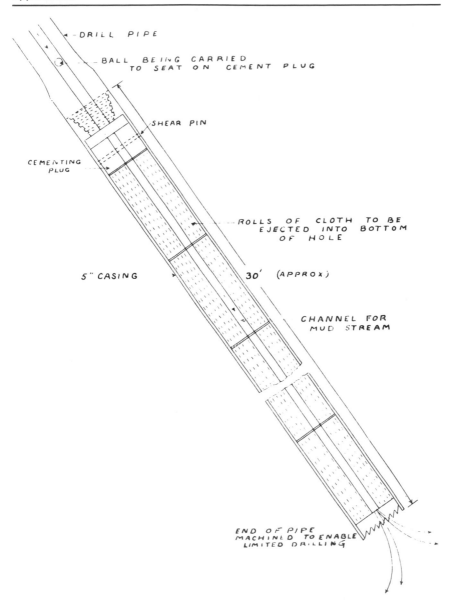

Bazooka: tool used to aid in cementing off Atlantic No. 3 from the D–3 zone.

pleted. These were Atlantic #1 and #2. It was decided to direct part of the flow from Atlantic #3 back to the producing zone via these two wells. The balance went to Nisku, from where it could be removed by rail.

On May 27, 1948 equipment had been moved into position to begin injection of water from the Saskatchewan River, some two miles distant, into Imperial Leduc #48. This equipment included four large pumps at the river, which forced water into two four inch lines which stretched for four miles before being brought together into a seven inch line which carried the water another three–quarters of a mile. It was at this point that the tracer was added. Two more pumps forced the water over to the well head and down Imperial Leduc #48. This well was located 1,400 feet west of the wild well. The idea was to flood the D3 zone around Atlantic #3 and try to make the wild well produce water. The pressure at depth was sufficient to support a column of oil and gas emulsion 5,000 feet high (the depth of Atlantic #3 well) but not enough to support a correspondingly high column of water.

This measure brought no success. Indeed, by June 21st it was found that the well was producing more oil than ever (13,200 barrels). So the water injection was discontinued. During the period of water injection more than 750,000 barrels of water were pumped down Imperial Leduc #48.

Sodium Thiosulphate had been used as a tracer in the injection water and continual tests were taken for this chemical from samples obtained at the well head. In spite of the fact that this process was carried out over the entire period of injection, not once was a positive test for Sodium Thiosulphate found.

Soon after the Government stepped in it was decided to drill two relief wells, the drilling to be done directionally by means of whip–stocks and controlled by Eastman and Homco surveying. A difficulty was experienced here in that no surveys had been taken during the drilling of Atlantic #3 and therefore the exact location of the bottom of the well was not known. A number of Totco surveys had been run, however, and from these it was realized that at no point could the hole be more than 25 feet off the vertical. Consequently the directional drilling was to be done in such a fashion that the relief holes would terminate directly below the derrick left standing over the wild well. In this area a characteristic drift to the North–West had been observed in drilling other wells. It was assumed that Atlantic #3 had followed this pattern...

...At Relief west, the hole had been completed to casing depth. After very careful reaming and conditioning 5,228 feet of 7 inch casing was run and cemented. Seventy–two hours later the cement core was drilled out of the bottom end of the casing and drilling was continued. The casing had been set just above the D3 zone in the impervious Green Shale. On August 30th the hole at Relief west had been completed and water was being forced down the hole at the rate of one barrel per minute at a well head pressure of 2,100 pounds per square inch. By next day the rate had increased to two barrels a minute but in the days that followed the rate of pumping could not be increased substantially without fear of bursting the well head. Its rated working pressure was 2,000 pounds per square inch.

When pumping was discontinued, a great deal of the water that had been forced down in the well came slowly back up. It is believed that with a pressure of 2,100 pounds per square inch at the top of a column of water a mile in depth, pressures at the bottom of the column had been created that were great enough to force the various beds upwards. When the pressure was released, these beds tending to settle back into their original positions had forced the water from the zone. Accordingly, the formation was acidized using 1,500 gallons of 15% hydrochloric acid. Following this the formation took the water at 550 barrels per hour or about 5 times as fast as before.

This was September 6th, and it was on this day that Atlantic #3 caught fire. The excessive cratering under the derrick had removed all support and the derrick had fallen into the hole on September 5th. It is believed that stones striking the fallen steel caused sparks that started the fire.

Relief west was acidized each day for three days and on September 11th the formation was taking 900 barrels of water an hour at 300 pounds per square inch. It was on the third day that Atlantic #3 was choked off. Where a raging inferno had been, there were now only occasional small fires from the oil and gas seeping out of the saturated ground.

A tracer consisting of a copper salt had been used in the water pumped down Relief west and again tests of the material from Atlantic #3 showed no indication of this chemical. However, considerable whiteness had been noticed in certain portions of the flames and when this was observed through a spectroscope a definite green flame was noticed which lasted only a short time.

Relief south, having reached casing depth at this time, had run 7 inch casing to 5,228 feet and was standing cemented. Upon drilling only 18 feet of new hole, and while still in the Green Shale, it was found there was no weight on the bit and the string had to be lowered over 6 feet until weight reappeared. At the same time circulation was lost suddenly. The original Atlantic #3 hole had been actually intersected...

...Then a new method was used which proved successful. A piece of 5 inch casing was prepared with teeth cut in one end to enable limited drilling and with the other end adapted to fit the conical drill pipe threading. This barrel was then loaded with ten rolls of wire cloth forming cylinders end to end and linked together so they would unroll and spread out to form a matting when ejected from the barrel. A continuous channel of small diameter was left running the length of the pipe. At the upper end of the barrel a cementing plug with a hole through it was held in place by a shear pin. When this was run in on the end of the drill string to the bottom of the hole, mud could be pumped through the entire string. When everything was in place, a plastic ball was inserted in the top of the drill pipe. This ball followed the mud stream down and seated on the hole in the cement plug sealing it off. Pump pressure was then used to break the shear pin and force the plug with the rolls of cloth ahead of it out of the barrel and into the bottom of the Atlantic #3 hole. This was done six or seven times before it finally held. More cement and plugging material followed to form a permanent bridge which sealed Atlantic #3 off from the D3 zone...

...In the meantime Atlantic Relief west had been constantly flooding the formation with water at an average rate of 550 barrels per hour, at an average well head pressure of 500 pounds per square inch. The total amount of water forced down Relief west was over a half a million barrels.

As conditions stand now, Relief south is connected to the original hole at the plug and tubing pressure at the well head is zero. Relief west is connected to the D3 below the plug and tubing pressure is 1,500 pounds per square inch. This indicates a permanent solid seal between the producing zone and Atlantic #3. Equipment at both wells has been winterized and is ready for immediate action should such be necessary.

At the surface there is a cone resembling a small volcano, around the Atlantic #3 hole, some 30 feet in diameter and 20 feet deep. The volume of material in the crater rim has been measured and found to be over 5,000 cubic yards. Some of this material has come from as deep as 1,500 feet.

This then, is the story of Atlantic #3 from the viewpoint of one who was in contact with much that happened. The story may not be as colorful as that presented by the newspapers to their general readers. Instead it aims to give a factual account of the pitting of technical skill and ingenuity against the forces of Nature out of control in probably the most serious mishap in Alberta oil production to date.

List of Additives Used on the Relief Wells

Atlantic Relief West

Wyo–Jel	9,000#	Quebracho	1,360#
Aquajel	89,300#	Anhydrox	12,100#
Alta Mud	1,000#	Soda Bicarbonate	370#
Caustic Soda	530#	Oil	1,200 gals.

Atlantic Relief South

Wyo–Jel	9,200#	Quebracho	860#
Aquajel	62,100#	Anhydrox	18,700#
Caustic Soda	625#		

Plus the following amounts, after Relief South intersected the original Atlantic #3 hole, to regain circulation:

Aquajel	43,000#	Cement (Calseal)	8,659 sacks
Alta Mud	87,800#	Sawdust	2,348 sacks
Calcium Chloride	3,200#	Plastistone	400 sacks
Zonolite	995 sacks	Hardwall	100 sacks
Lime	148 sacks	Cotton Seed Hulls	44 sacks
Jelflake	20 sacks	T.V. Shale	340 loads

Note: The additives used at Atlantic Relief South, are purposely split up so that the reader may obtain an idea of the quantity of material that was lost completely to the producing zone. Further, the figures presented are from the Daily Drilling Reports from each Rig. These figures will be in error, but will be on the low side due to a reticence on the part of most.

APPENDIX L

This land–mark meeting brought together the three main players: Atlantic, Imperial Oil and the Board. Its main purpose was to discuss the merits or otherwise of the "Proposal" (Appendix N) and let the other operators in the field "have their day in court". Misspelled names are noted here: Neil McQueen, W.J. Maughan, W.D.C. Mackenzie, F. McMahon, G. McMahon.

     A meeting was held at the offices of the Board at 10 a.m. January 26th, 1949, to consider a proposal submitted by Atlantic Oils Limited to the producers in the Leduc Field.

Present were:

Gordon Webster	– Home Oil Co. Ltd.
Neil MacQueen	– Central Leduc Oils Ltd.
Harold Herron	– Okalta Oils Ltd.
W.J. Mahon	– Leduc Consolidated Oils Ltd.
J. Phillips	– Leduc Consolidated Oils Ltd.
F.A. Schultz	– Continental Oil Co. of Canada
W.D.G. McKenzie	– Imperial Oil Limited
V.J. Moroney	– Imperial Oil Limited
W. Kemp	– Gas & Oil Products Ltd.
W. Jeffries	– Gas & Oil Products
F. MacMahon	– Atlantic Oil Co. Ltd.
G. MacMahon	– Atlantic Oil Co. Ltd.
A.P. Bowsher	– Atlantic Oil Co. Ltd.
G.H. Allen	– Atlantic Oil Co. Ltd.
J. Boyd	– East Leduc Oil Co. Ltd.
C.C. Cross	– Globe Oil Co. Ltd.
J. Godfrey	– Leduc West Oil Co. Ltd.
H.J. Wilson	– Deputy Attorney General
C.E. Smith	– Counsel for the Pet. and Nat. Gas Cons. Board.
I.N. McKinnon	– Pet. and Nat. Gas Cons. Board
D.P. Goodall	– Pet. and Nat. Gas Cons. Board
G.E.G. Liesemer	– Pet. and Nat. Gas Cons. Board

Mr. McKinnon acted as Chairman and Mr. Liesemer as Secretary of the Meeting.

     In opening the meeting the Chairman introduced Mr. Moroney and Mr. Wilson and requested Mr. Moroney to review the final stages in the history of Atlantic #3 well and the present status of the two relief wells and the entire lease. His report was substantially as follows:

     "The South directional well had been drilled into the well bore of Atlantic #3 and it was here that the final cement job took place. During the numerous attempts to establish a bridge, diminishing quantities of water were pumped into the west well. A bridge was finally placed in the lower part of the green shale using wire screen and various plugging materials. Subsequently a cement plug was squeezed on top of the bridge to 2800 psig. This plug was then drilled to just above the bridge, the hole filled with light mud and the drill pipe pulled (resulting in a drop in fluid level of 300 feet). The west well was filled with water. As a final step (completed Nov. 15th) all pipe lines were buried and equipment such as pumps etc., winterized and left in condition for immediate use if any emergency arose. Since that date the surface pressure at the west well has risen to 1500 psig. or the equivalent of the gas cap pressure below the bridge while the pressure at the south well stands at zero. It is accordingly believed that the well is now effectively sealed off.

As a further step toward cleaning up the oil saturated surface and the various thief sands that were presumed to have absorbed considerable oil, three shallow wells were drilled. The first well spotted about 300' west of Atlantic #3 now produces on pump about 2 bbls. per day with varying amounts of water from a sand about 50' below the surface. The second well located 300' south of Atlantic #3 bailed 2 bbls. per day on test, but no pump has as yet been installed. The third well drilled 400' east of Atlantic #3 has not as yet been tested. This would indicate that the shallow sands do carry some oil. As a further precaution a deep ditch has been dug on the north and west sides of the crater to drain any seepage into the sump. The object of all this work is to drain any oil out of the shallow aquifers and, if possible, keep any oil from draining toward the outcrop along the ravines and thus keep it from reaching the river and contaminating the water supply of Edmonton. Currently operations are proceeding on an intermittent basis due to weather conditions.''

The Chairman then asked the meeting to take into consideration the proposal submitted by Atlantic Oil Co. Ltd., copies of which were made available to all persons present. During the course of the discussion the following information was brought forward.

Firstly: It appeared that the actual costs of the entire operation would be $900,000.00 rather than $800,000.00 as first estimated. (McKinnon)

Secondly: No attempt had been made to appraise how much would be available from the various salvage items. (McKinnon)

Thirdly: Tentative amounts ($100,000.00 in each case) had been set aside as compensation

Fourthly:

for Leduc Consolidated #2 and Royalite (Imperial) #48 wells. (F. McMahon) No final settlement had as yet been made on the insurance for equipment damaged or destroyed. (F.McMahon)

Fifthly:

Royalite #48 is now in position for a complete test. (McKenzie and Moroney)

Mr. McKenzie of Imperial Oil Limited briefly reviewed the proposals submitted at several previous meetings and then offered the following comments on the proposal under discussion:

(a) That the final adjusted figure (565,195 bbls.) for over–production expressed as approximately 72% of the actual over–production (784,686 bbls.) seemed fair and reasonable.

(b) That this over–production be made up strictly in form of barrels rather than dollars as is customary for all cases of production in excess of the legal allowable.

(c) That the proposal to make up over–production on a "living wage" basis was acceptable provided that the production rate for the entire lease (i.e. 4 wells) be cut from the proposed 50% to 33⅓% of the allowable for all other D3 wells.

The Chairman asked for comments on the proposal as amended by Mr. McKenzie and there being no discussion it was requested that the matter be put to a vote. The Chairman then called for an individual expression of opinion on the part of each and every representative regarding the amended proposal. With one exception all persons present signified their approval of the proposed terms of settlement. Mr. Webster of Home Oil Co. Ltd. stated that he was present only as a spectator and did not have the authority to speak for his Company. Mr. Doze, representing the Saskatchewan Federated Co-operatives, was unable to attend the meeting but it was understood that he had already expressed himself as being satisfied with the original proposal.

Mr. Wilson, the Deputy Attorney General, requested the opinion of the meeting regarding enabling legislation. The majority of the producers were in favour of legislation being enacted to implement the proposed settlement.

After further discussion the meeting was adjourned.

(Signed)
G.E.G. Liesemer,
Secretary.

(Signed)
I.N. McKinnon,
Chairman.

APPENDIX M

ATLANTIC OIL COMPANY LIMITED
SUMMARY

I. Funds held by Board after payment of all costs and claims and provision for emergencies (Schedule 1) $ 617,183.00

II. Production of No. 3 Well from
April, 1948 (Sechedule 2) 988,460 Bbls.
Total sales of production, No. 3 Well (Schedule 3) $2,932,353.00
Total costs of production (Schedule 3) $1,338,078.00
or $1.35 per bbl.

III. Actual production from lease (Schedule 4) 996,186 Bbls.

IV. Normal production Atlantic lease to
April 1, 1949 (Schedule 5) 211,500 Bbls.

V. Over–production from lease
(Actual less Normal Production) 784,686 Bbls.

VI. Adjusted over–production:
Assuming reduction of 65 cents per bbl.
in lifting costs (Schedule 6) 565,195 Bbls.

VII. Recommendations:

1. That funds in the hands of the Board after payment of all approved claims and costs and reserve provided be turned over to Atlantic Oil Company Limited upon passage of enabling legislation.

2. That the Atlantic lease be allowed to produce as from April 1, 1949 at 50 per cent of allowable based on 4 producing wells and that neither the No. 3 nor the No. 4 location be approved for drilling for such time as the Board may determine.

The Petroleum and Natural Gas Conservation Board
Atlantic No. 3 Well Trust
Statement of Revenue and Expenditure

Revenue
Sale of Crude Oil (949,229 Bbls.) $2,818,584.01
Bank Interest 13,276.48
$2,831,860.49

Expenditure
Control and Other Costs $946.645.95
Royalties 606,674.41
Damage Claims 227,447.45
Oil Wells $200,000.00

Surface Damage   27,447.45

                                                    $1,780,767.81

Excess of Revenue over Expenditure
Paid to Atlantic Oil Company Limited $1,051,092.68

The Petroleum and Natural Gas Conservation Board
Atlantic No. 3 Well Trust
Statement of Payments made to Atlantic Oil Company Limited

May 11th, 1949	$ 500,000.00	
September 2nd, 1949	100,000.00	
March 8th, 1950	200,000.00	
March 27th, 1951	199,600.00	(bonds)
February 27th, 1953	24,950.00	(bonds)
	26,542.68	
	$1,051,092.68	

The Petroleum and Natural Gas Conservation Board
Atlantic No. 3 Well Trust
Statement of Royalties and Damage Claims

Royalties:
National Trust Company re Rebus
gross royalties $352,323.00
Imperial Oil Limited re royalty
agreement $254,351.41
                                                    $606,674.41

Damage Claim
Oil Wells:
Leduc Consolidated Oils Ltd. re
Leduc Consolidated No. 2 Well $100,000.00
Imperial Oil Limited re Imperial
Leduc No. 48 Well   100,000.00
                                                    $200,000.00

Surface Damage:		
John Rebus	$ 10,996.40	
Mike Bara	9,687.03	
J.S. Halwa	2,277.32	
Lukas Smith	1,804.00	
Anton Bawol	959.00	
Harry Charko	746.80	
Andrew Rebus	501.90	
Alex Halwa	450.00	
Mary Yaremko	25.00	
		$ 27,447.45
		$834,121.86

MEMORANDUM
Re: Atlantic No. 3 Well

In presenting this proposal as to the settlement of claims, the disposition of funds now held and the future operation of the Atlantic Lease the following points should be emphasized:

1. The blowout of the Atlantic No. 3 Well must be considered not as a purely localized matter, but as something which was of importance to the whole Field; that the experience gained is of benefit to the whole Field and that, in assessing its value or cost, this point of view must be maintained.
2. The blowout was not the result of negligence or malpractice on the part of the owner or its contractor. Considerably more than minimum precautions were taken at all times and the advice and approval of the Conservation Board Engineers was sought on all points.
3. The experience gained has placed information in the hands of operators which has materially reduced the risk of the recurrence of such an accident, although the recent blowout at the Mercury Well at Nisku has demonstrated that such things can happen at the most unexpected of times or places.
4. The Atlantic Oil Company has at all times co-operated with operators and Board Officials and has repeatedly stated that it had no wish to profit financially from this unfortunate occurrence.

A review of the situation indicates that Atlantic has suffered considerable loss and, regardless of what disposition is made of funds now on hand, cannot recoup more than a small proportion of that loss. During the period in which the well flowed out of control more than 1,000,000 barrels of oil was produced and sold and almost an equal volume was returned to the formation through its wells No. 1 and 2, which, unlike other wells in the Field, were restrained from producing during this period.

Exhibit "A" (attached hereto) sets out the amount of revenue the Company would have received had it been allowed to complete its wells at normal intervals. It will be noted that adjustment has been made in respect of production which was saved during the period and for an amount of $90,000 which would have been expended on the Drilling of the No. 4 Well.

Costs incurred by the Company include the value of material and equipment damaged or destroyed during the blowout and the fire, and are subject to adjustment in the amount of salvage which may be obtained.

It will be noted that the production deficiency as set out in Exhibit "A" amounts to $338,411.51.

Exhibit "B" sets out details of the revenue and estimated expenditures made by the Conservation Board in connection with its operations at this well. It will be noted that it is estimated that after settlement of all claims and payments of all costs there will remain, on the basis of the estimates, a balance of $1,105,261.01 which it is proposed to distribute in the manner set out in the statement. Assuming the accuracy of the estimates and accepting the proposal to set up a fund for repressuring in the amount of $200,000, there will remain for payment to Atlantic the sum of $655,261.01.

From the amount of $655,261.01 may be deducted the sum of $338,411.51 as set out in Exhibit "A", leaving an apparent surplus of $316,849.50 which is, of course, subject to adjustment in respect of unforeseen items or in excess estimates of liabilities, or in respect of the net value of additional oil which may be salvaged.

It is suggested that this apparent surplus is the only benefit which Atlantic may receive at this time. It is also suggested that this, in itself, is small recompense for the loss from its lease of more than 1,000,000 barrels of oil.

The net amount of $316,849.50 received by Atlantic Oil Company Limited after such adjustments as are necessary have been made thereto should be converted into barrels at current prices and that amount should be considered to be the measure of the over-production taken from the Atlantic lease.

Atlantic Oil Company Limited submits the following proposal for consideration:

1. Atlantic No. 3 Well to be effectively abandoned.
2. The Atlantic lease to be permitted to produce one-half of the normal allowable for four D3 wells which would have been allotted to it by the Petroleum and Natural Gas Conservation Board, until such time as assumed over-production from the No. 3 Well has been made up.
3. Drilling of additional D3 zone wells on the locations selected for Wells No. 3 and 4 to be allowed, provided however that the drilling of such wells will not serve to increase the allowable production as set out in (2) above.
4. The net amount realized from salvaged oil to be added to the amount of the assumed over-production and converted into equivalent barrels at the current price from time to time posted in respect of formation production, which will serve to prolong the period of restricted production from the lease.
5. The methods of salvaging, treating, storing and shipping of oil now lying in surface soils to be subject to the approval of the Petroleum and Natural Gas Conservation Board.
6. The deposit of $200,000 to be held in Dominion of Canada or Province of Alberta Bonds to guarantee Atlantic's contribution of its share of the cost of any repressuring or water injection scheme which may be required in the future. In the event of such a scheme being introduced it is suggested that Atlantic should pay only its proportionate cost and that the length of time that this deposit is to remain intact and its subsequent disposition should be the subject of mutual arrangement between the Government and Atlantic Oil Company Limited.

Adoption of the foregoing as a principle to be followed in this matter will, it is submitted, place all operators in the same comparative position they would have enjoyed had this accident not occurred, with one notable exception, viz. the loss by Atlantic Oil Company of more than $2,000,000 in ultimate recovery from its lease.

Such a loss spread over a field of the size of the Leduc Field is a minor item but when such a loss is to be deducted from the ultimate production of a quarter section it is of major importance to the operator concerned.

It is submitted that, in view of the fact that all assessable damage claims will have been settled liberally and that Atlantic will be allowed only restricted operations for a period to make up for an assumed over–production, all operators in the Field may be said to enjoy the same comparative positions and to compensate for any delay they may have experienced Atlantic will suffer a not inconsiderable loss in ultimate pro–duction.

In conclusion it may be advanced that the blowout was not an unmixed blessing. The value of the publicity which the Leduc Field in particular and the Alberta Oil Industry in general received during the approximately six months duration of the well's activity was tremendous. There can be no doubt of this, although it is not suggested that such a spectacular event should be re–staged as a "publicity stunt".

Exhibit "A"

ATLANTIC OIL COMPANY LIMITED
Statement of Deficiency in Net Production for Period
ending December 31, 1948
Based on Assumed Completion of Wells 1 to 4
at Normal Intervals.

1948	Well #1	Well #2	Well #3	Well #4	Accum.
April	4,500	4,500	4,500		13,500
May	4,650	4,650	4,650	1,650	15,600
June	4,500	4,500	4,500	4,500	18,000
July	4,650	4,650	4,650	4,650	18,600
August	4,650	4,650	4,650	4,650	18,600
September	4,500	4,500	4,500	4,500	18,000
	27,450	27,450	27,450	19,950	102,300
October	4,650	4,650	4,650	4,650	18,600
November	4,500	4,500	4,500	4,500	18,000
December	4,650	4,650	4,650	4,650	18,600
	13,800	13,800	13,800	13,800	55,200
	41,250	41,250	41,250	33,750	157,500

Value of above production:	102,300 bbls. at $3.45	$352,935.00
	55,200 bbls. at $3.47	191,544.00
		$544,479.00
Less Gross Royalty (Rebus)	$ 68,059.88	
Imperial Oil	95,283.82	163,343.70
		$381,135.30

Deduct
Value of sales actually made:

Well No. 1 April	$12,016.66		
Well No. 1 May	3,061.12	15,077.78	
Well No. 2 April		13,579.55	
Well No. 3 May		113,769.35	
			142,426.68

Less Gross Royalty	$17,803.30		
Imperial Oil Limited	24,924.67	42,727.97	99,698.71
			281,436.59

Deduct

Assumed operating expenses at $600 per month per well	21,000.00
	260,436.59

Add:

Expenditure on controlling Well No. 3 including loss of equipment and material	167,974.92	
Less allowance for drilling Well No. 4	90,000.00	77,974.92
Net Deficiency		$338.411.51

Exhibit "B"

ATLANTIC OIL COMPANY LIMITED
Statement of Operations Well No. 3 as Supplied by Petroleum and Natural Gas Conservation Board

Sales of Oil		$2,818,584.01

Estimated Disbursements:

Gross Royalty (Rebus)	$352,323.00	
Imperial Oil Limited (85,736 bbls.)	261,000.00	
Drilling relief wells, etc.	800,000.00	
Compensation (Imperial Leduc #48)	200,000.00	
Compensation (Leduc Consolidated #2	100,000.00	1,713.323.00
Balance		$1,105,261.01

Suggested Distribution:

Contribution to gas or water injection scheme	200,000.00
Reserve for contingencies	250,000.00
Payment to Atlantic Oil Company Limited	655,261.01
	$1,105,261.01

Production from the N.W. ¼ 23–50–26 W. 4th Mer. owned by the Atlantic Oil Company to be regulated as follows:

(a)   Atlantic No. 3 well to be effectively abandoned.

(b)   No further drilling to obtain production from the D3 zone to be permitted on the N.W. ¼ 23–50–26 W. 4th Mer.

(c)   Atlantic Nos. 1 and 2 wells to be permitted to each produce one third of the allowable which would be normally allocated to these wells by the Petroleum and Natural Gas Conservation Board until such time as the over–production from the Atlantic No. 3 well be made up.

(d)   Provided however that as long as oil is being salvaged from the N.W. ¼ 23–50–26 W. 4th Mer. at a rate equal to or exceeding the allowable set forth in (c) above for Atlantic Nos. 1 and 2 wells, the said wells shall not be produced.

(e)   Oil salvaged in excess of the total allowables for Atlantic Nos. 1 and 2 wells as set forth in (c) above shall be treated as over–production and shall be considered as part of the over–production from Atlantic No. 3 well.

(f)   All salvage operations undertaken by the Atlantic Oil Company to recover oil from the N.W. ¼ 23–50–26 W. 4th Mer. must receive the approval of the Petroleum and Natural Gas Conservation Board.

APPENDIX N

1949

CHAPTER 17.

An Act to determine all Claims Arising from the Atlantic No. 3 Oil Well Disaster.

(Assented to March 29, 1949.)

WHEREAS the Atlantic No. 3 Oil Well of the Atlantic Oil Preamble
Company, Limited blew out of control and subsequently
caught fire causing extensive loss and damage; and

Whereas pursuant to the provisions of *The Oil and Gas Resources Conservation Act,* being chapter 66 of the Revised Statutes of Alberta, 1942, the Petroleum and Natural Gas Conservation Board entered upon, seized and took possession of the said well for the purpose of bringing it under control and conserving the flow of petroleum and natural gas; and

Whereas further loss and damage was caused and expense incurred as a result of measures taken for the purpose of bringing the said well under control; and

Whereas there are numerous claims arising directly or indirectly from the Atlantic No. 3 Oil Well disaster and from the measures taken to bring the same under control, whether recoverable as debts, damages or otherwise howsoever; and

Whereas the proceeds of the sale of the petroleum recovered from the said well have been deposited in a trust fund in the name of the Petroleum and Natural Gas Conservation Board and it appears desirable and expedient that the said trust fund be used to pay the said claims; and

Whereas due to the nature of the disaster and the resulting claims there are technical and engineering problems involved in the determination of liability and the assessment of damages which are common to many of the claims; and

Whereas the claims are so inter-related that it is not feasible or practicable to deal with them individually; and

Whereas it appears desirable and expedient in the public interest to determine all such claims; and

Whereas on the invitation of the Board several meetings were held in the City of Calgary, in the Province of Alberta, attended by representatives of the Atlantic Oil Company,

Limited and other producers in the Leduc field affected by
the disaster for the purpose of determining all such claims;
and

Whereas at such a meeting held in the offices of the Board
in the City of Calgary, on Wednesday, the twenty-sixth day
of January, 1949, representatives of the Atlantic Oil Company,
Limited and of the majority of the producers expressed
their approval of the settlement of claims adopted by the
meeting and no objection to the proposed settlement was
registered by the representatives of any of the said producers;
and

Whereas it is deemed desirable and expedient to implement
the settlement of claims adopted by the said meeting;

Now therefore His Majesty, by and with the advice and
consent of the Legislative Assembly of the Province of
Alberta, enacts as follows:

Short Title.

Short title   **1.** This Act may be cited as *"The Atlantic Claims Act"*.

Interpretation.

Interpretation   **2.** In this Act unless the context otherwise requires,—

"Board"   (*a*) "Board" means the Petroleum and Natural Gas
Conservation Board;

"claim"   (*b*) "claim" means a claim arising directly or indirectly
from the Atlantic No. 3 Oil Well disaster, whether
recoverable as a debt or damages or otherwise howsoever,
and includes a claim of a holder of a gross
royalty payable by the Company out of the production
of the petroleum and natural gas from the Atlantic
No. 3 Oil Well;

"Company"   (*c*) "Company" means the Atlantic Oil Company, Limited;

"person"   (*d*) "person" includes a corporation;

"trust fund"   (*e*) "trust fund" means the trust fund in the name of
the Petroleum and Natural Gas Conservation Board,
being the proceeds received by the said Board from
the sale of petroleum produced from the Atlantic
No. 3 Oil Well.

General.

Powers of Board   **3.**—(1) The Board is hereby authorized to retain from
the trust fund for a period not exceeding two years from
the date of the passing of this Act any moneys which in its

discretion may be required for further expenses in connection with bringing the Atlantic No. 3 Oil Well under control, and conserving the flow of petroleum and natural gas therefrom or for any other purposes connected with the Atlantic No. 3 Oil Well disaster that the Board deems necessary.

(2) The Board is hereby authorized to pay money out of the trust fund for any of the following purposes:

> (*a*) The costs and expenses of and incidental to any action which has been taken or may hereafter be taken by the Board for the purpose of bringing the Atlantic No. 3 Oil Well under control;
>
> (*b*) The costs and expenses of carrying out all investigations and conservation measures that the Board has taken or deems necessary to be taken in connection with the said well;
>
> (*c*) The payment of such sums of money as may be required to give effect to any settlement approved by the Board and arrived at between the Company and any claimant who may have a claim against the Company, provided that if the parties cannot agree upon a settlement the Board may, in its discretion, pay to the claimant such amount, if any, in settlement of the claim as the Board may consider to be just and equitable;
>
> (*d*) The payment to the Company from time to time of such sums of money as the Board in its discretion deems it advisable to advance, having regard to the protection of the interests of claimants under this section of whose claims it has notice in writing prior to such advance.

(3) The money remaining in the trust fund, if any, after payment of all claims, costs and expenses authorized to be paid pursuant to this Act shall belong and be paid to the Company.

4. The Atlantic No. 3 Oil Well shall be deemed to have over-produced to the extent of five hundred and sixty-five thousand one hundred and ninety-five barrels of oil during the period it was flowing out of control and the Board may,— *Restrictions as to production and drilling*

> (*a*) restrict the production of the Company's No. 1 and No. 2 wells to an amount which shall not exceed two-thirds of the normal allowable production as set from time to time by the Board; and
>
> (*b*) prevent the drilling of further wells on legal subdivisions 11 and 12 of section 23, township 50, range 26, west of the 4th meridian;

until such time as the Board may consider it necessary in order to compensate, in the opinion of the Board, for the over-production of Atlantic No. 3 Oil Well.

Commence-
ment of
action

5. No person shall commence any action against the Company or the Board, or any other person in respect of any claim unless such person has first obtained the consent in writing of the Attorney General.

Additional
powers of
Board

6. The Lieutenant Governor in Council may vest in the Board such additional powers and duties as are deemed necessary or advisable for the purpose of enabling the Board to perform its duties under this Act, and may make such regulations as are deemed necessary or advisable for carrying out the provisions of this Act according to their true intent.

Validation
of O.C.
1495-48

7. A certain Order in Council dated the twenty-first day of December, 1948, intituled O.C. 1495/48, and set out in the Schedule hereto is hereby ratified, validated and confirmed and shall have the same force and effect as if the same had been enacted by this Act.

Coming into
force

8. This Act shall come into force on the day upon which it is assented to.

Schedule

SCHEDULE

Approved and Ordered,

(*Sgd.*) J. C. BOWEN,
Lieutenant Governor.

Edmonton, Tuesday, December 21st, 1948.

The Executive Council has had under consideration the report of the Honourable the Minister of Lands and Mines, dated December 20th, 1948, stating that:

Whereas by the terms of section 46 of *The Oil and Gas Resources Conservation Act*, being Chapter 66 of the Revised Statutes of Alberta, 1942, it is provided as follows:

"**46.**—(1) The Board may take such steps and employ such persons as it considers necessary for the enforcement of any order made by it and for the purposes thereof may forcibly or otherwise enter upon, seize and take possession of the whole or part of the movable and immovable property in, on or about any well or used in connection therewith or appertaining thereto together with the books and offices of the owner thereof, and may, until the order has been complied with, either discontinue all production or may take over the management and control thereof.

"(2) Upon the Board taking possession of any well and so long as such possession continues, every officer and employee of the owner thereof shall obey the orders of the Board or of such person or persons as it places in charge and control thereof.

"(3) Upon possession being taken of any well the Board may take, deal with and dispose of all petroleum produced at the well as if it were the property of the Board, subject to the obligation to account for the net proceeds thereof to the persons entitled thereto.

"(4) The costs and expenses of and incidental to proceedings taken by the Board under this section shall be in the discretion of the Board, and the Board may direct by whom and to what extent they shall be paid.";

and

Whereas Atlantic No. 3 Well of the Atlantic Oil Company Limited, blew out of control and the Petroleum and Natural Gas Conservation Board deemed it necessary to enter upon, seize and take possession of the movable and immovable property in, on or about the said well for the purpose of bringing it under control and conserving the gas and flow of oil under the terms of an Order of the Board; and

Whereas during the time that the Board has been in possession of the said well it has marketed the oil derived from the well, the proceeds from which are held in a special trust account in the name of the Board; and

Whereas it is deemed necessary and expedient to pay out of the said trust account to the persons hired by the Board the costs and expenses of and incidental to the work of bringing the said well under control; and

Whereas it is also deemed advisable and expedient to endeavor to settle any claims against the Atlantic Oil Company, Limited, other than claims arising from an interest in mines and minerals and to settle claims of persons entitled to a royalty on production from the Numbers 1, 2 and 3 wells of the Atlantic Oil Company, Limited; and

Whereas there is no statutory provision enabling the said payments to be made or settlements effected and it is proposed to make the said payments and settlements subject to ratification by the Legislature at its next ensuing session. Therefore, upon the recommendation of the Honourable the Minister of Lands and Mines, the Executive Council advises that the Petroleum and Natural Gas Conservation Board be and is hereby authorized to:

(1) pay out of the fund now held in the name of the Petroleum and Natural Gas Conservation Board in trust and representing the proceeds of the sale of petroleum from Atlantic No. 3 Well the costs and expenses of and incidental to the proceedings taken by the Board to control the gas flow in the said well and the flow of petroleum therefrom.

(2) pay out of the said fund such sums as may be required to give effect to any settlement approved by the Board arrived at between the Atlantic Oil Company, Limited and any claimant or claimants who may have a claim against the Atlantic Oil Company, Limited arising directly or indirectly from the Atlantic No. 3 Well blow-out whether recoverable as a debt or damages or otherwise howsoever, other than a claim arising from an interest in mines and minerals.

(3) pay out of the said fund to any person entitled to a royalty on production from the Numbers 1, 2 and 3 wells of the Atlantic Oil Company, Limited, such royalty as, in the opinion of the Board, would have been received by such person if the Atlantic No. 3 Oil Well had not blown out of control and if the said wells had produced at a rate equivalent to the actual rate of production allowed by the Board to similar wells belonging to other companies in the same field at the same time.

(*Sgd.*) ERNEST C. MANNING,
Chairman.

APPENDIX O

Chapter 15, "Measuring the Loss" discusses the implications of this report:

LEDUC D–3 A POOL RESERVES DATA
Discovery Date: May 1947
Location: 20 km (12 mi) southwest of Edmonton
CRUDE OIL RESERVES DATA[1]

Area	21770 acres
Average Oil Pay	35.4 feet
Porosity, %	10
Water Saturation, %	14
Shrinkage Factor, %	75
Initial Oil in Place	386×10^6 bbl.
Recovery Factor	63.7%
Total Recoverable Reserves	246×10^6 bbl.
Cumulative Production to Dec. 31, 1985	242×10^6 bbl.
Remaining Oil Reserves at Dec. 31, 1985	4×10^6 bbl.
Current Production Rate (July 1986)	3460 bbls/day
Forecast Abandonment Year	1996

[1] Data from ERCB and Esso Resources Canada Limited, December, 1985.

LEDUC D–3 A POOL RESERVES DATA
NATURAL GAS RESERVES[1]

Original Gas in Place	
Solution Gas	185 Bcf
Gas Cap Gas	412 Bcf
Initial Recoverable Raw Gas Reserves[2]	
Solution Gas	138 Bcf
Gas Cap Gas	338 Bcf
Initial Recoverable Marketable Gas Reserves	
Solution Gas	110 Bcf
Gas Cap Gas	309 Bcf
Cumulative Marketable Gas produced to Dec. 31, 1985	
Solution Gas	83 Bcf
Gas Cap Gas	23 Bcf
Remaining Marketable Gas Reserves	
Solution Gas	27 Bcf
Gas Cap Gas	286 Bcf
TOTAL GAS	313 Bcf

[1] Data from ERCB and Esso Resources Canada Limited, December, 1985.
[2] Does not include 30 Bcf lost from Atlantic No. 3 blowout.

LEDUC D–3 A POOL
COMPARISON OF RESERVES ESTIMATES, THEN AND NOW

Date	Oct 1948	Dec 1985
Estimated by	Ted Baugh, Cons. Bd.	ERCB and Esso Resources
Area – acres	11570	21770
Porosity – %	13	10
Water Saturation – %	12	14
Shrinkage Factor – %	70	75
Oil Recovery Factor – %	75	63.7
Initial Oil in Place, 10^6 bbl.	231	386
Recoverable Oil Reserves, 10^6 bbl.	173	246
Initial Gas Cap Gas in Place – Bcf	393	412

The above indicates that, in October 1948, the gas cap was quite well defined, but only half of the areal extent of the oil zone had been delineated. Also, the expected oil recovery efficiency was somewhat overestimated in 1948, due to the early stage of development of the pool and the resulting lack of production performance data. The recovery losses that would be related to the oil "sandwich" being squeezed by the encroaching gas cap and water zones and the coning problems that would occur as the pool became depleted were probably not fully recognized in 1948. Taking all of these factors into account, the 1948 estimates were as good as could have been made at that time.

SUMMARY OF OIL AND GAS RESERVES LOSSES
RESULTING FROM ATLANTIC NO. 3 BLOWOUT

CRUDE OIL – Barrels

ESTIMATED TOTAL OIL PRODUCED		1,407,000
PUMPED TO NISKU	998,000	
REINJECTED TO D–3 ZONE	244,000	
TOTAL OIL SAVED		1,242,000

OIL LOST:

– non–treatable	10,000	
– burned in pits	30,000	
– burned in flare	25,000	
– lost to thief horizons	50,000	
– lost to spray and seepage	50,000	
TOTAL OIL LOST DURING BLOWOUT		165,000

ESTIMATED FUTURE OIL RECOVERY LOSS
(from oil zone moving up into gas
cap 1½ feet)   2,500,000

TOTAL OIL LOST BY BLOWOUT   2,665,000
(slightly over 1 percent of the total
recoverable oil reserves of 246 x 10^6 bbl.)

NATURAL GAS – Bcf
TOTAL GAS LOST DURING BLOWOUT   30.1 Bcf
(6 percent of total recoverable solution
gas and gas cap gas reserves)

CONCLUSION: Considering the magnitude and seriousness of the blowout and its 6–month duration, these oil and gas losses would seem to be relatively minor.

RESERVOIR MANAGEMENT OF THE LEDUC D–3A POOL

The innovative way in which production operations at the Leduc D–3 A Pool have been managed by Esso Resources, operator of the two principal units in the pool, has resulted in ensuring that the maximum amount of economically recoverable oil will be produced. The production strategy of controlling injection of gas into the overlying gas cap and water into the underlying water zone to maintain reservoir pressure and mini- mize adverse effects of gas and water coning as the oil zone became depleted has been extremely successful.

The Leduc–Woodbend D–3 Unit was formed in 1960, and the Leduc D–3A Southeast Extension Unit was formed in 1975. Together, these Units contain most of the productive area of the Leduc D–3 A Pool, and this has enabled the efficient operation of the pool.

With the pool having reached an advanced stage of depletion, Esso applied to the ERCB in April, 1983 for approval to blow down the gas cap and concurrently produce oil and gas from the Leduc D–3 A Pool. The gas cap had been shut in since the pool was placed on production, in order to maximize oil recovery.

The ERCB approved the blowdown plan and blowdown was sched- uled to commence in November, 1985. Esso initiated a program aimed at accelerating oil production prior to the start of blowdown. This program was timed to be complete by November, 1985. The program was so successful that not only was the oil production decline arrested, oil pro- duction increased from 3800 barrels per day to 4400 barrels per day, and this rate was maintained for about 1½ years. The program consisted of: optimization of completion intervals on existing producing wells, reactiva- tion of suspended wells, and a re–look at wells previously considered uneconomic.

In summary, the program was aimed at maximizing all short–term oil production opportunities.

Some of the recent recompletions have used a 6 inch completion interval. The oil zone, which originally was 38 feet thick between the gas– oil and oil–water contacts, has now shrunk to about 4 feet. The oil zone now remaining is above the initial 5 foot major completion interval used in most wells in the pool. The 6 inch completion interval is placed in the bottom of the existing oil zone, since gas tends to cone more easily than water.

With the better than expected results of the well workovers and reactivations, in the interest of conserving more oil, the blowdown of the gas cap has been delayed, and is now anticipated to commence in 1987, after the oil production has declined. A continuing effort to maximize oil recovery is still underway (in 1986) and the delay in starting the blowdown is expected to add oil reserves in the order of 2 million barrels.

Harry S. Simpson, 1986

GLOSSARY

Acidize: a treatment by acid (usually hydrochloric) of a producing forma–tion (usually a carbonate rock) by which the porosity and permeability of the formation is increased, thereby improving its producibility.

Barefoot: a completion technique in which the production string is landed and set above the formation to be produced. The casing shoe is drilled out and the producing formation below is cleaned up so that its contents can flow into the production casing.

Boilers: steam boilers; the source of power for steam rigs.

Bonding: the tight, impermeable "bond" formed between cement and the outer wall of the casing and cement and the irregular wall of the well bore itself. A poor "bond" may allow fluids from one formation to migrate (leak) into another formation.

BOP: Blow–out Preventer. Equipment, mounted at the top of the surface casing, with which to control oil, gas or water flows from a well while drilling.

Casing Head: equipment mounted at the top of the production casing string through which production can be regulated by means of valves.

Casing Shoe: equipment run on the bottom end of a casing string, through which cementing takes place.

Cathead Man: the man who works at the cathead(s) when "spinning in" or "snapping up" with rope during the running of casing.

Cement Plug: a batch of cement run into an extremely porous and permeable formation in an effort to plug it and regain circulation.

Choke: production from oil and gas wells is regulated through various sized orifices (chokes) in valves.

Circulation: drilling mud (occasionally water) is pumped through the kelly and down the drill pipe, through ports in the drill bit and back up the annulus between the drill pipe and the hole wall. It cleans the bit and flushes the drill cuttings out of the hole; it is absolutely essential in order to keep the hole clean, and prevent sticking of the bit or the drill pipe.

Coring: the operation which, by the use of a special (diamond) core bit and barrel at the bottom of the drill string, results in obtaining a sample of the formation that was cored.

D–2, D–3: Devonian dolomite formations (fossil reefs) that produce oil and gas in many parts of Alberta (later named Nisku and Leduc, respec–tively).

Daywork: a drilling contractor contracts with the operator (owner) to *drill* him a hole in which he, the operator, can do further operations (such as completion for production). Any operation, such as coring, dril–lstem testing, fighting lost circulation, that is not *drilling,* is usually done on *daywork,* and is charged differently to the owner.

Derrick: the wooden or steel structure raised over the drawworks of the drilling rig, in which the drill pipe is stacked in racks when it is pulled from the hole. The drilling line passes from the drum of the draw-works through the crown block at the top of the derrick and through the travelling blocks to raise or lower drill pipe (or casing). A huge block and tackle mount.

Derrickman: the man who, standing on a platform up in the derrick, handles and racks the drill pipe while tripping in or out of the hole or handles casing. He also has some responsibility for the drilling mud. No. 2 man on a drilling crew.

Dog House: the shack attached to the drilling rig in which is kept (in the "knowledge box") day to day information regarding operations at the well.

Drill: to "turn (the bit) to the right" and make hole.

Drill Bit: a 3 or 4 roller toothed bit used for drilling rock formations. Also includes "fishtail" bit, which is really a gouge used to drill unconsolidated surface formations.

Drill "dry": to drill ahead without mud returning to surface. Means that there may be no hydrostatic pressure against potentially productive formations, and can result in a blow-out. Very dangerous.

Driller: the man on each crew who operates the drilling rig, stud hand of a drilling crew. "The man on the brake."

Drilling Rig: generally speaking, all of the machinery and constructions assembled with which to drill a well. Includes draw works, rotary table, pumps, motors (boilers and steam engines in the case of steam rigs), derrick, shale shaker, etc.

Drilling String: the "string" of hollow steel drill pipe with special taper-threaded couplings, at the bottom of which is the bit that drills the hole.

Drillstem Test: the operation by which a porous, possibly productive formation is relieved of its formation pressure so that its contents (gas, oil, water) can flow into and up the drill pipe to give an idea of the productive potential of the formation.

Dry Hole: a bore hole in which no oil or gas productive horizons are present.

Dutchman: a broken piece left inside a threaded connection.

Flash-set: where a quick setting chemical (e.g. Calseal) is added to cement to speed up the setting time of the cement. Used in lost circulation situations.

Geophysical: most commonly, an exploration technique by which energy waves originating at the surface (in seismic shot holes, or by other means) are reflected back to the surface by sub-surface formations, thereby enabling structural mapping of the formations. Also includes earth-gravity, magnetic, and electrical techniques.

Halliburton (and Dowell): service companies whose specialty is in cementing services on wells.

Hinderliter: a manufacturer of well head equipment.

Hosmer Button: an early, extremely simple BOP tool by which some blow–outs were contained, (see illustrative advertisement in Chapter 6).

Kelly: a long, square, hollow, steel tube that is attached to the top end of the drill string. It fits in the square hole in the rotary table; when the rotary table is "turned to the right", the drill string and bit are also turned. Mud is pumped down the kelly and drill pipe, out through the bit, and returns up the annulus between the wall of the hole and the drill pipe, thus flushing the drill cuttings out of the hole.

Lead–pipe Cinch: a "100%" chance of success.

Lost (Loss of) Circulation: the condition where the mud pumped down the drill pipe escapes into a very porous and permeable rock formation instead of returning up the annulus. Very serious.

Lost Circulation Material: a large variety of usually fibrous material that is mixed in the mud for the purpose of plugging extremely porous and permeable formations in efforts to control lost circulation. Sawdust is most common, but feathers, walnut shells, gel–flake (containing small pieces of cellophane) and many innovative items have been used.

Lsd: one of 16 sub–divisions of a 640–acre section of land. In the Leduc Field one well was drilled on each lsd (40–acre well spacing).

Macaroni String: a term generally used for a string of tubing that is equipped with a bit and used to drill out obstructions inside drill pipe or casing.

On Vacuum: the condition where fluids (e.g. mud, water) introduced into a well bore disappear (go away) down the hole without the application of pressure (i.e., pumping).

Perforation: the shooting of holes through the casing and cement opposite a formation to be produced, so that fluids (oil, gas) in the formation can flow into the casing, from which it can be taken out (by pump, or natural flow). "Bullet" or "Jet" perforating guns are used.

Permeability: where the void spaces in a porous rock are interconnected so that the fluid contents (oil, gas or water) can move through the rock.

Porosity: the void or open spaces (pores), usually microscopic in size, in an otherwise solid looking rock. In the D–3, the pores range up to cavernous in size (vugs). The presence of porosity enables a rock to contain oil, gas or water.

Power Rig: a drilling rig powered by diesel (or gasoline, or propane, rarely) engines. May also include diesel–electric rigs, where the motors drive electricity generators that power the rig.

Production String: the string of steel casing that is *cemented* at the bottom of the hole, and through which the oil or gas may be produced.

Psi: pressure measurement in pounds per square inch.

Psia: pressure as calculated.

Psig: pressure as measured by gauge.

Push (Tool Push): the man in charge of the management of a drilling rig.

Reefing: to exert a great strain on something, e.g., drill pipe, to pull on it when stuck.

Rough Hands (Roughnecks): the lowly hands doing all the dirty work around a rig.

Round Trip: pulling drill pipe (or casing) out and running it back in the hole.

Schlumberger: a service company whose specialty is producing logs of wells. Electrical, radioactivity and sonic properties of the formations are measured and recorded for interpretation by specialists.

Separator: equipment through which the oil produced with its contained gas from a well is passed, to separate the gas from the oil. It renders the oil much less explosive.

Shearing Ball: device used to trip, or release another piece of equipment that is already in the hole (or in the drill pipe or casing) so that that piece of equipment can perform its function or be removed from the well.

Side Track: the operation of drilling new hole, starting at depth, just beside the "old hole" that has deviated badly, or has become full of junk and cannot be cleaned out. A form of directional drilling.

Single: one length (approximately 30 ft.) of drill pipe.

Sinker Bar: a weighted steel bar used to carry light weight instruments or tools down through the heavy viscous mud in drill pipe, casing or the well bore.

Snipe: a length of pipe slipped over the handle of a wrench to enable more strain to be exerted. The reason most wrenches around rigs are broken.

Steam Rig: a drilling rig powered by steam.

Sump: a disposal pit that gets all the waste during the drilling of a well.

Surface String: the string of casing cemented from bottom to top in the surface hole. It should be bottomed in consolidated rock formation so that the flow of drilling mud, or an uncontrolled flow of water, gas or oil cannot escape into the area surrounding the well, as happened at Atlantic No. 3.

T.D.: total depth, at any given time, of a well bore.

Treater: equipment through which oil produced from a well is passed, to drop out any water produced with the oil.

Triple: 3 lengths of drill pipe together (approximately 90 ft.) for racking in the derrick during trips.

Tubing String: a string of small diameter pipe that is *hung* inside the production casing, and through which oil and gas production may be taken. The tubing can be removed from within the casing.

Viking: a Lower Cretaceous sandstone formation that produces gas and oil in many parts of Alberta.

Wildcat: an exploratory well drilled far from known production.

ACKNOWLEDGEMENTS

The list of resource persons will be found in this section rather than the preface, mainly because of their sheer numbers. Although there is some repetition, on the other hand there may be a few omissions. For those who have been left out, the author can only plead forgiveness.

The "staff" set a hectic pace immediately preceding going to press, and additional recognition is due them:

Evelene Watson who kept her "cool" while "finalling" the discs and making them perfect for the printers.

Deborah Maw, who, besides doing months of research, turned out two exquisitely written "grey pages".

Don Glass, Editor, who simplified syntax, weeded out redundancies and organized the final assemblage; indispensible!

The Working Committee, who met with the author and proffered their wise counsel:

Bryan Corbett	Vivian Templeton,
Willis J. Gibson	George Warne
Harry S. Simpson	Vicki Williams

The Shadow Committee, all experienced professionals in their own right, who kept pushing the author:

John Andrichuk	Ralph W. Edie
Andy Baillie	Oscar Erdman
Cliff Demetrick	Bill McDonald

Glenbow Archives:

Doug Cass	Georgeen Klassen
Hugh Dempsey	Bill McKee
Lori Everett	Pat Molesky
Tania Henley	

Glenbow has provided excellent support throughout the past two years. They have kindly agreed to retain films, photos and documents pertaining to this project. They already hold tapes of interviews generated by the Petroleum Industry Oral History Project. Some of these have been transcribed and extensively accessed.

Alberta Provincial Archives (Edmonton):

Diane Carey	Alan Ridge
Jean Dryden	Bryan Speirs
David Leonard	Marlena Witschl

The author's first attempts to assemble historical material on the oil industry began in 1977 with the assistance of the then Provincial Archivist, Alan Ridge, O.C. More recently, this body has provided most valuable assistance in the form of historical records and photographs.

Dominion Archives (Ottawa):

A. Kesteris	Bennett McCardle
Yvan Goudreau	Rod Young

This agency assisted in identifying sources of information.

Energy Resources and Conservation Board:
Murray Blackadar
Usha Dosaj
George Johnson
Frank Manyluk
Howard Stafford
George Warne (also a committee member)
Floyd K. Beach (posthumously), author of the Board's 1949 Schedule of Wells, an indispensible reference.

This tribunal played a key role in the Atlantic No.3 drama. It was able to provide valuable historical material.

Alberta Historical Resources Foundation:

This body made it possible for the author to found the Petroleum Industry Oral History Project in 1980. He interviewed many informants, some of whom were directly connected with Atlantic No. 3. Out of PIOHP has emerged another organization also dedicated to oil industry historical research: Centre for Petroleum Industry History (CPIH).

Canadian Broadcasting Corporation:

A chain reaction was set up in May 1985, thanks to Edmonton's CBC–AM "Good News". A former CBC radio announcer, Ralph Horley, heard of the program through his wife and advised the author that he had made a tape of the fire. The author finally located a copy, thanks to CBC Ottawa headquarters. It forms an invaluable addition to the book.

CKRD, Red Deer, gave valuable publicity via both radio and televised interviews.

CFCN–TV, Calgary, provided coverage in the early stages, thus assisting in bringing in more informants.

Resource Persons

Taped interviews have been conducted for those marked with asterisks. The tapes therefrom are on deposit at Glenbow Archives.

Ackerley, Duff
*Alger, Harry
Andruski, Harry
*Angus, Jean
*Anthony, Raymond E.
*Atkinson, W.L. (Pete)

Bagot, Harry
Baker, Dorien
*Ballachey, John
Bara, Kenneth
Bara, Norman
Bara, Reginald
Barlow, C.B.
Barris, Ted
*Barroll, Ed
*Baugh, J.E. (Ted)

*Bedard, Paul
Beland, Francine
Bell, Anita
Bell, Elgin D.
Bergen, Henry
Berthiaume, Frank
Bessemer, Art
Black, Frank
Blackadar, Murray
*Blain, Mark, Sr.
Blanchard, Howard
*Bohme, Cal
Bonnet, Hank
Borchert, E.
Bott, Bob
Bowsher, A.P. (Pat)

Branscombe, Art
Bray, Bill
Brown, Esther
Bulk, Marius
Bullivant, Norm
Burge, Ed
Burn, Ian and Ivone St. G.

Campbell, Kae
Cantwell, Toby
Carpenter, P.C.
*Caspell, Lyle
Clare, Barney
Clark, W.F.
*Collins, Myrtle
Connell, Gordon
Cook, G.D.
Copeland, Juanita
*Corey, Bert
Cotter, Buzz
*Couture, Roger
Covey, C.H. (Cliff)
Craig, Bill
Craig, Murray
Cummer, Bill

Daniel, Katie
Davis, G.M.
Dawe, Barry
*De Mille, George
Deinum, John
Dickau, Erwin
Dickson, Terry
Diemert, Paul
Douglas, Keith
Doze, Ken
Dranchuk, Peter
Dufresne, Leah
Dunn, Kay

*Edwards, Garnet
Ekvall, Herb
Ellert, Sye
Elliott, Bob
*Erdman, Oscar
Essery, F.A.
Evans, Bill
Evanson, Kathy

Fandrick, Paul

Finn, Frank
Fogarty, Howard, J.
Franke, Cal
Fraser, J. Keith
Frew, John

Gamble, Don
Gammell, Graham
Getty, Roberta
Gibson, Laurence B.
Gilbert, E.E.
Gobin, Paul (P.J.)
*Goodall, D.P. (Red)
Goodman, N. (posthumously)
Goudreau, Yvan
Gould, Billie
Graham, Gloria
Grainger, Al
Graves, Roy
*Gray, David
*Gray, Earle
Greiner, G.A.
Guthrie, Paul

Hall, Dorothy
*Hall, E.T. (Jeep)
Hallett, Tom
Ham, Ken
*Hancock, Willis P.
Hankel, Rory
Harris, Cliff
Harris, Dorothy
Harvie, Jim
Harysh, John
Hautzinger, Roy
Hawkins, Gordon
Hedberg, Rudy
*Hemstock, Alex
Hewitt, Wes
Horley, Ralph M.
Horsfield, Roly
Hughes, Doug
Hunter, Mrs. V.H. (Beatrice)
*Hunter, V.H. (posthumously)
Hyslop, Andy

*Irwin, Jim

*Jackson, Johnny
Jaremko, Gordon

Joyce, Bill
Johnson, Del
Johnson, Arnold F.

Kerber, Bill
Kerber, Vern
*Kinghorn, Bill
Kinley, J.C.
Kinley, Mrs. M.M.
Kirkpatrick, George H.
Klinck, Norm
Kohlman, Dennis
Kohlman, Joe

*Laborde, Ed
Lane, Murray
*Langston, J.F. (Spi)
Larmour, Jim
*Layer, D.B. (posthumously)
LeBlanc, Sandra
*Leiper, Hugh
Lemire, Ann
Leslie, Mary Jo
*Lewis, D.E.
Lindseth, Roy
*Lineham, Fin
Loudoun, N.G.
Luczi, Jane
Lyle, Johnnie (posthumously)

Macfarlane, Catherine
MacKenzie, R.W.
*Mackenzie, W.D.C.
*MacMillan, Harry
Madill, Floyd
Maguire, Ross
Maloney, Harvey
Mann, Stan
Manning, Ted
*Manyluk, Frank
Matthews, F.R.
Mendl, Dido
Milner, Stan
*Moore, Carl (Mr. and Mrs.)
Moore, Jack
Moroney, Mrs. B.
Moroney, Jerry
*Moroney, V.J. (posthumously)
Morris, A.J. (Bud)

*Moseson, Paul
McAuley, Patrick
McCourt, G.B.
*McDonald, D.P.
McDonald, Jack
*McKellar, Bill
*McKinnon, Fred
McLachlan, Dugald
McLaws, I.J.
McLocklin, T.R.
McMahon, Bill

Nelner, Stan
*Nelson, Reg
*Newell, Matt

Oakes, Billy
Olson, Cliff
*Orman, Jack
Owre, L.G. (Ben)

Pahl, Bob
Patterson, Ellen
*Paulson, M.P.
Peacock, Ralph
Pearson, Lorne
Perry, Fraser
*Pettinger, Jack
*Phillips, W. A. (Al)
Planche, Hugh
Pope, Mel
*Porter, Jack
Powell, Bob
Pshyk, H.L.

*Rae, Gordon
Rahemtulla, Iqbal
Rankin, Chuck (posthumously)
Rathwell, John
Rees, Jim
Rennie, Jim
Ronaghan, Frank
Ronaghan, Walter

Sanderson, Mrs. J.O.G.
Sands, Andy
Schwarz, Bob
Scollard, Doug
Sellers, Don
Sereda, W.
Sevick, Len

Schaffer, Don
*Siferd, C.C.
Simmons, Dale
Sketchley, Bruce
Skov, Ed
Sluzar, R.D.
Snyder, Lois
*Somerville, H.H.
Spencer, Aileen
Spencer, Dyrl
Stafford, Howard
*Stafford, Jimmy
*Stafford, Lloyd
Starozik, George F.
Stevenson, D.W. (Doug)
Stimson, Stan
Stoian, E.R.Q.
Strauss, Arden
Streeter, Joe
*Sturrock, B.J.A.
Swan, F.R. (Slim)

Tait, Bill
Thompson, Jim
Tod, Jim
Tosh, G.
Turnock, Elinor

Van Zant, Mr.
Varty, Murray

Vestal, Mr.

Wagar, Howard
Wark, Bob
*Wark, Tom
Warnick, Bill
Weaver, Carol
*Webb, C.T. (Bill)
*Webster, Gordon
*Webster, Harry
Wedderburn, Bill
Welch, Gordon
Welch, Larry
Welch, Ruth
Welsh, G.A. (George)
Whitney, Don
*Wilkin, Don
Wilkinson, Norm
*Will, Ralph
Williams, Patricia
Wilson, George
*Wilson, Lloyd
Wood, Chris
Wood, David
Wright, G.A. (Al)

Yaworski, Clarence (Curley)
Yeo, Johnny
Youell, Len

Zessner, Michael

INDEX